29/300

In Search of Plainsong

Ian Clayton

route

First published by Route in 2022
info@route-online.com
www.route-online.com

ISBN : 978-1901927-87-0

First Edition

Ian Clayton asserts his moral
right to be identified as the author of this book

Edited at Olympic cross-country skiing pace by:
Ian Daley
Isabel Galán

Cover Design:
John Sellards

Cover Photograph:
Gijsbert Hanekroot

Images on the inside pages are drawn from the archives of Iain Matthews and Andy Roberts, several of which were taken by Andy and Harry Isles. We're grateful also to Nick Lambert for permission to include his photos of Plainsong at Palais de Danse, Nottingham.

Typeset in Bembo by Route

Printed and bound by CPI Group (UK) Ltd, Croydon, CR0 4YY

All rights reserved
No reproduction of this text without written permission

Foreword by Clinton Heylin   5

Introduction | A Poem of an Album   9

PART I: CALL THE TUNE
1. My Front Pages   17
2. A Picture from the Cover of Melody Maker   37
3. If You Saw Thro' My Eyes   49
4. It Never Rains in California   61
5. Along Comes Mary, Sandy, Bobby and David   81

PART II: FACE THE MUSIC
6. Plainsong Take Off   95
7. Against the Prevailing Wind   106
8. A Change of Direction   115
9. In Search of Amelia Earhart   135
10. Rock and Fucking Roll   156
11. Weighed Down by a Concept   167
12. Everybody Had a Say in What Went Down   177
13. Now We Are 3   189
14. Like Icarus Ascending   203
15. Fallout   217
16. Reconciliation   222

Plainsong Concert Dates 1972   232
Plainsong Radio and TV Appearances 1972 1973   235
Acknowledgements   239

Foreword

It's a rare privilege when a music historian gets to interview two protagonists for a given narrative simultaneously, and sees the dynamic that exists between them up close and personal. It has happened to me only twice: once was with two ex-members of Van Morrison's Them, Billy Harrison and Ronnie Millings, who hadn't seen each other since the band imploded in 1966. I just turned the tape recorder on as they sat and regaled me for two hours with stories of the young (but still gobby) Van, rarely flattering, invariably funny. That band ended badly, with recriminations on all sides and everyone, even the singer, left high and dry. But what a great band they were, even if they left but two albums' worth of evidence to that effect, and a few radio and TV sessions. Sounds like another band, or ten...

The second occasion was in Brighton, not so long ago, when I was doing the interviews for *What We Did Instead of Holidays*, a ludicrously ambitious attempt to tell the story of English folk-rock through the Fairport prism, one only Route saw the need for – God bless 'em. This time I was there for four hours, drinking copious amounts of tea and rolling tape. Actually, not. It's all digital now, so no danger of running out of tape – only memory. My hosts were the inestimable Iain Matthews and Andy Roberts, back together again as Plainsong [Redux], touring with the Richard Fariña tribute album they began making in their minds in 1971, when first they crossed paths.

As a so-called folk-rock expert, I knew something of their collaborations then, and the remarkable outpouring of product that resulted in five terrific albums in two years (1971-72): *If You Saw Thro' My Eyes, Tigers Will Survive, Journeys from Gospel Oak, In Search of Amelia Earhart* and the second Plainsong album (two of which – albums #3 and 5 – would only be released after the fact). I would still put *If You Saw Thro' My Eyes, Journeys from*

Gospel Oak and the *Amelia* album up there, worthy to sit alongside some pretty remarkable competition in the aftermath of Richard Thompson's departure from Fairport and Joe Boyd's departure from these shores: *No Roses, Bright Phoebus, Sandy, Henry the Human Fly,* even chunks of *Marc Time.*

But what I didn't know – not really, anyway – was the real Plainsong story. How that band was born out of the ashes of Thompson's (understandable) refusal to join Matthews and Roberts in a brave new band at the end of 1971; the negotiations required to extract Iain from his irksome Vertigo contract (one result of which was the surprisingly coherent, nay delightful *Journeys from Gospel Oak*); and the way Plainsong itself came together and oh so quickly fell apart, the victim of the usual 'musical differences', Iain's single-mindedness (perhaps, back then, with a soupçon of bloody mindedness) and Jac Holzman's wholly misguided belief that he a) understood folk-rock and b) knew what was best for Iain.

Caught in the crossfire was redoubtable record producer Sandy Roberton, who had assumed the mantle of folk-rock factotum when Boyd fled west, having already produced – and managed – Steeleye Span in the Ashley Hutchings era (1970-71), thus producing three folk-rock classics; as well as Marc Ellington (RIP), Shelagh McDonald and the Albion Country Band, before he became the third essential cog in the Plainsong wheel of fortune, extracting them from Vertigo and setting the wheels in motion for a future with Elektra.

I had yet to interview Sandy that Brighton afternoon, and little did I know his side of the story. So, as Iain and Andy talked about what happened to the original Plainsong, a sense grew that they had never really talked much about this before; that the scars were still there, but so were the bonds of an unbreakable friendship. Remarkably, I discovered that those bonds still bound Sandy, too. Yes, it was possible to not carry the burden of past resentments like a cross, Mr Morrison.

And yet there is real blood on the Plainsong tracks, released and unreleased, delivering fleetingly on the promise of those earlier Iain Matthews solo albums (in truth, the first flowering of the Matthews/Roberts alliance, after the original producer for *If You Saw Thro' My Eyes*, that fine technician Paul Samwell-Smith, realized which side his bread was buttered, and threw his lot in with Cat Stevens, preferring to record the timeless *Teaser and the Firecat* across the way).

For four hours the USB rolled, as I listened rapt to the tale of Plainsong unravelling. Inevitably, and somewhat reluctantly, I came away convinced that what the world really needed was a whole book about the Plainsong saga – just as I left Bangor twenty years ago, convinced someone should tell the real *Story of Them* in volume form – but I, shameless hack that I am, had other fish to fry. Maybe someone would trawl the waterfront, maybe not.

Well, I'm delighted to say someone did, and someone as immersed in English folk-rock as could be. Ian Clayton has brought it all home and, most importantly, constructed a narrative which sends the reader back to the music. Because that is where, lest we forget, the magic resides. And though the original Plainsong four-piece – and indeed the Happy Blunderers before them – have gone the way of all flesh, the Matthews-Roberts alliance endures. Go see 'em while you still can, and meantime, return to a time when there were more than three record labels, when record bosses listened to the music, and producers and musicians just wanted to make the best record they could; oh, and artists, real artists, made more quality music in two years than Adele and her management team can manage in ten...

Clinton Heylin, author of *What We Did Instead of Holidays*,
No More Sad Refrains and so much more...

Introduction | A Poem of an Album

On Sunday 19th December 1971, a group of four young musicians convened at a second-floor flat at Altior Court in the fashionable North London suburb of Highgate. After circling one another for most of the year, the four finally came round to the idea that they might be a band. They set themselves a task. They would sing a song called 'Along Comes Mary', a notoriously difficult piece in the Dorian mode that had been an American Top 10 hit for The Association in 1966. They decided that if by the end of the day they were satisfied with their harmony, they would form themselves into a band.

The four friends were Iain Matthews and Andy Roberts, who were both 25 years old; Bobby Ronga, a New Yorker, then just four days shy of his own 25th birthday; and David Richards, a Londoner who was 24. Despite their tender years, all four were vastly experienced musicians. Bobby had grown up in the New York songwriting factories and played bass, electric guitar and twelve-string acoustic in various teen bands. David played piano and guitar from boyhood. He had found work both on the road as an accompanist and in bands. Andy worked as a session guitarist for hire after working with the anarchic Liverpool Scene alongside the poet Adrian Henri. Iain Matthews, having been lead singer in Fairport Convention, went on to form Matthews Southern Comfort and by that day in December had recorded seven highly-praised albums in just four years.

The singing went well. By late afternoon, the four declared themselves happy with their arrangement. They called another friend, Sandy Roberton, manager and record producer, and asked him to come and listen to a tape they had made. He was delighted with what he heard. The five of them had dinner and over wine they searched for a name for their group. They randomly leafed through *The Concise Oxford Dictionary of Music* and landed on a page that contained the word Plainsong. All agreed it was a good name for a band that planned to put harmony first and foremost.

Plainsong spent the first month of 1972 in rehearsal refining that harmony and then took their show on the road. By the time they recorded the album *In Search of Amelia Earhart* in the summer of 1972, the musical harmony was sublime. Everything seemed set for Plainsong to fly. What wasn't widely known at the time was that they were arguing amongst themselves about which direction to take and that they were being weighed down by the emotional baggage they had brought with them.

The band that recorded *In Search of Amelia Earhart* was active for just twelve months between January and December 1972. They released that one album and were working on a follow-up when they fell apart. *In Search of Amelia Earhart* made it onto many of the critics' album-of-the-year lists and should have been a launch pad for the band, instead it led to fallout and disharmony. Plainsong, like the heroine they named their record for, couldn't find where they wanted to be and disappeared.

In Search of Amelia Earhart is a poem of an album with sincere, heartfelt songs, sublime vocal harmony, gentle acoustic guitars and understated piano. It was released on Jac Holzman's Elektra label and flew mainly under the radar at the time, but over the years it has gradually gained attention from the record-buying public. It has long been a respected album amongst the music cognoscenti and fellow musicians alike. Iain Matthews tells a story about how he once met Lou Reed in a club in Greenwich Village and Reed sang to him the words to 'Call the Tune' with its refrain 'If you're gonna try, you gotta face the music'. Perhaps now, as the record approaches its fiftieth anniversary, it's time to have a searching look at the band that made it.

I was introduced to Plainsong and *In Search of Amelia Earhart* by a friend of mine who went by the name of Trapper. In 1977 we shared a house. Trapper told stories about the time he had been a roadie for The Sutherland Brothers & Quiver and Osibisa. He told me that he had worked for Pink Floyd as well. I always thought he was slow timing me with that tale, until one day his sister told me it was true. Trapper had a collection of battered

LPs; I winced when I saw him putting his vinyl back into the cardboard sleeve without first sliding it into the paper inner. The Plainsong album was scratched on every track, but even through the pops and clicks it was clearly a very beautiful record. I also heard and fell in love with Joni Mitchell's *Hejira* album through Trapper and Al Stewart's *Year of the Cat*. I can't be certain, but I think I heard Iain Matthews's *If You Saw Thro' My Eyes* album for the first time at Trapper's house too.

A good few years went by before I came back to Iain Matthews's music. It was a CD called *Joy Mining* by Iain and the Searing Quartet released on the Fledg'ling label that rekindled my interest. That and a subsequent live album Iain did with the Dutch pianist Egbert Derix called *Afterwords*. Since then I have collected almost everything from Iain's vast back catalogue; this is a man whose work ethic has seen him release original music in almost every year since 1967.

In 2010 Iain and I met for the first time when I organised a gig for him at a music-loving pub near where I live. We became firm friends. In 2012 he asked me to write the sleeve notes for a recording he made for the Verve label. I jumped at the chance; after all, this was the label that released Billie Holiday and Ben Webster records back in the 1950s. Iain then asked me at least twice a year if I might help him write his memoir. In 2017 we finally got around to it. I travelled to his home in the south of The Netherlands and we sat at his kitchen table as he told stories. One day I asked him to tell me his personal favourite records from that back catalogue. Plainsong's *Amelia* album was still high in his top ten. The tales he told about the band that made that record were fascinating: stories of huge record deals, the tensions caused by differing personalities within a small unit, the constant touring and promotional work, the pressures of commercial success versus the pursuit of the muse, and the inevitable creative differences. All set against the exhilarating atmosphere of the early 1970s music business. Worthy perhaps of a book of its own.

But how to tell the story of a band from fifty years ago who released just one album and then fell apart? Are there enough people around who can really remember what went down? Sadly,

David Richards and Bobby Ronga are no longer with us, but Iain and Andy's friendship and collaboration continues and I have been fortunate to utilise their first-hand accounts for this book, as well as the memories of Sandy Roberton who managed and produced the band. Andy gave me access to a wealth of archive material housed at Liverpool John Moores University that has helped me join together all the various dots, including a diary kept by the band's road manager, driver and photographer, Harry Isles, that details day-to-day activity. Further material comes from a scrapbook of press cuttings that Iain has kept. Andy also put me in touch with John Cornelius, who had worked as Plainsong's roadie. John died not long after I started corresponding with him, but he gave me an unpublished memoir with a large section on his days with Plainsong which he kindly gave me permission to use.

Once the story started to unfold, I made contact with a whole host of musicians, fans, agents and journalists who were around at the time. Richard Thompson was generous with his time, as was the man who founded the Elektra label, Jac Holzman, who wrote to me in lockdown from his home in Hawaii. And the fans, those who actually witnessed Plainsong in concert, went the extra mile to help, some of them rooting around in attics to find handwritten diaries.

Unless otherwise stated, all contributions that follow are taken from personal correspondence I've gathered during the research for this book and the stories Iain told me for his memoir *Thro' My Eyes*. I have also drawn from contemporary reviews and media reports, as well as press comments from the band members in the years that followed. Taken together they have helped me weave a tapestry that illuminates a particularly interesting time in the history of popular music, the heady days of the early 1970s.

1972 was a leap year. It was also a year when two seconds were added to the extra day in order to synchronise time with the rotation of the earth. This made it the longest year yet recorded. 1972 was a pivotal year in popular music; the giants of the 1960s continued to perform and release important new records – The Rolling Stones unveiled *Exile on Main St.* in May, and Van Morrison put out *Saint Dominic's Preview* in July. In America,

Neil Young released the *Harvest* album, Steely Dan recorded *Can't Buy a Thrill* and The Nitty Gritty Dirt Band collaborated with the cream of the old-time country players to create *Will the Circle be Unbroken* which proved that the young, long-haired hippie generation could hit it off with players from the 1940s. At the other end of the scale, Lou Reed came to Trident Studios in London to record the pop art/glam rock classic album *Transformer*. The pop charts in Britain reminded us that this was indeed the year of glam rock. T. Rex released *The Slider* album, David Bowie unleashed Ziggy Stardust and Roy Wood, having moved on from the Electric Light Orchestra, formed Wizzard. Beyond the brashness of glam, beneath the make-up and sequins, Plainsong flew in the face of much that was going on at the time. There was a distinct lack of the use of electricity, no pyrotechnics on stage, certainly no make-up and mirrored top hats, and no encouragement to see my baby jive or advice about how driving Rolls-Royces is good for our voices. Plainsong were never going to fall for rock'n'roll excess. Theirs is a story of the eternal conflict between making good art and the commercial and personal pressures that come to bear.

The first part of this book tells the story of the band's origins, leading up to their formation at Iain's Highgate flat just before Christmas in 1971. The second part follows Plainsong's adventures throughout the whole of 1972. When I first spoke to Iain about the possibility of this book, I suggested that the story should be told warts and all. 'It can't be anything other then that,' he said. Andy and Sandy agreed that a lot of water had flowed beneath the bridge since 1972 and it was time to set the record straight.

Ian Clayton, Featherstone

PART I
CALL THE TUNE

Overleaf: Andy Roberts, Bobby Ronga, Iain Matthews and Richard Thompson with a Mercury Records rep (centre) backstage at The Troubadour in Los Angeles, August 1971.

1. My Front Pages

Saturday 28th November 1970 was a cloudy day in England; an area of low pressure had arrived from America to sit over the west coast, bringing with it occasional rain carried on a gentle breeze. At three o'clock in the afternoon, if you dialled your radio to 247 meters on the medium wave, you'd find John Peel and his producer John Walters presenting *Top Gear* on BBC Radio 1. Featured on the show was a session from the band Matthews Southern Comfort, current darlings of the airwaves and music press. Their performance included a Neil Young song 'I Believe in You' and an Iain Matthews composition called 'And Me' from the band's recently released album *Later That Same Year*. In Manchester, music fans were preparing for a live performance at Manchester University Students' Union headlined by Matthews Southern Comfort with support from the psychedelic folk band Dando Shaft.

Peter Cowley, a 16-year-old music obsessed son of a tobacco and confectionary shopkeeper, wrote in his diary that evening: 'Worked at Dad's shop. Went to see Man Utd. Went to see Matthews Southern Comfort.' Now retired to the Cotswolds, Peter remembers the day.

Peter Cowley: I went to work in my dad's shop on Stockport Road in Levenshulme. I left there at lunchtime and travelled to Old Trafford to see United play against Huddersfield Town. It was a 1-1 draw and George Best scored for us. His teammates that day included Bobby Charlton, Dennis Law and Brian Kidd. Then I went to the university to see Matthews Southern Comfort. The only trouble was the Matthews Southern Comfort I saw was without Matthews. The rest of the band did show up but they seemed demoralised and stunned by his absence, especially as the 'Woodstock' single had so recently been number one and was still in the charts. I remember some unfavourable comments being made about Iain Matthews by some of the band members. The word went round that he had walked out on the band that very day or perhaps it was the day before. The performance wasn't very good and a lot of people in the audience, myself included, felt short-changed.

Iain Matthews was 200 miles away in London, holed up in his bedroom with his head under the blankets, refusing to answer the phone or knocks at the door. He had walked out of the band during the soundcheck at a gig in Birmingham the day before. He'd put his guitar back into its case, walked down to the railway station, caught the first train back to London, headed straight to his bedroom and bolted the door behind him. He hid himself from the world for over a week. When he emerged he told the *NME*, 'Matthews Southern Comfort had gone as far as it can and wasn't getting any better. When the horse is dead, you have to get off it.'

★

Matthews Southern Comfort as a concept was the brainchild of Iain Matthews, a young singer-songwriter born in the mainly rural English county of Lincolnshire on 16th June 1946. Iain grew up in the steel town of Scunthorpe where his dad worked in the furnaces. After school he was apprenticed to a local firm of painters and decorators. Outside of work he sang in local beat groups; first in the Classics and then in The Imps, a band who covered songs by The Hollies and The Everly Brothers. A chance meeting in a local coffee bar inspired him to seek the bright lights himself.

Iain Matthews: One evening in The Buccaneer I was introduced to a couple of girls who were from Scunthorpe but had moved down to London the previous year and were home for the weekend. They had a flat in Highgate in North London. One of them worked at Chanel on Bond Street in the West End. They talked about the music, the fashion, the shopping, the culture, the people and the need to escape from small-town mentalities. I listened intently, quietly excited by the conversation. I saw them as adventurers and admired that in them. I was intrigued by their naive worldliness. By the end of the evening I felt convinced that I had to go down to London and find out for myself what all the fuss was about and told them that. They said if I was serious about going I could stay with them a while and check out job possibilities. If it didn't work out I could always come home again. On the outside I remained calm and nonchalant, but inside I was bubbling with excitement. It was exactly what I wanted to do, but I told them that I needed to think about it. I was very nervous, it felt akin to jumping into the deep end of a swimming pool without knowing how to swim. The one thing I knew for certain was that I couldn't wait to get the hell out of Scunthorpe and down into the centre of all that action. I packed the one bag I had, took a bus to the railway station, bought a one-way ticket and was gone.

As a fresh-faced nineteen-year-old, Iain landed in London in the spring of 1966. Following a stint as a shoe salesman at Ravel's on Carnaby Street, he had a spell in the South London surf music trio, Pyramid. In August 1967, he was invited by producer Joe Boyd to meet up with the group Fairport Convention at Sound Techniques studio in Chelsea. They were recording their first single 'If I Had a Ribbon Bow'. Without any great ceremony, Iain joined the band that day and found himself sharing vocal duties with singer Judy Dyble. Fairport Convention had started out making interesting takes on the songs of North American writers like Leonard Cohen, Bob Dylan, Joni Mitchell and a particular favourite of Iain, Richard Fariña. Iain sang on their eponymous first album, after which Judy Dyble was replaced by Sandy Denny. Iain and Sandy shared vocal duties on the second album, the eclectic *What We Did on Our Holidays*. It was on this album that Fairport started to develop their own brand of folk rock with their takes on the traditional songs 'Nottamun Town' and 'She Moves Through the Fair'. Under Sandy Denny's growing influence, the band began to switch their attention to songs from the British folk tradition.

Iain Matthews: Sandy brought a wealth of unsung traditional material to the table and I was both puzzled and threatened by that. The music was alien to me and the band was embracing it wholeheartedly. I had been perfectly happy with the direction we were moving in. I wasn't an instrumentalist back then, I only had my voice to fall back on. The band had no fear of improvisation, so it was left to me to thump around on a conga drum, trying to contribute something of my own to that alien music.

The artistic differences piled up as Fairport continued to pursue and reinvent that 'alien music'.

Iain Matthews: I felt I wasn't putting any more into it. It was like Fairport were standing at one end of the stage and I was standing on my own at the other. I left knowing I didn't want to do what they were doing, but not sure what I was going to do.

Iain was asked to leave Fairport Convention just as they were starting work on their third album, *Unhalfbricking*, in the spring of 1969.

Iain Matthews: It's the first and only time in my long career that I've been asked to leave a band. I silently vowed there and then that it would be the last.

Iain continued to live in the house at Brent in North London that he shared with Fairport bandmates Richard Thompson and Simon Nicol. He took guitar lessons from Richard and sought advice from the DJ John Peel as to what to do next. He sat with Peel in the office of his mews house in the West End of London. Peel asked him what he was currently listening to. Iain said he liked the contemporary American songwriters. Peel said, 'You know what it's like to be on a stage, you know how to sing and you have studio experience, don't let any of that go to waste.'

Iain found himself some managers in the shape of Ken Howard and Alan Blaikley. After tasting success by writing pop hits for The Honeycombs and Dave Dee, Dozy, Beaky, Mick & Tich, Ken and Alan had been looking to investigate other forms of music in order to pursue artistic and critical acclaim. Within weeks Howard and Blaikley organised for Iain to become the first British artist to sign to a label called Uni, a division of MCA, with a three-album deal. By June of 1969, Iain was in the studio making his first solo album. He pulled together a stellar cast of players, a mixture of old mates from Fairport — Ashley Hutchings, Simon Nicol and Richard Thompson — and the cream of the folk-rock scene in England: drummer Gerry Conway, Dolly Collins and Pete Willsher, plus the steel guitar player Gordon Huntley, who at the time was making a name for himself as the go-to session man on that distinctive instrument.

In the autumn of 1969 Iain wrote a letter to his mum and dad:

> [The record] will be coming out on January 3rd which is a drag because it means waiting a couple more months, but the company said the earliest it could be put out was the middle of December, but it would be lost in the Christmas rush (plus the fact that the cover takes five weeks to be printed). It's a beautiful cover. I had my own way with every bit of it, it's one which opens out like a book. The photographs are really great. There's one on the front, one on the back, and one right across the inside. Remember Steve Hiett (Pyramid) well he took the photos, he's a full-time photographer now. Anyway, I got an advance in royalties of, would you believe, £3000. By the way don't worry about Fairport, they're doing ok. All our love, Ian and Chris.

Iain referred here to the recovery the members of Fairport were making after a horrendous crash on the M1 motorway after a gig at Mothers in Birmingham. While driving back that night, their van overturned and drummer Martin Lamble, who was just nineteen, and Jeannie Franklyn, a girlfriend of Richard Thompson, were killed. The rest of the group were badly injured, particularly Ashley Hutchings who suffered severe facial injuries and a broken pelvis. Iain himself ended up in the same hospital ward as his mates after collapsing on seeing the extent of their injuries.

Iain Matthews: After the Fairport road accident it didn't feel right living in the Brent house with them anymore. I needed to break away from Richard and Simon and that whole Fairport thing and find a life of my own. My girlfriend Chris was uneasy there too and the accident was the final straw. Chris lived half at home with her mom and half with me. We needed to feel more like a couple and be independent of all that. Chris found a house in Hampstead. A rental. It was just the top floor really, but cosy and secluded. She really liked it and the rent was affordable, so we moved to Hampstead.

In the letter to his parents, Iain doesn't tell his mum and dad what name was on the sleeve of his new album. When he'd seen the first draft of the cover and saw the name 'Ian Matthews' he realised he wasn't yet ready for a solo career. It brought him out in a panic and he asked his managers if it could be changed. Ken and Alan gave him 24 hours to come up with a new name. Iain drew inspiration from a song called 'Southern Comfort' by Canadian folk duo Ian & Sylvia and added 'Matthews' to the front of it to come up with something that he felt sounded like a band name. Ironically, having decided on a solo career after moving on from Fairport, Iain was steering himself towards a band, almost by default.

The album was released at the beginning of January 1970 and was critically well received. Chris Welch in his review for *Melody Maker* wrote:

> Undoubtedly the best album released by a British crew for some time. It features a happily refreshing new band based on country rock and led by singer Ian Matthews. One is immediately struck by the unpretentious quality of the music.

In 2007, Iain talked to David Wells who was compiling sleeve notes to a CD reissue of a Matthews Southern Comfort album.

Iain Matthews: It was always understood that I would tour on top of the album. Gordon Huntley said he would like to get out and gig and I had friends who I wanted to play with, like the guitarist Mark Griffiths and the drummer Roger Swallow who had been in a band called Harsh Reality.

Roger Swallow: There has been connective tissue between Iain and I ever since the morning I woke up bleary eyed and shivering in Hell Field on the Isle of Wight, back in 1968. Smile, the band I was in that day with Mark Griffiths, performed their one and only gig, save for a long forgotten Granada TV show. We awoke in the early hours. The dawn light fell on activity on the stage and a vaguely seductive, jangly sound bathed our ears. I wandered close to the stage attracted by this new idea and approach, a male/female soaring lead vocal and a subdued, unsmiling mystery band that mesmerised even at that ungodly hour. This was my introduction to Fairport Convention. I first met Iain in 1969 when Marc Ellington introduced us in a fast-food cafeteria at the bottom of Edgware Road near Marble Arch. Iain told me of his intentions to form a band. I liked him immensely and I enjoyed his clear insight into, and deep knowledge of, the California counter-culture. Marc, being American, hosted a Thanksgiving feast at the flat in Upper Norwood he shared with his wife Karen. The party coincided with the release of Fairport's *Liege & Lief* album. I drove down from my parents' house in rural Northamptonshire in a milk van and picked Richard, Simon and Iain up in North London to drive them over the river. It was at that party that I approached Iain and asked him if he might consider my best friend and bandmate Mark Griffiths and me for the band that became Matthews Southern Comfort. Coincidentally, before I got the chance to sit with Iain at the kitchen table to broach the subject, there was a note telling me to call Ashley Hutchings. I called him from a payphone at the bottom of the stairs. Ashley too had decided to move on from Fairport and wondered whether I might join him in a new band. I thanked him but said I had to decline and I gave him the reason why. I then went up the stairs to the kitchen and asked Iain. To mine and Mark's delight, Iain agreed.

Around that time I inherited a flat in Golders Green from Richard Thompson complete with a four-foot tall poster of Joni Mitchell.

Mark Griffiths: When the offer to join Matthews Southern Comfort came, I was working with Roger Swallow and the banjo player Keith Nelson. We had an idea to form a bluegrass band with an American musician called Carl Barnwell who lived at Norwood with his wife. We were going to call ourselves Chilcott Green.

Iain's cold feet about being a solo artist meant that the band was put together with great haste. Roger Swallow and Mark Griffiths were joined by Carl Barnwell on guitar, a student called Peter Watkins came in on bass, and the veteran steel guitar player Gordon Huntley, who had already expressed an interest in touring, was the sixth member. The album was released as *Matthews' Southern Comfort* and the title that Iain had suggested 'sounded like a band name' then became, without the apostrophe, the name of the touring band.

Matthews Southern Comfort had not only recorded an album before they actually existed as a band, but they also appeared on television before they appeared in public. On 24th January 1970 they performed alongside the band Chicken Shack on a late night BBC Television show called *Line Up's Disco 2* presented by the DJ Tommy Vance. *Disco 2* ran for two series and was a forerunner to the celebrated *Old Grey Whistle Test*.

On 1st February 1970, Matthews Southern Comfort were booked to play their first ever concert at Mothers in Birmingham. They shared the bill with Fairport Convention and Fotheringay, the new band Sandy Denny had formed after she too had flown the Fairport nest. Iain gave a press conference in a London pub a few days before the gig. He told one of the journalists there that he was full of apprehension about Matthews Southern Comfort's debut concert. 'It'll be all down to me,' he said. He went on to give a detailed interview with Chris Welch of *Melody Maker* which appeared under the heading 'A drop of Southern Comfort'. Welch reported that on the way to the interview at a city pub, Iain had 'been threatened by two youths of a violent disposition in a public railway carriage, he retained his cool and resolve to beat the obstacles put in the path of the ambitious by Man and the fates'. He described Iain clenching a great mug of ale firmly by the handle and through clenched teeth saying, 'I know it will succeed, I know it will.' Looking towards the gig at Mothers, Iain said, 'I'm incredibly nervous. Richard, Simon and Tyger played on the record, but I've got my own band together now. The drummer is Roger and there is Peter on the bass... and there's Carl and Mark.' Welch suggested Iain looked worried as he tried to remember their names. He added, 'Ian is confident that country rock will grow in popularity and he's going to sing that way anyhow. Shucks.'

Mothers was a rock venue on the High Street in Erdington, a suburb five miles to the north of Birmingham. Though it closed at the beginning of 1971, the building these days displays a blue plaque on the wall. It operated in a space above an old furniture store. Many of the biggest names in rock music visited, including Fleetwood Mac, Jethro Tull, Led Zeppelin and the American bands, Moby Grape and Canned Heat. Pink Floyd recorded parts of the live section of their *Ummagumma* album there.

When Matthews Southern Comfort arrived at Mothers that Sunday night, their minds must have been concerned with putting into practice what they had just days to rehearse. The band had driven separately from Iain as they realised how nervous he was to be playing his first real show as a leader. Ken and Alan had Iain travel with them in their white Rolls-Royce. The minds of the members of Fairport Convention must have been on the last time the band had played there, just nine months before, when they suffered the fatal accident on the drive home.

Chris Welch was at the Mothers gig. He wrote:

> Three rousing yihahs for a fine new group. Matthews Southern Comfort impressed with a beautiful set of tasteful country rock and folk of a kind rarely produced by English bands. Ian Matthews can be proud of his new band, and his old friends from the Convention were obviously pleased at his success. The band maintained an intelligent volume level which enabled us to hear the steel

guitar playing of Gordon Huntley and the most groovy lead wailing of Mark Griffiths.

The band drove back to London straight after the show and less than 24 hours later they recorded a BBC Radio 1 *Top Gear* session for John Peel. They played one of Iain's songs 'What We Say', a traditional shanty called 'Blood Red Roses' that Richard and Mimi Fariña had recorded, and an Arlo Guthrie tune called 'My Front Pages'. The session was broadcast on 14th February.

By March, Matthews Southern Comfort had replaced two members. Andy Leigh, who had played in Spooky Tooth, came in on bass for Peter Watkins, and Ray Duffy, an original member of the group Marmalade, was now behind the drum kit. Duffy's bass drum still bore the name 'The Gaylords', the name of the band before they changed to Marmalade. This new line-up began work on a second album against a background of buzz in the music press that suggested country music was going to be the next big thing. In his column 'Peter Cole's Beat', under the headline 'Country Cash-In', the journalist predicted that 1970 would be the year when country music would show itself in every department of popular music, citing the recent work of Bob Dylan, Johnny Cash and the Nashville group Area Code 615. Iain told Peter Cole that after listening to Rick Nelson and some Everly Brothers country music he realised this was what he wanted to sing and write himself. Peter Cole suggested that this might be a following of fashion. Iain told him, 'I'm afraid people will think that I'm doing it because it's hip to sing country, but for me it's 100 percent genuine.'

The band were to play at the very hip Friars Music Club in Aylesbury on Monday 23rd March. For the princely sum of eight shillings, Friars management promised in their press release 'an incredibly beautiful band… They have some superb four-part harmony vocal arrangements' and added 'we will certainly never be able to afford them again so don't be a twit and miss them'.

A few weeks later in a press interview with Caroline Boucher of *Disc and Music Echo*, Iain offered insight into a band that had now been together for just three months.

Iain Matthews: Within the group I'm not terribly easy to get on with. If somebody's not playing very well I have a terrible habit of making them play worse. I was really getting on top of everyone. We said, 'Okay, we'll do three more gigs and call it a day.' But the second of the three gigs was great, the best we've ever done, and it's just got better and better. So we sat down and talked about things we should say to each other and things we shouldn't, because no one would say anything before, I didn't know I was upsetting everyone. So it won't happen again. It's nice being the leader, because everything we do I more or less choose. I don't like to have total say, I take notice of everyone, but there's only me that knows the direction I want to go in, so I've got to dominate in most things. When a group starts initially it goes through stages of getting off the ground, then there's something pretty big that happens, then there's a spasm when nothing really happens and you just go along and get tighter and tighter, which is what we're doing now.

On 5th July, Matthews Southern Comfort had fun at a traditional country fair at Oakwood Park in Maidstone, Kent. The filmmaker Tony Palmer made a short documentary of a performance that featured Fairport Convention, a troupe of performing chimpanzees and a team of helicopters. There were jigs, reels, balloons and ice cream galore, and an eclectic audience of picnicking families and hippies. The two songs that feature on the film are 'My Front Pages' and a good version of 'Southern Comfort'. In an interview conducted about the film, added as an extra to the DVD issued in 2007, Tony Palmer recalled that the director Michael Winner had been asked to make a film with Matthews Southern Comfort, but knowing little about contemporary music had passed the idea on to him.

The appropriately named second album, *Second Spring*, was released that month. It was partly recorded at Morgan Studios with engineering by Robin Black, and at Sound Techniques with John Wood behind the desk. The record had more than a country tinge to it and kicked off with a song Iain composed in the bluegrass style called 'Ballad of Obray Ramsey'. Ramsey was an old-time banjo picker whose music Iain had discovered and liked. The journalist Jim Bickhart gave a warm review for the LP.

> It is another testimony to Mr Matthews's increasingly evident tastefulness. MSC's version of James Taylor's ballad 'Something in the Way She Moves' is rivalled in appropriateness by the composer's own version. It is easily the best cover version yet afforded to a Taylor number. The group manages the tricky feat of adapting well to American folk music.

Bickhart also mentioned the shifting rhythms and melodic lines on the last track 'Southern Comfort', the song by Sylvia Tyson that had given Iain the idea for a band name in the first place.

The album had a cover design based on the Southern Comfort liqueur bottle label. Somehow Iain's managers Ken and Alan had struck a deal with the makers of the drink. Iain recalled in his memoir that cases of the stuff would show up from time to time. The rumour was that a similar deal with Janis Joplin in America had afforded her a $2,500 lynx fur coat.

Despite Iain's previous assurances that the tensions within the group had been resolved, they soon reappeared over financial as well as creative matters.

Iain Matthews: The band were on a wage and I paid them a fair weekly amount as our profile grew, but still they wanted more. Ken and Alan thought they were a very good band and that I should hold on to them at all costs. I understood the thought behind that. They wanted me to consider giving the band a share of the action. I listened patiently and eventually agreed to give each of them a ten percent share of my royalty. Fifty percent in total. They still complained. By then Carl Barnwell, a more than decent songwriter, had visions of being a lead singer. His songs were included on the album and, as a gesture of faith in his talents, I also let him contribute a couple of lead vocals. He was already ahead of the others financially and visually, but he seemingly wanted more. At a certain point, in order to bring sanity back to the band, I reluctantly let Carl go. We played a couple of shows without him and spent the entire evenings looking across the stage at each other wondering what the hell we'd done. There was a piece of the puzzle missing and we all knew what it was. Mark Griffiths said, 'I think we've made a mistake letting Carl go. Do you think we can ask him back?' We asked him the question and thankfully he re-joined us.

Mark Griffiths: Carl was a peaceful, understanding guy from California. Iain was never sure what he wanted to do, but it was his band. We were all a bit green really, unprepared for the fame.

The band went straight back out on tour and started to build an enthusiastic following. One reviewer signing off simply as 'Mark' mentioned Iain's spoken introduction to an encore at one of the shows: 'Ian Matthews commented, "I don't know what you're getting excited about, we're only a group."'

Iain and his 'only a group' recorded almost monthly radio sessions for the BBC throughout the summer of 1970. On one session in June they were told that there was room for one more song. Earlier that week, Iain had been out to buy the latest Joni Mitchell album *Ladies of the Canyon*. He liked a song on it called 'Woodstock' and suggested that the band work up their own arrangement. This radio recording has never found a commercial release, unlike many of the other radio sessions, so we may never know what the arrangement sounded like. It must have impressed because within days the BBC were inundated by requests from listeners who wanted to know where they could buy the record. With such obvious demand, Howard and Blaikley persuaded the band into Morgan Studios in Willesden Green where they recorded a second arrangement of the Mitchell song. Crosby, Stills, Nash & Young had already recorded a hard rocking version, Matthews Southern Comfort's take on it was much gentler.[1] The single was released on 24th

---

[1] Iain has always claimed that he prefers the Crosby, Stills, Nash & Young version of the song. At the beginning of August 2019, the modern day line-up of Matthews Southern Comfort played at Wickham Festival in Hampshire on the same bill as Graham Nash. Iain bumped into Nash backstage. Five decades after both musicians had covered the same song, Nash told him, 'Your version of "Woodstock" was the best.'

Top: Iain Matthews and Sandy Denny line-up of Fairport Convention.
Bottom: Matthews Southern Comfort with Joni Mitchell.

July and the following day the band performed it on TV with a second visit to the Tommy Vance presented *Disco 2*. On the same day, the record label took out an advert in *Melody Maker* announcing the single as a 'special release'. A fortnight later, with the song hovering on the edges of the Top 50, the band were singing on *Top of the Pops*, Britain's popular chart music television programme introduced that evening by the DJ Tony Blackburn. Despite this early media exposure, sales of the record stalled. Then, during October, Tony Blackburn, who at the time presented BBC Radio 1's popular breakfast show, made 'Woodstock' his record of the week. Sales increased sharply and promotion on two more episodes of *Top of the Pops* meant the record started selling 30,000 copies a day.

On Sunday 25th October, Matthews Southern Comfort were invited to share a bill at the London Palladium with James Taylor. Taylor brought along his then girlfriend, Joni Mitchell. The expectation was that she would join Taylor on stage, instead she sat knitting in the wings. Four days later Joni came to a recording of *Top of the Pops* and agreed to pose for photographs with the band. She then travelled the short distance from BBC TV Centre to the Paris Theatre in Lower Regent Street, where she performed with the help of James Taylor. The show was recorded for an *In Concert* BBC radio broadcast. It is a splendid recording and gives the listener a real idea of the laidback style of show that performers of that ilk were giving at the time. Two days later on 31st October, the day a monsoon called Louise swept through Indochina and all but put a stop to the Vietnam war, Matthews Southern Comfort's version of 'Woodstock', with Joni's verse about jet bombers 'turning into butterflies', replaced Freda Payne's 'Band of Gold' at number one in the British pop charts. 'Woodstock' had featured on *Top of the Pops* almost every week throughout October and this run continued into November. The band also appeared live on a BBC2 television show fronted by country singer George Hamilton IV.

In an interview with *Melody Maker* published on 21st November, Iain talked about the meeting with Joni.

Iain Matthews: I apologised to her for changing the melody of 'Woodstock' because I couldn't reach the high notes. She said it was all right, and that she preferred it that way.

In the same *Melody Maker*, Iain was asked for his views on country music. 'I'm not sure I want to play it anymore. I found playing country is so limiting. There are three basic country rhythms. The rest of the band are just getting into it and I'm starting to get out of it.'

Getting out of country wasn't Iain's only problem. He was tiring of Gordon Huntley's steel guitar and tiring of all the hype and publicity that a number one hit carried with it. In an interview with Roy Carr, published in the *NME* on 21st November but conducted at least a week before (it was trailed in the previous week's issue), Iain spoke of his frustrations. Carr had come to talk to Iain about the success of 'Woodstock' and the possibility of a follow-up. He got more than he bargained for.

Iain Matthews: If I was really silly about things I could quite easily destroy my career. The trouble with me is I'm far too self-critical. Success has made me more of an introverted person, I even find myself not wanting to answer the phone when it rings. On the last few gigs I've found that after we have played 'Woodstock' we just can't go wrong. Up until we play it, people kinda hold back. I'm sure that the majority of them only come along to hear us do it. I didn't realise at the time that leading my own band could prove to be such a strain. I suppose I could start by realising that there's more than just me in the group. Everyone could see that it was getting a bit too much for me.

There exists some rare film from this time made for a French programme *Pop Deux*. The band sing 'And When She Smiles'. Iain looks pale and worn out and he's certainly not smiling.

In the days following this bombshell interview, Iain's managers found themselves having to issue press releases to explain the situation, hinting that in future Iain and the band might record separately. There was also a matter of a new contract. Iain had originally been contracted for three albums and, with the third album about to be released, his managers were looking to secure a new deal. They had been in talks with The Beatles' label, Apple, and The Rolling Stones' own label. The managers were talking about six figure sums and claimed things were looking promising, though the Rolling Stones label were backing away. It seems that Marshall Chess who was then president of the label liked Matthews Southern Comfort, but Mick Jagger thought that they weren't funky enough.

Matthews Southern Comfort's third album in eleven months, *Later That Same Year*, was released on 20th November. In an interview with Chris Welch for *Melody Maker* published just before the release, Iain said, 'Lately I have realised that you can play soft music louder.' Iain invited Welch to his home in the leafy suburb of Hampstead and squatted on the floor as he talked through a tape of the album track by track. Meanwhile, back up in Scunthorpe, the local newspaper *The Scunthorpe Telegraph* visited Iain's parents and reported that steelworker Allan MacDonald and his wife Dorothy of Enderby Road were feeling pretty proud of their lad's breakthrough and that Matthews Southern Comfort would be playing at Cleethorpes Winter Gardens on 15th November. In an another feature in *Melody Maker,* Iain was asked again about his hit record. He said, 'It's a stepping stone. It's disturbing to me that people come to see us now because of the hit.'

Then the balloon went up. Those music fans out early to the newsagent on Thursday 26th November to pick up their copy of *Disc and Music Echo* were greeted with the headline 'Matthews Quits Southern Comfort'. Iain had told the paper, 'I can't say anything because I have been told not to, but I am not denying it.' No doubt his colleagues in the band read that paper and by the time of the soundcheck at Birmingham Town Hall the following night we can easily imagine the atmosphere. Iain only got as far as the soundcheck before walking out, heading home and locking his bedroom door.

Mark Griffiths: When Iain disappeared during the soundcheck, we had no idea where he had gone. I took a phone call about two or three hours later. It was Chris, Iain's girlfriend. She said, 'Iain has just come home and he has told me to tell you that he is not coming back.' I had to tell the management at the venue. I think we made up a story about Iain not being well and somehow we did the gig with Carl taking lead vocals. Gordon couldn't get it, he just couldn't understand what was going on.

The following week the music press had a field day. The band's drummer Ray Duffy told *Melody Maker*, 'We had talked about it earlier this year and thought we would stay together until the New Year. But last week Iain suddenly decided that he would do no more dates and we had to do two by ourselves. We went down well considering we had to rehearse our act in the car on the way to the gig.' Iain's managers Howard and Blaikley commented in the *NME*, 'Anyone who knows Iain Matthews will realise that he is a very impetuous person, he always wants to move to pastures new.'

Mark Griffiths: The number one took us all by surprise, but what should have been the happiest time of our lives didn't work out that way. It was a big regret for me. Matthews Southern Comfort was my first real band.

Iain Matthews: It felt that everyone wanted a little piece of me and very little of it had to do with music. It became all about promotion, when in my mind it should have been about creation. I lived in a fantasy world where I thought I could just write, record and play. If I could have hired someone to do the talking for me I would happily have given them the job. I had Howard and Blaikley telling me I needed to do this, do that, go there, say this, don't say that, don't worry you can do that later. Ad infinitum. I then began taking those frustrations home with me at night. I became dark and moody with lots of deep unresolved anger and that in turn affected my relationship with Chris. She couldn't seem to comprehend what I was feeling when everything appeared to be going so well and began to back away from me. I had no one I could speak to about it and what should have been a joyful period in my life became an unbearable load.

The teenager Peter Cowley, who had leapt to his feet on the Old Trafford terraces to cheer Georgie Best's equaliser on that overcast afternoon in November, couldn't have known then that on their way up the M6, the band whose single he had bought and enjoyed and who he was going to see that very evening, were rehearsing an improvised show without their lead singer. And he could never have known the torment that singer was going through behind locked doors, with blankets over his head, in his leafy suburban apartment.

Iain Matthews: When Ken and Alan called I insisted that Chris answer it and refused to speak to them. I let Chris do my talking and when she'd eventually had enough, we stopped answering the phone altogether. They reverted to slipping messages under my door, to which I didn't or couldn't respond. I was in a very dark and confused state. I saw no light. That was more or less it for Matthews Southern Comfort. I couldn't face the band. Remarkably, all this was happening with 'Woodstock' still in the Top 10. Mark Griffiths later told me that the rest of the band let it go and moved on, but apparently Gordon had told them he was going to kill me. Knowing of his physical abilities, I believed it and that scared me. It was well and truly over and the band made the decision to carry on without me. They signed a deal with Harvest records, eventually changed their name to Southern Comfort and made three more albums.

The Jimi Hendrix single 'Voodoo Chile' had replaced 'Woodstock' at number one on the pop charts. It stayed at the top for just one week and, in the very week that Iain locked himself in his house, Dave Edmunds replaced it at number one with a cover version of a New Orleans rhythm and blues song. He sang 'I hear you knocking, but you can't come in'.

Iain remained grounded for nine days. He ventured out to

watch The Flying Burrito Brothers in concert at The Lyceum on Sunday 6th December. The morning after the gig he talked to *Melody Maker*. He told them, 'It's hard to explain why I left. I saw The Flying Burrito Brothers in London last night, Southern Comfort should have been like that.' *Melody Maker* asked him if he thought quitting would damage his career. 'I don't think so. There was a lot of mental strain on me being in a band. I'm not cut out to be a member of a group. I'll make a solo album and maybe next April or May do some acoustic concerts with some friends. Do it that way instead of having a permanent group.'

2. A Picture from the Cover of Melody Maker

When Iain started work on his solo album, he would meet and work with a musician who was to become a lifelong friend and collaborator. 'Brothers from another mother,' in Iain's own words.

Andy Roberts was born just four days before Iain in Hatch End, near Harrow in Middlesex on 12th June 1946. He studied violin from the age of nine, got hold of a plastic ukulele at ten because he wanted to play skiffle, and on his thirteenth birthday he was presented with a Spanish guitar. A year later he had an electric guitar.

Andy Roberts: My dad worked in the legal department for the Post Office. Mum was head of filing at the Institution of Electrical Engineers. She worked in a building on the Embankment that fronted onto The Strand, two doors away from The Savoy Hotel. Before the war she had worked at the Foreign Office, from where she was recruited to assist the then Prime Minister Stanley Baldwin. She worked for him during the abdication crisis. At the age of 25 she caught polio and it affected her for the rest of her life. She had been Foreign Office tennis champion several years running and she was a great horse woman, a real spark. The polio left her with little feeling down her right-hand side. She met my dad on a train at the start of the war. They were married within ten days and then he went off to be a sub-lieutenant in the navy; first on the Atlantic convoys and then on a gunboat in the Mediterranean. He hadn't been back from the war long when Mum found herself pregnant with me and not long after that they decided they didn't really like one another. I was brought up by an elderly housekeeper called Mrs Wakeley. She told me that when she was a girl she had seen horses cooling off their hooves after pulling stage-coaches down the hill at Stanmore.

Andy's parents were well enough off to pay for his early education. He later obtained a scholarship and studied at Felsted, an ancient private boarding school near Braintree in Essex founded in 1564 by the Baron Richard Rich. He was the villain who did for Thomas More.

Andy Roberts: At school there was a band called Flash Sid Fanshawe and The Icebergs. They played guitars they had made themselves in school workshops. The guitarist was a lad called Rick Brown who went on to play with Screaming Lord Sutch. I sat and watched them rehearse. They were all lanky lads with quiffs. I thought it was the coolest thing I had ever seen. In the school holidays I went to stay with my grandpa in Merthyr Tydfil. Grandpa loved America; he had been born in Cheyenne, Wyoming. He played 78rpm records for me on an old wind-up gramophone. I loved a record made in 1929 by Jack Hylton and his Orchestra called 'I Lift Up My Finger and I Say "Tweet! Tweet!"'. The B-side was 'Shinaniki Da', I liked that even more. I guess I developed a liking for tunes and harmonies by listening to Grandpa's record collection. Then I heard The Everly Brothers and Buddy Holly's Crickets.

Andy formed his own school band, Monarch T Bisk and The Cherry Pinwheel Shortcakes.

Andy Roberts: I was a music scholar, so it was expected that I should perform. Our band had a psychedelic name but we covered mainly Howlin' Wolf and Muddy Waters stuff. We played school concerts and we were once hired by Henry Reekie, the headmaster, to play for his daughter's birthday party. In 1964, when the school celebrated its 400th anniversary, there was a big ball and we were invited to play at that. After school, when the band split up, some of us amalgamated with guys from another band called The Princes. In 1965, before I started university, we performed at The Eel Pie Island and had a short residency at the Eros Club. By then we were called Blues en Noir, which was a play on the term 'Blousons Noir', the French name for Teddy Boys.

The brother of the drummer in the school band wrote a revue for the 1965 Edinburgh Festival, which gave Andy his first opportunity to perform music in front of a paying audience. That same year Andy got a place to study law at Liverpool University. He took his guitar with him.

Andy Roberts: On the day I got there I bumped into the poet Roger McGough in a bookshop on Renshaw Street. Roger suggested that we might collaborate on poetry and music stuff. In February 1966 I did a thing with him at The Bluecoat Theatre in Liverpool. It just took off from there. Within a couple of months I was doing poetry events at the Everyman Theatre and playing with a band at the university.

By early 1967 Andy had recorded an album with Roger McGough and Adrian Henri entitled *The Incredible New Liverpool Scene*.

Andy Roberts: We recorded it at Regent Sounds in Denmark Street after a gig. The whole thing took just two hours. When I came home from university for the summer, I heard John Peel's pirate radio show *The Perfumed Garden* for the first time. It was broadcast from a ship called *The Galaxy* in the North Sea just off Clacton, on a station called Radio London. The signal didn't reach me in Liverpool, but I could tune in at my parents' house in Middlesex. Peel played an eclectic pick of folk, blues, Captain Beefheart, Jefferson Airplane, and he mixed it with poetry and readings from *Winnie-the-Pooh*. One day he played some of the album I'd done with Adrian and Roger. I was a student, just twenty years old, and I was on the radio. I saw in a music paper something about an underground night at the Roundhouse. The advert mentioned the DJ would be John Peel. I wanted to meet him, so I just turned up and introduced myself. I said, 'Sorry, I believe you're John Peel.' He looked at me. I said, 'I'm Andy Roberts, the guitarist on the Liverpool album you've been playing on your show.' He smiled and said, 'Oh! Brilliant!' At that time Peel lived in a basement flat off the Kings Road. I used to visit him there. We drank whisky and talked about music. On Friday nights he got sent the new releases schedule from record companies. I liked to sit watching him play them. As soon as he came to something he didn't like he whizzed it like a Frisbee straight into the coal fire. There was a flow of black tar under the grate in his hearth. He came up to Liverpool to hang around with us. I lived in Canning Street with Adrian. John wrote an article after his visit for *The International Times*. It appeared under the headline, '64 Canning Street. A Modern Day Parnassus'.

In the spring of 1968, Andy swapped his modern Parnassus for Paul McCartney's house in Cavendish Avenue, St John's Wood. Paul's brother Mike McGear and Roger McGough were recording some demos – later released under the title *McGough & McGear* – at De Lane Lea Studios with Paul McCartney producing. Andy played guitar on all the tracks.

Andy Roberts: Mike wrote the tunes, but he wasn't a player, so I became the conduit between him and the other players, jotting down the chords. We recorded a suite of poems called 'Summer With Monika', which Roger and I had first done for our first poetry event at the Bluecoat. Every time the door opened in the studio a picture from the cover of the *Melody Maker* walked in. Graham Nash came to do backing vocals, as did Paul's girlfriend Jane Asher. I think Paul just went round to The Scotch of St. James or The Bag O'Nails and said to whichever musician he found there, 'I'm doing a record with our kid.' In that way he brought in Jimi Hendrix and Dave Mason from Traffic, who turned up with a sitar. Paul played piano on some of the album. I used to get a ride back from the studio to St John's Wood in Paul's Aston Martin with him and Jane Asher. On another occasion I was meeting Mike at Paul's house, so I took the tube to St John's Wood and walked up to the house. I had no idea I would have to run the gauntlet of gangs of teenage girls to ring the bell on the electric gate. All this and I was still a law student wondering how I was going to make my living.

Andy graduated with a law degree in July 1968. He immediately set out to be a professional musician. On 6th September he signed a publishing contract with Chappell and Co. and went into the recording studio with The Liverpool Scene, a band that comprised Andy on guitar and vocals, Adrian Henri on poetry, Percy Jones on bass, Mike Hart on guitar and vocals, Brian Dodson on drums, and Mike Evans on saxophone and poetry. He also found himself playing on a record that went to number one in the pop charts. Mike McGear, Roger McGough and John Gorman had for some years been members of a modern day music hall group called The Scaffold. They'd had a hit with 'Thank U Very Much', a comedy song sung in the Scouse accent. In 1968 they became the Christmas number one with a cleaned-up version of a bawdy song called 'Lily the Pink'.

Andy Roberts: I actually wanted the B-side to be the A-side. It was a lovely little song called 'Buttons of Your Mind'. Nicky Hopkins played harpsichord on it and I played an intricate double time bit. I was really proud of that. We recorded it at Abbey Road Studio 2 with top session men; Herbie Flowers was on bass and Clem Cattini on drums.

Liverpool Scene approached John Peel and asked him to produce their first album, *Amazing Adventures Of*.

Andy Roberts: John built a small stable of acts that he liked. Whenever he was asked to do DJ work at the clubs he would virtually insist that one of Tyrannosaurus Rex, Principal Edwards Magic Theatre, Davy Graham or The Liverpool Scene would be on the bill. John introduced me to Sandy Roberton. The introduction was quite formal, we handwrote letters to one another. It was Sandy who came through with the RCA deal for The Liverpool Scene album Peel produced. John had no idea about the technicalities of producing a record, but we wanted his name on it.

The album that followed was called *Bread on the Night*. This time Sandy Roberton was the producer. The closing track was a very funny skit on the British blues music boom called 'I've Got Those Fleetwood Mac Chicken Shack John Mayall Can't Fail Blues'. In June 1969 they toured on a three-band bill with Blodwyn Pig and Led Zeppelin. In August they played the Isle of Wight Festival on the same day as Bob Dylan. The following month they set off to tour America. They stayed for three months and came back £5,000 in debt.

Andy Roberts: The American tour was a strange experience. As part of the reciprocal agreement between musicians' unions either side of the Atlantic, I think we went there when Duke Ellington and His Orchestra came here. Adrian Henri and I had gone over two weeks in advance to put our ears to the ground, get a feel for the place and write some new material. Most of our show relied on parochial Liverpool humour and landmarks like Sefton Park. We knew we couldn't do Sefton Park jokes there. There was a worry amongst us that the Americans wouldn't understand us and whether they would get the humour and philosophical standpoint – where we were coming from in all senses. The promoter was a man called Dee Anthony, a big, thickset bloke with a strong Brooklyn accent. He handled Joe Cocker and Ten Years After. We walked into his office and he said, 'You can call me Uncle.' His agency was called Bandana. On his desk there was a pot of pencils and on each pencil in gold leaf was the word 'Bandana'. Adrian drew one of the pencils out of the pot and said to Uncle, 'Would you mind if I take one of these?' Uncle said, 'Sure, go right ahead.' Adrian took one and then asked, 'Have you got any bandanas with Pencil on them?' Uncle just looked blank. The surrealist transference never quite transferred. It was at that point that we both realised we might have difficulty with our brand of humour. We did. We still had fun, but we came home with nothing to show.

In 1976 Andy gave an extended interview for the winter edition of a small circulation quarterly music magazine called *Fat Angel*. He reflected on his experience of the tour Liverpool Scene made to America.

Andy Roberts: Dee Anthony saw us play one of our usual lunatic gigs at a pub in Welwyn Garden City and said, 'Yes, okay, I'll take you over.' So we went over and he proceeded to promote us exactly as he promoted Savoy Brown or Blodwyn Pig. Of course, for a band doing what we were doing, it was the kiss of death. In Detroit at the Grand Riviera Theater we played two nights on a bill that was topped by The Kinks, then Joe Cocker, then Grand Funk Railroad, then Liverpool Scene, and the opening act was The James Gang, with Joe Walsh on guitar. It was crazy, very few people even noticed us. You think when you're going there that you're going to be a star – 'Good Lord, somebody actually asked us to go to the States, we've made it!' – and when you get there you are the smallest fish in the biggest possible music scene in the world. You've got to play all the games, the only way you can get across is through hype and advertising and all that, and we weren't prepared to do that.

When they came back from America they stumbled on, touring and paying themselves £20 a week wages. One night at a show in London the stress of low wages, incompatible elements and constant touring came to a head.

Andy Roberts: Liverpool Scene broke up on stage at the London School of Economics on 6th May 1970. The arguments carried on into the dressing room, with me and Adrian on one side and Mike Evans and Percy on the other. As soon as I hit that dressing room I thought 'Fuck it'. We were all pulling in different directions. Percy wanted to be a jazz player, I wanted to be a pop star like Steve Miller, and Mike Evans had got married and his wife Sue had just had a baby while we were in America. As a mother she wanted to put a stop to his gallivanting. We phoned Sandy Roberton up and told him what had happened and we never played again. I went to Liverpool the next day and cleared out of my thirty bob a week room. I set off to my parents' house to lick my wounds. On the way back I dropped by to visit a girl in Wakefield and then called in to see my friends in Principal Edwards Magic Theatre.

Top: Liverpool Scene, New York, 1969.
Bottom: David Richards and Andy Roberts (sat with guitars) and Adrian Henri (stood) in Mölde, Norway, 1970.

This was a performance art collective, made up of musicians, poets, dancers, singers and light show specialists who lived communally at the village of Moulton in Northamptonshire.

Andy Roberts: I hadn't been there long when I had a motorcycle accident in the farmyard. I ended up at Northampton hospital. My mother drove up to collect me and I nursed more wounds than I had bargained for.

It was while Andy was recuperating from the accident that Sandy Roberton introduced him to David Richards at Sandy's September Productions office.

Andy Roberts: After the break up of Liverpool Scene there was still a contract we had to fulfil. It was a four-night tour in Norway organised by The Norwegian Book Club, a huge organisation that was run by the son of Thor Heyerdahl, the Kon-Tiki explorer. We made up a band of me, Adrian Henri, a lad from Liverpool called Alan Peters on trumpet, John Pearson on drums, and David Richards on bass. It was the first time I had worked with David. We were treated like superstars.

In 1969 David Richards was in a band alongside Paul Kent called P.C. Kent. The pair reached out to Sandy Roberton. Sandy had a deal with RCA Records to bring them new acts. He liked the demos that P.C. Kent brought with them and signed them up. Sandy then produced their album *Upstairs Coming Down* at Trident Studios with the engineer Ken Scott, who had worked on The Beatles' White Album. Although still just 21 years old, David was a versatile musician; as well as acoustic guitar, he played bass, piano, harpsichord and sang on the P.C. Kent record. The band broke up after just one album.

David's younger sister Hazel recalled how important music was to her brother.

Hazel Richards: David was passionate about music as far back as I can remember. Our mother played rudimentary piano, she came from that generation where everybody had a piano in the parlour and they would gather round to sing the old songs. So, even though we grew up in post-war austerity and we weren't a wealthy family, we had a piano at home. David played the piano and the organ at our local church. In the 1960s David decided to turn the family piano into a honky-tonk instrument by pressing drawing pins into the hammers so they hit the strings. He also took up guitar and practised in what we called the summer house at the bottom of the garden. We lived in Perivale, not far from the famous Hoover factory. Our garden backed onto a railway cutting. On my way home from school it always thrilled me to hear music crossing the railway line from our summer house. David was a very good guitar player and gave lessons to other budding guitarists from home. David was a bright lad too. He made it from the wrong side of the tracks to grammar school and continued to progress his music. He was also an extremely sensitive and kind person. When it came to my time to study A-levels at grammar school, I struggled a bit at first. Everybody seemed to have their own friendship groups and, because I came from a different school, I felt left out, a bit of a non-entity. I was sixteen then, David would have been twenty-two. He saw that I was unhappy. One day he brought a picnic and his guitar and sat with me at lunchtime on the green in front of the school. We ate our picnic and then David played his guitar for me. When I went back into school the other girls suddenly became interested in me. They all wanted to know who was the handsome young man with the guitar.

Andy got on well with David. On returning from Norway they decided to work together.

Andy Roberts: David played bass but was also a fine high harmony singer. We took an old stone cottage in Amesbury in Wiltshire to work on some ideas. It was the era of getting it together in the country. My solo album *Home Grown* had been released earlier in the year by RCA. After Liverpool Scene broke up, Sandy recovered the rights to it and reissued it on B&C

Records – Beat and Commercial – in a re-sequenced and remixed form. David played bass on the record. I also fancied some steel guitar on the title track. I had heard Gordon Huntley's work with Matthews Southern Comfort, so I hired him to play on that album too. David and I then put a band together that we called Everyone. We had John Pearson on drums, a guy called John Porter who I met in Newcastle was another guitarist, and he introduced Bob Sargeant, an organ player with a big bluesy voice.

The band recorded one album with Sandy Roberton producing.

Andy Roberts: We played our first gig on the Thursday at the Isle of Wight Festival, so that dates us to August 1970. In November 1970 we had a gig at Southampton University. We had two roadies, Andy Rochford and Paul Scard. Andy had met up with a girl and decided to stay in Southampton with her. Paul drove us and the band's gear back to London. We went to John Pearson's flat to come down. We drank some tea and smoked some dope. The phone rang. It was Andy Rochford. He said there had been a change of plan. He wanted to bring his girlfriend back to London and asked Paul if he could drive back to Southampton to pick them up. Paul agreed. On the way back, near a roundabout on the A30 at Basingstoke, a lorry with a flatbed trailer hit some ice. It jack-knifed and hit the van that Paul, Andy and the girl were in. Andy and the girl were laid down in the back and escaped the worst of the impact. Paul was killed outright. He was just nineteen years old.

Everyone folded following the car crash. All of their equipment was destroyed and the band were too distraught to continue.

Andy Roberts: The whole band was deeply in shock. I can barely remember Paul's funeral. A doctor dosed me with something and I was in a trance. Up to then my life as a musician had been one of constant touring. I was adamant that I wouldn't ever tour again.

Andy reflected on the trauma of the accident in an interview with Rosalind Russell in *Disc and Music Echo* published on 6th November 1971.

Andy Roberts: I wouldn't want to be responsible again for anyone else. [Paul] was close to me and had a great personal loyalty towards me and I realised that in a way I was responsible for his well-being. If the crash had happened two years earlier, I might be sitting in a solicitor's office right now. I have a degree in law. But by then the music was ingrained in me and I couldn't imagine doing anything else. It's a pity in a way because sometimes I feel I'd like to have a band.

After the Everyone crash, Andy rented a cottage next to Moulton Grange, a couple of miles from where Principal Edwards Magic Theatre lived.

Andy Roberts: My mother found the cottage at Moulton while browsing through a copy of *The Lady* magazine. She suggested that I needed some thinking time and encouraged me to take it. I was there for about three or four weeks. I didn't socialise too much. I believe I went to a nurses' dance one night and then an old girlfriend, the actress Polly James, who was starring in *The Liver Birds* visited because she was concerned about my welfare. Polly was great. She had given me some surreal experiences over the years. She took me to Tommy Steele's New Year's Eve party in Richmond the night he hired a full Scottish pipe band and another time I had tea at the Savoy with her and Anthony Perkins. I could barely talk with the image of him in *Psycho* in my mind. Then David Richards came to stay and we started working on some songs.

Some of these songs later appeared on Andy's *Nina and The Dream Tree*, another album produced by Sandy Roberton that featured David Richards on bass.

3. If You Saw Thro' My Eyes

Iain's managers Ken and Alan had wasted no time in getting him a new recording contract after he left Matthews Southern Comfort, this time a three-album deal with Vertigo records, a subsidiary of Philips.

Iain Matthews: I liked the idea of Vertigo from the very first moment I walked in there with Ken Howard and saw a huge portrait of Rod Stewart hanging in the foyer. I thought, 'Yep, I want to be on the same label as Rod.'

Iain's attention now turned to making his first proper solo album.

Iain Matthews: My friend Marc Ellington had played me Cat Stevens's album *Tea for the Tillerman* and I loved the sound of the record. I noted that it had been produced by Paul Samwell-Smith. Paul was one of the first musicians I was aware of who had made the transition from player to producer. He had been the bass player in The Yardbirds and had now built a solid reputation as a producer. Cat Stevens was his current and most impressive calling card. I asked Ken and Alan if there was any way they could convince him to produce me. They said to leave it to them.

Ken and Alan got their man and it was through Samwell-Smith that Iain and Andy Roberts got together for the first time just before Christmas in 1970.

Andy Roberts: I talked on the phone to Mike McCartney who told me that Paul Samwell-Smith was looking for a guitarist to work with Iain Matthews. I had never met Iain, but of course I knew who he was. I talked to Paul on the phone, he said he had been brought in to produce Iain's first album and asked me if I would go to spend time with him to see if there was a chemistry. I went to Iain's flat in Hampstead. We talked some and we played some. Iain had a song called 'Desert Inn'. I worked out a little guitar motif for that and Iain liked it. Then we discovered that we both had a liking for backgammon, so we played that for the rest of the afternoon. I think it was the backgammon that cemented it.

The two young musicians also shared the recent trauma of having lost friends in road traffic accidents.

Andy Roberts: I was back at my parents' house in Old Church Lane, Stanmore and still trying to come to terms with the loss of Paul Scard when Paul Samwell-Smith called. I had to make a living, so I thought I could do it by becoming a session musician.

Andy joined Iain at Morgan Studios in Willesden to work on the album that Iain would call *If You Saw Thro' My Eyes*. At the same time and at the same studio, Samwell-Smith was also producing the latest work from Cat Stevens, an album called *Teaser and the Firecat*.

Alongside Andy, Iain assembled many familiar faces from the folk-rock scene. Keith Tippett played piano, Gerry Conway was behind the drum kit, Pat Donaldson played bass, Tim Renwick from the group Quiver and Richard Thompson were on guitars. The track 'Southern Wind' required backing vocals and a trio of Doris Troy, Liza Strike and Nanette Workman provided these. Doris and Nanette had sung backing to The Rolling Stones' 'You Can't Always Get What You Want'. Iain's old bandmate Sandy Denny came in to play harmonium and he persuaded her to add a sparse piano accompaniment as well as a vocal to the title track. This duet plus Tim Renwick with spare guitar backing created a startling and minimalist masterpiece. Iain describes it as 'a cry for understanding'.

Iain Matthews: 'Thro' My Eyes' came to me fully formed in a dream. I woke up in the middle of the night with it running through my head. I got out of bed and wrote all the lyrics down on a piece of paper. In the morning I'd forgotten about my dream until I found the paper on the coffee table.

Andy Roberts: At Morgan Studios I learned from masters. I didn't really know how to record or anything about how singer-songwriters worked. I learned everything about how to make a record from Iain. I had never met anyone who knew so much about songs as he did. We got there before 10am and stayed until around 7pm. I couldn't wait to get to work every morning. I learned how to sit down, because I had always stood up to record previously, how to behave, how to adjust microphones. There was a cafe upstairs. They used to do a special mixed grill. Danny Thompson the bass player was always there for one of those. He called it 'a plate of train smash'. No amount of money could have paid for the tuition I got from Richard Thompson and Iain. It was an education made in heaven. Iain knew so much about music and had the impeccable taste to find songwriters nobody else had heard of. He was also the obvious leader and nobody questioned that. He was the one with the ideas and moreover the one who'd had the global hit. If you did think that something he suggested might be not quite right, you just clenched your eyes and concentrated on the upside. With Iain you looked at the talent and then you gave in.

The making of the album wasn't without its problems. Just a few weeks into the recording sessions it became clear that Paul Samwell-Smith's mind was not on the job he'd been contracted to do.

Iain Matthews: He started coming in late to the sessions and one day he didn't come at all, he just called to cancel. I was disappointed. The album was important to me. I had a career to be getting on with. It transpired that Paul was having domestic problems and was also under pressure to work with Cat Stevens. I decided to soldier on without him and produce the album myself with the assistance of Robin Black our engineer.

After Samwell-Smith's departure, Andy suggested to Iain that if he needed help with the production he knew someone who might be willing to sit in and guide. Andy brought in his good friend, Sandy Roberton.

Andy Roberts: I said to Iain, if Paul can't do it I know a man who can. Sandy knew how to do everything, he was a brilliant organiser and never let you down. I thought Sandy was on Iain's wavelength.

Iain Matthews: Andy's instincts were spot on. On his own time and at his own expense, Sandy was invaluable on my first production. He came down to Morgan at the drop of a hat and solved whatever quandary we were in. In hindsight, I wish I had thought to credit him as co-producer.

Sandy Roberton: I'd first met Iain backstage at a concert. I had been using Matthews Southern Comfort's steel guitar player Gordon Huntley on sessions and he had invited me to a Matthews Southern Comfort show at Ewell Technical College. I was introduced to Iain, but it was just a 'hello' at that stage. Andy was the one I knew well, back to the days of Liverpool Scene. It was Andy who made the call to me to ask if I would help with the *Eyes* album, perhaps at the start of 1971. It was then that all three of us became properly acquainted.

Andy spoke about making the album to Lon Goddard of *Record Mirror* at the beginning of March.

Andy Roberts: Right now, I'm doing a session with Iain Matthews for his coming album and it's going to be great. The material is fantastic. There's nothing I can do to promote the Everyone record without a group. The prospect of being a solo guitarist isn't so bad. An acoustic guitar is like an orchestra at your fingertips. Of course, I'm not exactly the acoustic Alvin Lee, but I want to please listeners as well as impress myself. Davy Graham taught me 'the only person you should be in competition with today, is yourself yesterday'. In a sense, I am starting over again.

In the same month Iain did an interview with Jerry Gilbert for *Sounds*, just as he was putting the finishing touches to his album.

Iain Matthews: I'm going to use all the people I'm using on the album. I've asked everyone and they have all agreed that when it's time for me to do a gig, they'll do it with me. It's nice to work that way. I don't really want to be part of a band again because there's too much depending on one another to start with – and because everyone has a say in what you do, your own total ideas can never come across.

Within weeks Iain was telling the music press that he was thinking of buying a farm in Cornwall to spend more time with his girlfriend Chris and, if he's to be taken at his word, he'd already flipped on the idea of being in a band once again, having gathered together 'Andy Roberts and David Richards from the old Everyone group, and Richard Thompson'.

Iain Matthews: I'm thinking now in terms of an all-guitar line-up, some acoustic and some electric. We'll probably call ourselves the Pear Drops. I don't want to have to work live more than two nights a week, so I would have plenty of time to spend at the farm. I only want the house, not the farm.

Even before *If You Saw Thro' My Eyes* hit the shops, Iain was out on the promotional trail, being invited to do radio appearances to feature songs from the album. On 13th April, accompanied by Andy, Richard Thompson, Pat Donaldson, Gerry Conway and Ian Whiteman at the piano, he recorded a *Sounds of the 70s* for Bob Harris at BBC Radio 1. They performed 'Hearts' from the album and the Bob Dylan song 'It Takes a Lot to Laugh'. A month later on 17th May, they were back again to do a *Top Gear* show for John Peel as a trio of Iain, Andy and Richard. The session included the first public performance of 'Thro' My Eyes'. Songs from the session were broadcast on 5th June and repeated on 28th August, when Viv Stanshall stood in for a holidaying John Peel and offered surreal observations about Iain and his music.

The album *If You Saw Thro' My Eyes* was released on May Day 1971. 'Hearts' was released as a single a week earlier. The album was received well by the critics. Karl Dallas of *Melody Maker*, a long-time supporter of Iain's music, visited him in his Hampstead flat to listen to it.

> If I hadn't heard it myself with my own two ears I mightn't have thought it was possible: Ian Matthews has produced a hard, swinging, ACOUSTIC album. It swings like a bitch. Ian, who has always been his own toughest critic, is very happy with this new album. He has reason to be, for it is undoubtedly the best thing he has ever done. One always plays the first after-the-split album with mixed feelings of fear and hope. In Ian's case, for me this was also mixed with an anxiety that it was going to be another one of those boring folk-rock super sessions. After all, with Sandy Denny, Pat Donaldson and Gerry Conway, as well as Richard, it could almost have been Fairport-Fotheringay revisited, but when I suggested this as a remote possibility Ian looked really hurt. In addition to having produced the best songs he's done so far, and singing them better than ever before, it is very well produced indeed. The instrumental revelation of the album is Andy Roberts, who has come a long, long way since I first heard him playing Spider John Koerner-type stomping blues in the Edinburgh Festival. He can now afford to stand up and be recognised as a master of that difficult area, acoustic rock.

In June, Iain flew to America to do a series of press conferences in major cities to sell the album and talk up a tour that would take place in the autumn.

Iain Matthews: I took my girlfriend Chris with me on the press tour. We had a good trip and saw Philadelphia, Boston, Chicago, Detroit, San Francisco and of course New York. Before we went I made a film at Elstree Studios with the people who had worked on the album miming to the songs they had sung on. Sandy Denny was on it miming with me to 'Thro' My Eyes'. We had a film projector and showed that film at every press conference. The American journalists loved it.

On the trip, Iain was taken down to the Jersey Shore for a photo shoot by the pre-eminent sixties folk photographer, David Gahr. In New York, he met up with Paul Nelson. Nelson was originally from Minnesota, where he founded the *Little Sandy Review*, a magazine dedicated to the folk music revival, and went on to write for *Sing Out!*, *Village Voice* and *Rolling Stone*. In Los Angeles, Iain spoke with *Broken Arrow*, a small circulation Californian music magazine. The article they published gives a flavour of that press tour.

> He didn't have a permit to perform, but he shook a lot of hands, went to radio stations, and appeared at a few 'get-togethers' which Mercury put on by inviting both the press as well as disc jockeys. After Chicago, Detroit and San Francisco, he landed in Hollywood at the Continental Hotel on Sunset. There he chatted with about thirty people while that same evening across town Kris Kristofferson opened at The Troubadour. On one wall of the plush Continental banquet room a film was repeatedly shown. It showed Ian, his band and Sandy Denny singing and playing four cuts from his album. The highlight, amid all the visual effects, was watching Ian and Sandy weave their voices in simple harmony as they sat in total envolvement with the song.

The magazine described Iain as a man of few words, not shy but quiet and unassuming. He was probably tired of the constant probing by less sensitive journalists at that point. Witness the exchange between Iain and Bob Hamilton of *Radio Report* in Los Angeles.

> – Do you ever consider the impact a song will have on the people of the world after you have written it?
> No.
> – It never occurs to you?
> – No.
> – Have you ever met songwriters, are you yourself one, who are concerned with the situation in the world today?
> – Yeah.
> – Do you ever use your music to influence people toward what you think would be a better trip?
> – Well, maybe, very indirectly. I have never really written

about other people. I can't write about world affairs or anything like that.

– Let me take this from another viewpoint. The United States government, of late, has been involved with a certain amount of censorship of records because they say the records being played on Top 40 radio are influencing the young people toward drugs. They are saying songwriters are responsible for what will happen when people listen to these songs. Is it fair to a songwriter to carry this responsibility?

– Maybe some good songs will never get written.

Iain went across town to see Kris Kristofferson at The Troubadour. He was impressed. He spoke to Karl Dallas of *Melody Maker* just after he got back from his promotional tour. In an article published at the beginning of July, he told Dallas, 'People said it was the best he'd ever performed and I can believe it, just acoustic guitar with a very lightly played bass, an electric piano and another acoustic guitar.'

The article was notable for the forthright way in which Dallas started off. 'Here is an urgent message to the pop people of Britain: if you're not careful, you're going to lose Ian Matthews to America.' Iain was relaxing in a BBC bar after taping a performance for the TV show *Disco 2*, where he had played tracks from the new album. He told Dallas, 'After America, the music scene over here just seems so petty. At every level. Their radio set-up makes our BBC look like Noddy's Radio Station.'

It seems Iain couldn't wait to get back to the States. He didn't have to wait long. Howard and Blaikley had organised a tour to start at the end of July. In the meantime, Iain was back in the studio to start on his second album. Again he recruited Richard Thompson and Andy Roberts alongside guitarist Tim Renwick and drummer Timi Donald.

Iain Matthews: No sooner had we finished *If You Saw Thro' My Eyes* than Vertigo were asking for more and we soon began work on a follow-up, my seventh album in less than three years. I hadn't had time to conceptualise my thoughts and experiences;

I was still easing myself away from the previous album and these new songs were more a collection than a concept. A few of my tunes are about the struggles to come to terms with balancing a soaring career and a relationship; 'Morning Song' and 'Hope You Know' are blatant relationship songs.

Iain had also secured a couple of high-profile concert appearances over the summer. On Sunday 27th June he appeared at the 11th National Jazz and Blues Festival, known these days as the Reading Festival. It was the first time the festival had been held in that town. Andy and Tim Renwick backed him and he was sandwiched on the bill between Rory Gallagher and Medicine Head.

Tim Renwick: I had known Iain for a little over six months when we played Reading. I remember being very nervous because I believe we were under-rehearsed. I played alongside him and Andy Roberts on his first solo album. I don't know how he knew about me. He just gave me a call one day and came along to one of the many one-nighters I performed with the band Quiver. We hung out a little and he played me loads of great records by US country artists. He had a wonderful record collection. I also really liked Iain's voice.

Reading 1971 went down as a year of bad weather and aggressive tactics from the Thames Valley Drug Squad, who seemed to consider the festival a personal assault on their patch. The magazine *Frendz* reported:

> People arriving at Reading were stopped and searched as they drove into the town or as they got off the trains. The Thursday before the police had stated that no random searches would be made. But on Saturday the Assistant Chief Constable of the area, Mr Eric Gregory, when confronted with the facts, said that 'You could call these random searches.' The following week the police reaffirmed their statement that random searches had not been made. This implies that all the searches were made on reasonable grounds. Said ADE, 'It's going to be hard to

Tim Renwick, Iain and Andy at Reading (top) and Taverne de L'Olympia.

prove they had reasonable grounds to make 2000 searches when they only made 150 arrests.'

The weather was rough and the fields turned into a swamp, prompting *Frendz* to inform its readers that 'For three days, three thousand people sat in the mud and the rain listening to second rate groups over a very inadequate PA system.' The *News of the World* simply described it as 'a jamboree of pot and pop'.

Iain recalls little of the kafuffle at Reading that year.

Iain Matthews: I just remember playing my black Gibson J200. And I didn't have that guitar much longer, because later when I went on my American tour Glenn Frey saw it and just had to buy it. I went to America with a Gibson and came home with a Martin D-28.

Iain was still playing his Gibson when the trio of himself, Andy and Tim Renwick moved on to Paris to record a TV show at Taverne de L'Olympia for the *Pop 2* programme. The show was recorded on 30th June and transmitted on 24th July. They played, 'Close the Door Lightly', 'Desert Inn', 'Hope You Know', Andy's song 'Radio Lady' and 'Please Be My Friend'. Iain introduces the first song by telling the audience that it was a song he had sung in a band called 'The Fairport Convention'. Someone by the side of him chuckles, Iain apologises in case he hasn't said that modestly enough. He is nervous, this is only his second live concert since leaving Matthews Southern Comfort. He wonders aloud if the French audience can understand what he is saying. Later he tells them, 'We're not really a band or anything, we're just very good friends.'

Andy Roberts: After I met Iain I started doing my work for Musicians' Union rates. I was still living at my parents' house. Within six or seven months I had earned enough money to put down a deposit on my own first house. I looked in the *Evening Standard* at a section they had called 'Homes under £5,000'. I found a place at Bushey in Hertfordshire with farmland at the end of the road. I was able to put down a £2,000 deposit.

By the summer of 1971, as well as finding a new home, Andy had almost completed work on his *Nina and The Dream Tree* album. Iain's American tour was imminent and he asked Andy to leave his new home and his new album to join him along with Richard Thompson. It was then that Iain's girlfriend told him that she was pregnant.

Iain Matthews: I felt a little uneasy about going to America in the light of Chris's announcement. But I was bull-headed and single-minded, there would have been no stopping me.

4. It Never Rains in California

Iain, Andy and Richard Thompson flew to New York in the last week of July. There had been plans for Timi Donald on drums and Dave Richards on bass to join the tour, but that didn't come to pass.

Andy Roberts: It was going to be an electric band and then we decided, well Iain decided, that it wasn't going to be a very good electric band, which I think it would have been, but he didn't fancy all the rehearsing, so we went over as an acoustic trio.

The trio stayed in New York's bohemian Gramercy Park Hotel and spent a week rehearsing in Vanguard Studios. Vanguard was home to many of the great names of the folk revival; Joan Baez, Buffy Sainte-Marie, Hedy West and two acts who were already influencing Iain as a songwriter, Richard Fariña and Ian & Sylvia.

While Iain, Andy and Richard were ensconced in Vanguard Studios, just up the road in Midtown Manhattan on 1st August George Harrison along with his friend and mentor Ravi Shankar successfully organised The Concert for Bangladesh at Madison Square Garden. Money raised by the concert went to the relief of refugees from the old East Pakistan displaced by the war of liberation. It was an all-star affair supported by Eric Clapton, Leon Russell, the group Badfinger and Billy Preston amongst others. George's old bandmate Ringo Starr found himself gently tapping a tambourine on the heel of his left hand as he accompanied Bob Dylan on a rendition of 'Love Minus Zero'. Coincidentally, George and Ringo's old bandmate Paul McCartney chose this same week to announce that he was ready to fly with his new group, Wings. Meanwhile, the fourth member of the popular beat combo was involving himself in more direct political action. The Scottish firebrand union leader and communist party member Jimmy Reid organised a 'work-in' at the Upper Clyde shipyards to protect the jobs of thousands of workers. John Lennon and Yoko Ono declared themselves supporters of the cause and sent a cheque for £5,000. The joke amongst the shipyard workers that did the rounds at the time was that they thought 'Lenin' was dead.

At the time, Richard Thompson was just 22 years of age and had left Fairport Convention earlier that year.

Richard Thompson: I left Fairport as a gut reaction and didn't really know what I was doing, except writing. I was doing a lot of session work as a way of avoiding any serious ideas about a career.[2]

The first concert of the tour took place on Tuesday 3rd August at a youth community centre in Wheaton, Maryland. Wheaton, a small town once known for its sawmill and farm land, was hardly rock'n'roll central. Yet throughout the 1960s, the youth centre, based in a gymnasium opposite the local library, had proved the maxim 'If you build it they will come' many times over. Ron Fritts, who has researched the local music scene in Maryland and Virginia, believes that local promoter Bud Becker was approached by a talent agent called Richard Halem to take several of his acts for shows in the Maryland/Virginia area to support forthcoming album releases.

Iain Matthews: My managers Ken and Alan didn't really know anybody in America, so the tour was organised through the Philips label's agreement with their American outlet which was Mercury Records. I guess the plans for where I should play were quite vague. The scene for singer-songwriters hadn't yet developed in a big way and venues were used to hosting loud bands. Ken and Alan arranged for Bob Schwaid to look after us. Bob Schwaid had been Van Morrison's manager when Lew Merenstein produced the *Astral Weeks* album. A young guy called Bobby Ronga was working for them. One of the girls in Schwaid's

---

[2] *Richard Thompson: The Biography*, Patrick Humphries, Music Sales Ltd, 1997.

office heard about an English band flying in who needed a driver/roadie, and she told Bobby. Bobby volunteered. They gave him the job of road managing and driving us around.

Bobby managed to get the band lost on the drive to Wheaton. He got lost on the short drive to the second gig too, just a half hour drive away over the state border in Virginia.

Richard Thompson: We got lost a few times on the way. We got lost quite often on that tour.

The second concert was at Falls Church, an even smaller town than Wheaton. The venue was another gymnasium. Local woman Susan Sondheimer, who later became a go-go dancer on regional TV, was there.

Susan Sondheimer: I knew the promoter Bud Becker. I worked as a secretary for him. He had an office at a store called Giant Music, they sold instruments, sheet music and records. We were lucky enough through Bud's promotions to see national and international acts in our little town. They also put local bands on to support the big names. Around that time I saw Atomic Rooster, Bob Seger, Rory Gallagher and of course Iain Matthews. The gymnasium had bleachers to sit on and floor space for dancing. Iain played to a full house. I didn't know his music before I went but we kids were thrilled to have him there. He was dressed in yellow, I recall I wore a red peasant dress, hip for the time. It's long ago now, but I know I enjoyed the show because I bought Iain's album.

After the two gymnasium warm-up shows, Iain, Richard, Andy and their driver Bobby headed back to New York. They rehearsed some more and at that point it was apparent that Bobby wasn't just a driver with a poor sense of direction, he was also a fine musician. Iain invited him to join the band on stage.

Iain Matthews: Bobby had turned up at the rehearsals all bright and bouncy and began his tour managing duties. It became clear on day one that he was a competent bass player. He could also play guitar and piano. He was an enthusiastic talker, who clearly wanted to get something going for himself. I told him I couldn't afford to pay him any more but he was welcome to join us as a performer. I believe he went back home for his bass and amp that very same day. We tried a couple of songs with him and it felt good. He jumped at the opportunity for no extra money to play with us. So he tour managed, drove and played. He was very efficient at all three.

Robert R Ronga was born in Kingston, New York on 23rd December 1946. Kingston was an old settlement, badly burned by the British during the War of Independence. The young Robert graduated from Highland High School and formed a band called The Teddy Boys. He later joined Pinocchio & The Puppets for whom he wrote their only single 'Fusion', a psychedelic rock song released on the Mercury label in 1967. He also appeared on the soundtrack LP *We're The Banana Splits*, a bubblegum pop record released to cash in on the popularity of the American TV series of the same name.

Bobby Ronga: I really wanted to write. I did some gigs in New York clubs, until a girl in the agency heard that Iain Matthews needed a roadie for his solo tour. Then during the rehearsals I started playing bass and carried on when we went out on the road.[3]

There was a week in the schedule between the warm-up gigs and a residency at The Bitter End, leaving time to hang around as well as rehearse. In his memoir *Beeswing*, Richard Thompson recalled his time in The Big Apple.

Richard Thompson: New York was fine. The two girls from the agency who drove us around for the first few days doing promotion would crank up the soul station on the radio and

[3] Interview with *Let It Rock*, November 1972.

harmonise with everything, and I mean everything, every second of every trip, complete with dance moves, as far as it was possible while sitting and driving. It was thoroughly entertaining. I don't know if they ever had careers, but they were a great double act.

Iain Matthews: Richard bought himself some new guitars in Greenwich Village and I bought a Martin D-28 in Manny's Music store on West 48th Street in Midtown Manhattan. I played that guitar for the rest of the tour.

Andy Roberts: We made visits to the offices of *Cash Box* magazine. I had a friend there called Ed Kelleher. He had a cupboard in the office where all the review records that nobody wanted for themselves were deposited. Ed said I could choose any that I fancied. I did that thing of just going by the cover. There was one LP by Mason Williams, who I knew from his hit 'Classical Gas'. It had a jar on the cover which looked cool, so I took that one. There was a song on it called '(I'm A) Yo-Yo Man' which had a fantastic bluegrass groove to it, with an acoustic guitar part that was the perfect counterpoint to the vocal. Another record I got from the *Cash Box* cupboard was by a Texas band called Laramie. I think it might have been their one and only record. This record is not a musical triumph. In fact, some tracks are so out of tune and rough that it's laughable, but there was a song on there that I liked a lot. It was called 'Farewell First Lady of the Air'. It was about Amelia Earhart who I had heard of but knew barely anything about.

On Wednesday 11th August, the quartet opened for Dion at The Bitter End club on Bleecker Street in Greenwich Village. The shows were well received. Gregg Geller, who was present at the first night of a five-night residency, reviewed the gig for his Club Review:

> Ian Matthews has a past association with successful groups in the English folk tradition, namely Fairport Convention and Matthews Southern Comfort. Now a solo, he is

nevertheless the recipient of excellent back-up in the persons of fellow ex-Fairporter Richard Thompson and Andy Roberts. Ironically, aside from his own lovely tunes which can be heard on his first Vertigo album, *If You Saw Thro' My Eyes*, Matthews selects his songs from American folk singer-songwriters. On this occasion he offered reverent renditions of Richard Fariña's 'Reno Nevada', Eric Andersen's 'Close the Door Lightly' and Paul Siebel's 'Louise'. His voice is a pure, delicate, highly agreeable one. Andy Roberts contributed his own 'Radio Lady', a fine song that could be found on his first Ampex album *Everyone*.

In a review for *Cash Box*, Ed Kelleher referred to Thompson's 'extraordinary dulcimer playing' and asked 'if the thirteenth century was the golden age for troubadours, was Ian Matthews born too late?'

> Actually, although Ian would have functioned comfortably as a lyric poet in a mediaeval court, he is very much a contemporary artist. And while his compositions retain a traditional sound, they are garnished with elements of country and rock. His ventures into the catalogues of other songwriters reflects a strong interest in the best and most individualistic of present day composers, men like Paul Siebel and John D Loudermilk and women like Karen Dalton.

The *New York Times* sent its own reporter who filed a very formal review.

> Mr. Matthews sings and plays acoustic guitar and is backed by Bob Ronga, bass, and Richard Thompson and Andy Roberts, guitar. Mr. Matthews writes most of what he sings. His 'Please Be My Friend' and 'If You Saw Through My Eyes' tend toward being light, melodic and softly sung contemporary songs in the folk vein. There is no strain to Mr. Matthews's voice, just a simple, relaxed quality. In all, his music seems more like uncomplicated entertainment than either insightful poetry or aggressive musical artistry.

Andy Roberts: I adored New York. The bohemian lifestyle was still perfectly possible on a shoestring, compared with the hideous over-priced yuppie enclave that it is now. Greenwich Village in 1971 was the embodiment of an artistic area, with clubs, bars, stores, Washington Square, street life everywhere, and we opened at The Bitter End. Dion was terrific. He hung about outside the club between sets. One night, to Iain's disgust, we were invited to greet Helen Reddy who was sat in the back of a big car dressed like the Queen of Sheba. But the after-show get-togethers at The Gaslight when we hung around with the Mahavishnu Orchestra were incredible.

Iain Matthews: Dion was grounded and approachable. We got on. Right after that tour he recorded one of my songs, 'Please Be My Friend', in a medley on his *Sanctuary* album.

Iain told journalist Jerry Gilbert that he picked up some new songs while in New York, including a Dino Valenti song.

Iain Matthews: Paul Nelson was working at Mercury Records in the A&R department. He was my go-to person. He came to the Bitter End shows. He played me a lot of tapes he had of Dylan singing that few people had heard. Paul went on to be record reviews editor at *Rolling Stone* magazine. He introduced me to the top music journalists; Cameron Crowe who as a teenager was *Rolling Stone*'s youngest journalist, Bud Scopa and Stephen Holden who wrote music reviews for *Rolling Stone* and went on to be the film and theatre critic for the *New York Times*. Paul seemed to know everybody.

Sandy Roberton was in New York on a trip to meet with the Ampex record label at the same time as the residency. He recalled a photo opportunity with Andy in Record World offices and playing pool with Richard, Andy and Paul Nelson.

Sandy Roberton: I had signed a few acts to the Ampex label, my meeting with them coincided with Iain, Richard and Andy being in New York. I went to see them at The Bitter End. That's where I met Bobby Ronga for the first time.

Iain almost got to meet the subject of his song 'Ballad of Obray Ramsey', which he had written for Matthews Southern Comfort's second album. Obray Ramsey had been rediscovered during the folk revival and had recorded an album with the new generation of folk singers – Judy Collins and Eric Andersen among them – called *Fresh Air* that was released in early 1970.

Iain Matthews: We heard that Obray was in town. I would have loved to have met him, but by the time we knew, we were preparing to leave New York.

The tour moved on to Detroit and a club called Poison Apple. The four-night stay followed a similar residency held there the week before by Kris Kristofferson. Iain topped the bill and was supported by David Pomeranz, a 20-year-old New Yorker then promoting his own debut solo album *New Blues*.
Detroit was a city still recovering from the riots that took place in the predominantly black neighbourhoods in the summer of 1967, some of the worst street violence ever seen in America.

Iain Matthews: We stayed in an apartment above the Poison Apple. We were warned to be careful about going out. In Detroit in 1971 it wasn't advisable for a bunch of young white boys to stray too far.

Richard Thompson recalls that the club was on a short block with a 7/11 convenience store at one end, the club itself and a British pub. In his memoir *Beeswing* he suggests that the band thought they might feed themselves from the 7/11 and have the occasional beer in the British pub, where their Limey accents would get them through. He describes striding into the pub one day.

Richard Thompson: It was like one of those Westerns, where the piano player stops in mid-tune, the cowboy about to play the ace freezes in mid-air and all heads swivel towards the strangers who have dared to venture through the swinging doors. We suddenly felt long-haired and wrongly dressed. We got our beers. We drank them promptly. We didn't go back to the British pub.

Andy Roberts: The Poison Apple club looms large in my personal narrative, because that is where I met Karen Goszkowski. She was there on the first night, and we hit it off famously. I was seriously smitten with Karen for a few months. She worked in the travel industry and was taking a sabbatical from her husband.

On 22nd August the quartet flew on to Los Angeles for a six-night residency at The Troubadour. Iain, Andy, Richard and Bobby could not have anticipated the turbulence they were about to encounter. The group were sharing the bill with the soul singer Donny Hathaway. It looked like an incongruous pairing and that's exactly what it turned out to be.

The Troubadour, a nightclub on Santa Monica Boulevard, run by its charismatic owner Doug Weston, played host to the cream of the folk and folk-rock fraternity throughout the 1960s. By the 1970s it was attracting major names across the spectrum of popular music. Richard Thompson had played two residencies there in 1970 while he was still with Fairport. He was therefore known to Doug Weston, though what inspired Weston to pair the gentle acoustic sound of Iain Matthews with a full-on soul music revue was something that probably never escaped his own mind.

Iain Matthews: On paper and on stage he probably thought it looked an interesting combination. The thing he had forgotten to factor in was what the audience might think.

The club held around five hundred people. When the quartet took to the stage, the room was filled with anybody who was anybody in the Los Angeles soul fraternity.

Andy Roberts: That opening night was like the premiere of *Superfly*. Couples all blinged up, with white capes, big shoulders and gold-topped canes.

The skinny white English boys and their long-haired pal from Brooklyn started to play gentle acoustic folk-rock music. It seems that few in the audience realised they had started. If they did, they didn't bother to acknowledge it and carried on talking. Iain and the band tried their best. The talking got louder and then there was one or two cat-calls and some booing. This escalated until the sound from the seats was overwhelming that from the stage.

Iain Matthews: I slowly slouched off the stage, dragging my guitar behind me. The others realised I'd gone and followed suit. Richard, who was bolder than the rest of us, strolled to the front of the stage holding his dulcimer in front of him. 'Ladies and gentlemen,' he said, 'contrary to popular belief, this (meaning his dulcimer) and not the saxophone is your national instrument.'

The journalist Richard Cromelin writing for the *Los Angeles Times*, two days after the concert, reported:

> The Troubadour this week is the scene of one of those unfortunate billings, a pairing whose promise as one of the club's most attractive one–two punches is thwarted by a basic incompatibility between the two acts. Unfortunate Ian Matthews opened the show, but the room was stuffed with Donny Hathaway aficionados so eager to see and hear their hero that they simply trampled Matthews's set under the sharp hooves of their rudeness. Which is a shame, because the former leader of Matthews Southern Comfort is one of the most lyrical singers and interesting songwriters in the British folk-pop genre. In addition, he is accompanied on this trip by two of British folkdom's finest guitarists, Andy Roberts and Richard Thompson. But between entreating the crowd for a bit of quiet and then struggling through the noise when none was forthcoming, he never really got a chance to be as impressive as he can be.

Another journalist present that evening, 't.e.' of *Cash Box* magazine, was scathing about the audience who were described as the most boorish in recent memory.

> Throughout the set, members of the audience (largely on record company tabs, compounding the felony and casting dark aspersions on the manners of the industry as a whole) talked, greeted one another, and made enough noise generally that Matthews twice asked the house to please quiet down. His request was to no avail: things got so bad during the second set, that, after 2½ numbers, the group left the stage entirely. The audience was terrible (providing a strong argument against press parties) even though Matthews and his group performed quite nicely.

The journalists enjoyed listening to Iain's song 'Thro' My Eyes', a version of the Richard Fariña song 'Reno Nevada' and an a cappella version of 'Souling Song', a traditional folk song made famous by Peter, Paul and Mary. 'Souling Song', with the lyrics 'If you haven't got a penny, a ha'penny will do, if you haven't got a ha'penny then God bless you', is a simple song usually sung unaccompanied by groups of children around All Saints Day and Christmastime.

Iain, who idolised the music of West Coast America, thought that he had blown his chance to shine there, but was taken aback by Doug Weston's reaction. Doug cancelled the next five nights, but realising his own faux pas, took full responsibility and proposed that the band come back in a few weeks time to share a bill with the singer-songwriter Randy Newman.

The band had another residency booked to start in Vancouver on 1st September at Gassy Jack's, but the Troubadour cancellation meant that they now had an unexpected week off.

Iain Matthews: Richard liked to drink beer in those days, so he and Andy drank beer and played pool. I tried to do some promo for my album.

Iain's promo duties were not helped by some negative press from a bad case of mistaken identity and his recent past coming back to haunt him. Southern Comfort were touring the East Coast on a bill with Rod Stewart and Deep Purple at the same time as Iain was in Los Angeles. The reviewers were lazily writing that Iain was still fronting the band.

Iain Matthews: I was reading reviews in the press of shows on the East Coast by Southern Comfort. They had continued touring without me and their shows were getting awful reviews, but what made me furious was that I was the one taking the beating in the press. It was bad enough having a difficult time out west, but at least I was actually there on the stage.

Andy Roberts: We were staying in The Tropicana Motel. It was a rundown place, scruffy as hell, the air conditioning didn't work and there was a crack in the swimming pool where all the water had run out during an earthquake. We watched daytime TV, hung around in the bar and rehearsed a little. That area was heaven to me, from The Troubadour down to The Tropicana and Barney's Beanery, it was a proper scene.

Iain Matthews: I believe Andy had heard about The Tropicana, it was what you might call a rock'n'roll hotel. It was on Santa Monica Boulevard, near to The Troubadour. At the time Tom Waits was living there and you could bump into anybody at breakfast. They had a great breakfast cafe called Dukes.

Andy Roberts: We met Don Everly in Dukes and one time Richard and I got talking to a night porter who told us he played poker every week with Moe Howard of The Three Stooges. Through him we got to meet the great man, who looked exactly like we remembered him from the old shows, except his pudding basin haircut was greyer. He told us he got nothing from all the TV reruns. One day two young musicians from Linda Ronstadt's band turned up out of the blue. Richard had met them the previous year when Fairport came to The Troubadour. We had a few beers and got on really well. They were Glenn Frey and Don Henley. They liked Richard's playing. It was Glenn Frey who told me that when Linda had seen Fairport at The Troubadour she had asked him to join the band. They told us that they were forming their own band, they hadn't got a name yet or a settled line-up, but of course it was the beginnings of the band that became the Eagles. They had got some money from David Geffen to make an album and they were hoping that Glyn Johns would produce it. They were rehearsing behind a Mexican restaurant. Bobby drove us down there, somewhere out in the boondocks, and Richard played with them on some of the songs they were working on for their album.

Iain Matthews: We had a rehearsal space in Hollywood. Glenn and Don came to see us there. They kept saying to me 'Play us a song, play us a song!' Eventually I sang 'Please Be My Friend'. It was only when I finished singing that I realised they were less interested in me than they were in Richard's guitar playing. They asked him to join their band.

In his own memoir, Richard merely states that there were rumours that he had been asked to join the Eagles. He certainly jammed with them behind the Mexican restaurant. 'I got to jam with them on a song, borrowing Glenn's electric guitar, but the strings were like steel cables on a suspension bridge, so I'm not sure I did myself justice.'[4]

Joe Boyd, through whose auspices Iain had joined Fairport Convention, was at his home in Los Angeles that week. He had gone back to America the previous year to work for Warner Brothers on film music. One of his first jobs had been to produce the soundtrack to *A Clockwork Orange*.

Andy Roberts: Joe Boyd took us all to the Warner Studios. We saw the Camelot Castle that Warners had built for the Richard Harris film when he played King Arthur and Vanessa Redgrave was his Guinevere. I didn't really know Joe, though he once booked Liverpool Scene when we were first starting in 1967 for a

---

[4] We can only speculate as to which songs Richard Thompson played on, but the Eagles' debut album had on it 'Take it Easy', 'Witchy Woman' and 'Peaceful Easy Feeling'.

UFO night held at the Blarney Club off Tottenham Court Road. He billed us as 'Liverpool Love Festival'.

After the studio tour the quartet ended up in Joe's back garden, singing and playing music according to Iain; playing table tennis and drinking beer according to Richard. The lads ended the day singing a cappella. Somebody suggested they try the old Crystals song 'Da Doo Ron Ron'. Bobby joined Andy and Richard on harmony vocal. They had great fun singing it, so much so that Iain proposed that they ought to form a band. Earlier in the year, when Iain, Richard and Andy did the BBC radio session for John Peel on *Top Gear*, when asked what the name of the group was Iain gave a jokey reply to a relatively serious question. He looked at the three guitars and said, 'We are The Performing Gibsons.' This time, even though the afternoon of music making had been a few young musicians messing around in the late August sun in a Californian back garden, Iain was serious.

The band of friends travelled north to Vancouver to start another residency, this time at Gassy Jack's bar for a six-night run. Gassy Jack's was a venue where loud, brash acts like the rock'n'roll revivalists Flash Cadillac and The Continental Kids played. The eponymous Gassy Jack was John Deighton, a sailor and bar owner, originally from Hull in England. He was known for his storytelling and constant talking. It seems that the bar that bears his name had a similar reputation. An eyewitness on the first night, Peter Wilson of the *Vancouver Sun*, wrote a story that was starting to become a familiar one under the headline '4 Against 100 is Unfair':

> Ah, the sophisticated Vancouver rock club audience. You can't fool them for a minute. No sir, no way. But what is this? A ripple runs through the crowd. This is no rock'n'roll band. Where's the drummer? Where's the organist? Matthews seats himself on a stool and is flanked by guitarist Andy Roberts and bassist Bob Ronga. Thompson takes the outside stage-right corner. They begin with a quiet ballad. Their music is clean, clear and simple, a joy to the ear. Matthews's voice is soft and lyrical,

and the group works well together instrumentally. But they do not set feet to dancing. This is folk or country or country-folk or something, but it is not rock. At the end of the next piece, Matthews asks the audience to hold it down a bit. 'It would really help things if people didn't talk while we play,' he pleads. What's this? Not talk? Who is he telling us what to do? The music is smothered by half-screamed conversation. Matthews and the group ask if anyone would like to hear good old rock'n'roll. A yell of approval. Then Matthews and his men go and spoil it by doing a New York street singing a cappella. Finally six songs into the set, Matthews, Thompson, Roberts and Ronga quit the stage in enraged frustration. After an hour of negotiation over a bottle of wine it is announced the group will play their last set and then never darken the door of Gassy Jack's again. About half of the patrons leave but the rest stay and encourage the group to play an encore. It is decided then that they will try one more night.

Jeani Read wrote a review of the first night in her 'Nightscene' column under the headline 'Gassy Jack's swine get Ian's pearls'.

> While some music is like sheet metal and relatively impervious to outrageous audiences, some music is like rice paper, wondrous light and delicate in texture, but with little resilience. Do people really have to be numbed into silence by an overwhelming wall of sound? Wednesday night was opening night for Ian Matthews, formerly guiding light of Matthews Southern Comfort, which, if not sheet metal was at least aluminium foil and would have withstood adversity reasonably well. But Ian Matthews is now on his own, with some friends, and they are playing rice paper music, some of the most breathlessly lovely handfuls of melody and lyric that have been offered to a Vancouver club audience in a long while. The first set was something along the order of Pearls Before Swine, and it didn't seem worthwhile to keep going. So Matthews and his friends bowed out until the incessant roar had died down. I think they will stay until Monday night, if the audience that love Flash Cadillac will either stay away or learn how to be flexible. It was distinctly unfortunate that their audience Wednesday was so inexcusably moronic. They missed a tapestry of

Andy & Sandy

Stopping off at Record World during a Bitter End engagement with Ian Matthews are Andy Roberts, right, formerly of the Bonzo Dog Band, and his producer, Sandy Roberton. Roberts' first Ampex album, "Andy Roberts with Everyone," was recently released, as was a single, "Trouble at the Mill," from it.

4 against 100 is unfair

Nightscene
Gassy Jack's swine get Ian's pearls
By JEANI READ

IAN MATHEWS
... will try again

intimate guitar work, and a blend of vocal harmony that was magically lucid and transparent. The music makes you smile but the silhouettes of the notes last long into the night. But then everyone was talking so they probably didn't notice.

The band struggled to complete their six-night residency and walked off on subsequent nights until the audience quietened. Richard Thompson called them the lumberjacks.

Andy Roberts: Richard really didn't like the lumberjacks. There was a memorable Friday night when the lumberjacks came to town. By the next day Iain couldn't stand it anymore and we were cancelled again. Richard and I passed the week playing snooker in a hall down the street.

Iain Matthews: I went into that tour excited, but perhaps a little bit naive and certainly still a very shy person. I think the promoters tried to put us into cities they deemed to be important. I went along with it, I was far too unsure of myself to challenge them. We played Detroit because that was the first city in America to hear my version of 'Woodstock'. It broke in Windsor, Ontario, just over the border and floated on the airwaves across the river. I guess they thought that because I had a hit with Matthews Southern Comfort, that would translate to Iain Matthews as a solo singer-songwriter, but it didn't. I have no idea why we went to Gassy Jack's, because that was a full-on rock'n'roll venue. You wouldn't call it a great tour, but it was certainly an adventure.

On 7th September the band returned to Los Angeles and The Troubadour. This time they were on a bill with Randy Newman, still riding on the wave of success he had found with his second album, *12 Songs*. This was the album that featured his inspired piano playing and Ry Cooder's sublime slide guitar on the song 'Mama Told Me Not to Come'. With some justification, Iain and the lads in the band might have been wondering whether they ought to have come back themselves. They needn't have worried, the crowd that showed up to watch Randy Newman were much more amenable to Iain's gentle songs and interpretations and the reception was good.

Iain Matthews: Andy played as much guitar as Richard did, Richard played his dulcimer and Bobby anchored it all well with the bass. That quartet developed a style of its own on that tour, by the time we got back to The Troubadour, we had a sound.

Cash Box sent their reviewer 't.e.' back for another chance to hear the music without the cacophony of audience voices.

> Back again was Vertigo's Ian Matthews, after an aborted attempt a couple of weeks ago, second-billed to Donny Hathaway. The Newman audience was much more sympathetic to Matthews's quiet brand of British folk-rockish music. In return he and his pleasant little accompanying group performed an a cappella version of 'Da Doo Ron Ron' that was outtasite (if you know what I mean).

Iain Matthews: 'Da Doo Ron Ron' sounded and felt so good, as though we had been performing it for years. We were feeling pretty loose at that point so I said, 'What the hell, let's put it in the show.'

Andy Roberts: Karen Goszkowski flew out to LA when we played The Troubadour for the second time. Through her contacts in the travel industry, she seemed able to take flights to where she wanted to be. We spent some time together at The Tropicana. I wrote four songs about, or perhaps for her; all of them ended up on my album *Urban Cowboy*. One of them, 'Poison Apple Lady', is the true story of us going off with a carload after the show one night during the run at the Poison Apple. There was an abandoned house down by the Detroit river, and we hung out there – dope, booze, the usual – and made a night of it. The events are pretty much as described in the song:

> This is a song about a night and a house by a river
> I was taken there by Denny and Sandy and Karen
> who I'd only just met
> Nobody lived there then, maybe it's empty still
> But I can't forget the humming of the crickets
> and I probably never will.

Karen loomed large in my fantasies for a time. I hoped that she might come to England, but she went back to her husband. Then I fell in bed with Jacqui, my first wife, at Richard Branson's wedding. I had known her platonically since the Bonzos recorded at the Manor Studio in 1971, but once we were together we were inseparable. I stayed distantly in touch with Karen over the years, but I didn't see her again until I played Madison, Wisconsin, with Iain in 2017. She'd had a tough life, and was then living on Michigan's Upper Peninsula. She was unrecognisable as the object of my desires from 46 years previously, all smoker's voice and shotgun in the trunk.

Iain, Richard and Andy flew back to London on 14th September. Bobby drove them to the airport and waved them off. Looking back on the tour through the telescope of nearly fifty years, Richard struggled to remember much about the concerts.

Richard Thompson: The best part was hanging out extensively with Iain and Andy, discovering a wealth of music on radio and record, a lot of it country, and making new friends across America.

There was no rest when they returned. Andy was preparing to finish his album *Nina and The Dream Tree*, and Richard was to start work on his own first solo album, *Henry the Human Fly*. Iain had his second solo album to complete and he had a desire to continue working with Richard and Andy. There was also the small matter of an imminent baby.

Iain Matthews: The first thing I had to confront when I got back from America was a visibly pregnant girlfriend. When I'd set off on my tour in late July, her belly had been almost flat, but when she came to meet me at the airport in mid-September it caught me completely by surprise how big she had become during my absence. Of course we'd spoken by telephone while I was Stateside, but I'd no previous experience with visualising the stages of a pregnancy. On seeing her again, the realisation immediately hit me that music would have to take a temporary back seat while I focused on more important matters.

Since leaving his band Matthews Southern Comfort just ten months previously, Iain had performed, recorded and written continuously. On 28th September, Iain married Chris at Hampstead registry office. They then flew off to Portugal for a short honeymoon. Iain took his guitar with him just in case inspiration should strike. For ten days Iain revelled in a little white-walled cottage on a hill overlooking a fishing village in the Algarve. He woke up to birdsong and tried out some ideas to finish the album he'd started before he went to America. One lyric Ian worked out in Portugal was a song that would appear on the new album, a song called 'Never Again'.

5. Along Comes Mary, Sandy, Bobby and David

Three days after Andy got back from America on Friday 17th September he was support act to Procol Harum at the Queen Elizabeth Hall. He did that gig with David Richards on bass and Roger Powell on drums. The workload continued; he had to put the finishing touches to the *Nina and The Dream Tree* album and prepare for a tour as support to Steeleye Span, who, like himself, were under Sandy Roberton's management.

Sandy had also just returned from the States where he was negotiating deals for Andy's first solo album *Home Grown* and the record Everyone had made. Sandy was now firmly established as producer and manager, but he had started out as a musician himself.

Sandy Roberton: I was determined to be in the music business. By day I took jobs at Olivetti typewriters and at C&A to earn enough money to stay alive and by night I played with two brothers in a bar in Gerrard Street in Soho. It was a place called Dive Bar, which was in the basement below The Kings Head pub. My friend Rick used to sit in on our sessions occasionally. At one of those sessions when Rick was singing with me we were seen by some managers and they signed us. These managers made TV commercials and had TV connections, so Rick and I were on TV even before we had a record deal. Dusty Springfield's brother Tom signed us to his company, FXB Productions. FXB stood for Francis X Bushman, who had been a silent movie star famous for his physique. Both Tom and Dusty Springfield were crazy about Tamla Motown, Rick and I recorded a Hank Williams song 'Half As Much' in the Motown style. It was released on Mercury in 1965. Tom had real old-school showbiz parties at his house near the post office in Chelsea. When Tom decided to focus more on writing we moved on. We got signed to Decca and made three singles for them, the first being 'Lost My Girl' in 1965, produced by Les Reed. We played live a lot but much of the work was in working men's clubs up north and that wasn't going to help us break through into the pop world. When Rick decided to leave the music business I recorded a single, 'Solitary Man', for Columbia in 1966. 'Solitary Man' started off well but when London American released the Bang version by Neil Diamond I was toast.

Sandy moved into publishing and worked for Chess Records and their publishing companies, Arc, Conrad and Jewel, who were based at 52 Maddox Street in Mayfair, London.

Sandy Roberton: I got to know Peter Meaden, the manager who had suggested The High Numbers change their name to The Who. He was also managing Jimmy James & The Vagabonds. They recorded a song I published, 'Ain't Love Good, Ain't Love Proud' written by Tony Clarke, and it did pretty well; it was a big club hit in the UK in the late sixties. Peter started a production company with *Record Mirror*'s Norman Jopling. They called it New Wave Productions and I made a final single for them under an assumed name, Lucien Alexander. I used members of a band called Fleur de Lys to back me. It was a cover of Bob Dylan's 'Baby, You've Been On My Mind'. I used an assumed name because Chess wouldn't have been happy if their London manager was recording and releasing tracks. I left Chess' publishing companies and teamed up with Richard and Mike Vernon who had started the Blue Horizon Records label, and together we set up the two Blue Horizon publishing companies; Goodie Two Shoes Music and Uncle Doris Music. Eventually, in early 1970, I set up my own management and production companies and started producing full time.

Sandy first met Andy Roberts after he had read a book called *The Liverpool Scene* edited by Edward Lucie-Smith.

Sandy Roberton: I'd read Adrian Henri interviews where he talked about a band he was in that blended poetry and rock called

The Liverpool Scene and I thought that sounded pretty interesting. I tracked down Andy Roberts and asked him to call me. I ended up managing The Liverpool Scene. Chappell Ltd the publishing company did the admin for the Chess publishing companies and I got them to put up some money. In the autumn of 1968 we recorded *Amazing Adventures of*. John Peel produced it, I was the executive producer. It was released late that year after I persuaded RCA to put it out. In 1969 I produced Liverpool Scene's second album *Bread on the Night*. They then went on that tour of America which ended up with a large deficit. When the band scattered, I was left holding the debt and I was sued by the agents Chrysalis to repay the money. The American agents withheld Jethro Tull receipts in order to pass the debt onto the English agents.

By this time Sandy had started his own companies, September Productions and September Management. Through these, he secured a deal with RCA to sign acts to release on their label RCA Victor.

Sandy Roberton: In 1970 I signed the band P.C. Kent whose members were David Richards, Gavin Watson, John Ward and Paul Kent. I produced the album *Upstairs Coming Down*. RCA Victor released the album in 1970, the same year they released Andy Roberts's solo album *Home Grown*, which I also produced. My relationship with Andy was always strong and eventually Andy and David Richards got together and formed Everyone. They were a terrific band and had a huge future. I had been successful in organising a deal with Ampex in the USA to release their album but it all came to an abrupt end with the van crash. The insurance company fought us for a long time and in the time it took to get a settlement the band had collapsed. The *Everyone* album was released by B&C Records in 1971 but by then the band didn't exist and Andy had gone to work with Iain Matthews.

Another band Sandy signed to release through RCA Victor was Ashley Hutching's new band, Steeleye Span.

Sandy Roberton: When Ashley left Fairport Convention at the end of 1969, he and Terry Woods from Sweeney's Men came to see me at my office in St George Street in Mayfair. They wanted to form a new band. They were joined by Terry's wife Gay and the folk duo Tim Hart and Maddy Prior. I signed them to RCA Victor and produced the album *Hark! The Village Wait* that was released in 1970.

Sandy had organised a UK tour for Steeleye Span that ran throughout most of October 1971, with Andy providing the support. The tour started at Colston Hall in Bristol on 3rd October and played for sixteen nights, ending at Bournemouth Winter Gardens on the 27th.

Andy Roberts I needed a bass player for the tour. The obvious choice for me was David Richards. He was a very good musician, a very precise bass player and a lyrical pianist but the problem was that David was out on tour with Sandy Denny who was promoting her first solo album *The North Star Grassman and the Ravens*. I was looking around for someone and Bobby Ronga came into my mind. I liked Bobby's playing, a whole different way to what I was used to, very American, very rocky. I mentioned this to Sandy and he loved the idea. I got in touch with Bobby and he jumped at the chance. We had to get him a work permit, it wasn't easy to do that then. Strict Musicians' Union rules meant that reciprocal arrangements had to be made for American musicians to work here but Sandy worked his magic and sorted out a permit. Bobby came and stayed at my mum and dad's house and we went out on tour throughout October performing material from *Nina and The Dream Tree* and songs that would be released 18 months later as a new album called *Urban Cowboy*, plus other songs I'd learned recently. One of the first things Bobby bought with his first wage was an Afghan coat. They had been popular a few years before and were sold in the sixties hippy shops like Granny Takes a Trip. I guess Bobby thought if they were good enough for The Beatles then he needed one. I believe they are made of goatskin. The one Bobby had smelled like it had recently been removed from the animal that wore it before him, especially when it rained. Bobby couldn't be parted from his Afghan coat and wore it everywhere. The whole Steeleye tour was a joy. We all travelled together to the gigs. Tim Hart and Maddy Prior, and Peter Knight, were fantastic people, and Martin Carthy was as good as it comes in guitar terms. I was happy that my suggestion that he play a Telecaster on the tour was such a successful pairing. Everyone knew he had written the 'Scarborough Fair' arrangement that Paul Simon stole for the *Graduate* album, and it was wonderful to be around them all. Also Ashley's decision to go without drums chimed with the way we fashioned Plainsong.

At the beginning of October 1971, Iain sat in a Wimpy bar in the West End of London and gave a reflective interview to the journalist Jerry Gilbert.

Iain Matthews: I really want to work but I don't know how I am going to be able to, and I've never been in this position of not knowing what I've wanted to do before. I really don't know where I stand now in this country. For instance, I played the Reading Festival and the response was almost nil, so that's why I want to go back to the States. The tour was basically designed to see whether there was any hope for me over there. I originally wanted to do The Troubadour and The Bitter End and then come back, but as it was we were booked into all sorts of rock clubs, and I didn't know too much about the club thing there.

Iain was putting the finishing touches to his second album for Vertigo. He told Jerry Gilbert that he planned to record Eric Andersen's 'Close the Door Lightly' and 'Right Before My Eyes' by Peter Lewis of Moby Grape, as well as 'Da Doo Ron Ron'. The problem for Iain, wrote Gilbert, is what to do? Gilbert suggested that the band that toured America was formed specifically for that tour and now he was back on his own.

Iain Matthews: I've thought of all the possible choices; I'm not really good enough to play by myself, and I'm not sure if I

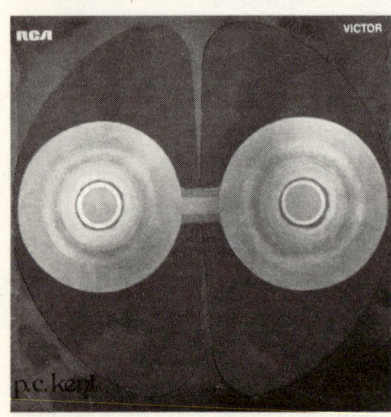

Album covers.
Top: Iain's *If You Saw Thro' My Eyes* and *Tigers Will Survive*.
Middle: Andy's *Home Grown* and *Nina and The Dream Tree*.
Bottom: P.C. Kent's *Upstairs Coming Down* and Everyone's *Everyone*.

want to join a band, so the only other alternative is to get other people to work with me; but I'm still not even sure I want to work electrically or acoustically and I'm not sure if I want all the hustle of a band again.

Iain had re-started work on his album after his honeymoon break in Portugal. On his return from America it had crossed his mind to scrap the stuff he had already done and start afresh. He changed his mind. He had already tried and tested 'Tigers Will Survive' and 'Please Be My Friend' and had solid songs in Richard Farina's 'House of Un-American Blues Activity Dream' and his own 'Morning Song'.

Iain Matthews: We added the Eric Andersen song, 'Close the Door Lightly When You Go'. Richard Thompson played accordion on that one. He didn't want a credit in his own name so he decided to call himself Woolfe J. Flywheel on account of his infatuation with the Marx Brothers. Another new song was one of mine called 'Midnight on the Water'. You can hear Bobby Ronga's piano playing on that. Bobby is also on backing vocal on our version of 'Da Doo Ron Ron'. We multi-tracked backing from me, Andy, Allan Taylor and Bobby, we even left the laughter on at the end.

Vertigo wasted no time in getting the new album out. Iain called the album *Tigers Will Survive* and it was in the shops by the end of November.

It was a busy few months for Iain, Andy, David and Bobby. Iain also sang on Andy's *Nina and The Dream Tree* album, adding backing vocals to the last track 'Dream Tree Sequence' alongside Mac and Katie Kissoon. David Richards played bass and piano on the same album. After Bobby had worked on Iain's *Tigers* album, he went on to find work on Allan Taylor's album *The Lady* where he played bass. Iain and Andy worked on that album too.

Iain Matthews: Andy and I got on well. In the space of just ten months we had recorded two albums together and toured

America. I liked his stories and the details he put in them. He could tune his guitar to DADGAD and play all kinds of things. It didn't take me long to realise I wanted to work with this man who I greatly admired. I wasn't thinking in terms of a band at the time, nor even a commercial proposition. I just thought we could do something with all the different influences we had.

In an interview with *Disc and Music Echo* during the Steeleye Span tour, Andy was clear that he wouldn't be joining a new band. But as the interview progressed, almost as an afterthought, he indicated that his position might not be as solid as he'd suggested.

Andy Roberts: I would perhaps join some group if the right people asked me. I feel I'm swimming up the same river as groups, but in the opposite direction. It's really strange going out onstage on this Steeleye tour and doing a whole set by myself.

On 19th October, Andy and Bobby arrived at Birmingham Town Hall with Steeleye Span. Iain was invited to join them on stage. It was Iain's first time back at the venue since the night less than a year before when he had packed his guitar into its case and walked out on Matthews Southern Comfort.

Iain Matthews: Chris and I were going to see Andy and Bobby play at Birmingham, but I got a call from Sandy Roberton saying, 'Andy is losing his voice, can you come up sooner than you planned and help him out?' So I went up and did about three quarters of the show with them and it felt good just working together in England.

A music fan called Chris Spicer of Solihull wrote a letter to *Sounds*, 'Back in October, I was lucky enough to see Ian join Andy in an unscheduled "jam" at Birmingham Town Hall. Their performance completely overshadowed Steeleye Span.'

The Steeleye Span tour finished on 27th October at Bournemouth Winter Gardens. David Richards's tour with Sandy Denny finished at the beginning of November. On 16th

December, Steeleye had a one-off concert at the London College of Printing. Andy was again asked to provide support and this time as well as Bobby, he took David Richards with him. David recalled this show in an interview he conducted with *Let It Rock*.

David Richards: The four of us lurched together. It was at a gig of Andy's at the London College of Printing. Bobby and I were playing with him and Iain appeared and suggested trying this band.

Iain Matthews: Andy and I had chatted backstage at Birmingham. We had been talking about forming a band while we were completing the *Tigers* album. We compared musical tastes and tried to visualise something different but didn't want to dive in. Then when we talked at the College of Printing, we thought that it should be an acoustic four piece with vocal harmony.

Andy Roberts: I guess you could say that the decision to form the band that later became known as Plainsong was taken backstage that night at the College of Printing in Elephant and Castle.

Iain spent much of November and December talking to the press about the new album *Tigers Will Survive*. On the home front, in preparation for the birth of their first child, Iain and Chris went house hunting. They found a big, two-bedroom flat on the second floor of a building in Altior Court in Highgate Hill, fell in love with it and moved in straightaway. Iain had also revealed to Karl Dallas that he had other plans to move too.

Iain Matthews: What I would really like to do is join a band again. Not to be a star with a backing group, but just the singer with the band. Like it was in the Fairport days.

In the week before Christmas 1971, there was a meeting at Iain's Highgate flat. Iain, Andy, Bobby Ronga and David Richards convened to sing together.

Andy Roberts: Iain had been talking to me on and off ever since the American tour about finding another two people to form a touring and recording unit. Maybe not a band in the traditional sense, but a loose collection of like-minded friends to play acoustic music. Bobby Ronga had played and harmonised well on the American tour. Richard and I in particular were curious about him. We got on. Bobby was a character. He always had plenty to talk about. I knew he could play piano, bass and guitar. He told us that he had worked alongside Aaron Schroeder in the Brill Building on Broadway. Schroeder had written a lot of hits. 'Because They're Young' for Duane Eddy, 'Good Luck Charm' for Elvis and 'Rubber Ball' for Bobby Vee to name just three. Bobby had been a staff writer at that songwriting factory and so had a connection to old-school, classic American song writing. He can't have been that successful at it because when we met him he was working as a driver. I think before that he had been writing songs for children's TV, half-a-dozen a day, a few words and a catchy chorus, until it was driving him mad. He was a very affable guy, quick to laugh and join in. He was a thickset lad and spoke with a strong Brooklyn accent. I suspect he was completely self-taught, he played the bass like a man used to playing lead guitar, and the piano like someone who had worked it out for himself. David Richards on the other hand was much more subtle, he had piano lessons as a kid and played it with great lyricism and his bass playing was equally precise. I was fond of David and I thought he would be a good addition.

At the get-together at Iain's flat, the four put themselves to the test by taking on the difficult Tandyn Almer song, 'Along Comes Mary'.

Andy Roberts: Iain's new place was quite a fancy flat. It had windows overlooking a park and a big work space. He also had a reel-to-reel player. It would have been Iain who suggested meeting there. It was also Iain who suggested we have a try out on 'Along Comes Mary'. It was a fiendishly difficult vocal arrangement, nobody in the UK was doing that type of material. By the end of the day we had nailed what I thought was a remarkable version.

Iain Matthews: It's a relatively complex song with an unusual chord progression, a wide vocal range and quite bizarre lyrics. It was a silly stunt really, but we agreed that if we could come up with a creditable version by dinner time then we'd become a band. The end result was effortless, surprising and very encouraging. By dinner time we shook hands on it.

Andy Roberts: I seem to remember that Sandy Roberton came over in the afternoon. If not then he certainly came over in the evening to listen to the tape of what we had done and he loved it.

Sandy Roberton: I listened to the tape and I thought it was great.

After dinner, Iain, Andy, Dave and Bobby, with the help of Sandy, discussed what they might call their band.

Iain Matthews: Over a glass of wine and on a whim, we randomly opened a copy of *The Concise Oxford Dictionary of Music*. Its pages fell open at 450-451, Pizzicato to Plainsong to Planets. It felt like a very significant moment for us. We had become a band. We were Plainsong.

Christmas 1971 was an unseasonably dry and mild one. After the holiday Plainsong reconvened to start work.

PART II
FACE THE MUSIC

6. Plainsong Take Off

The New Year brought bitterly cold weather. The newly-formed Plainsong went into intensive rehearsal. Andy made a call to an old acquaintance called Harry Isles, an art school teacher who as a young man had been one of the last generation to complete National Service. He had been a ground wireless service engineer in the RAF. Harry became the go-to man for all things Plainsong.

Andy Roberts: Harry had tour managed Liverpool Scene before moving on to work with Colosseum, who had broken up just a few months before I called him. We used a rehearsal place called The Cabin in Bamborough Gardens, Shepherd's Bush. Harry sat with us for a month working as a front of house engineer. I don't think Harry had done that before, but he could turn his hand to anything. He was a driver, a roadie, a photographer and he could build things, such as speaker cabinets. We had two mixing desks called Audiomasters, made by WEM, which was Charlie Watkins's company, Watkins Electric Music. From the start Harry was on the biggest wage. Once we started earning we paid ourselves £30 a week, we paid Harry twice that.

Harry Isles: We set up the gear and left it all in place for about a month. There were two column speakers and we linked two five-channel mixing desks together to make a ten-channel desk. We then had a PA made for us by a firm called Midas. Two huge bins with wooden flares and a big mixing desk. We paid a lot for that.

Andy Roberts: We worked hard in that month at The Cabin. I have spiral-bound notebooks from the time that show arrangements and keys for around forty or fifty songs, many of them Iain's own.

Iain Matthews: I had it in mind to blend my own songs with well chosen covers. The kind of music I was particularly interested in was the old-timey country tunes. I wanted to take the Appalachian songs, the ones that had travelled from Europe to America as folk songs, and give them a contemporary twist to make a new type of country music. Through Paul Nelson in New York I had met a record store owner who could source the material I was interested in at a reasonable price. He mailed records to me. When I was at Highgate Hill I made regular trips to the local post office to pick up parcels full of records from America.

The intensive rehearsals continued through January as the business shenanigans picked up pace. Iain's managers Ken and Alan wasted no time in fostering the band. They no doubt saw the concept as Iain's new group. Ken and Alan tried to sell the new band to Vertigo but came away disappointed. Vertigo simply reminded them that they didn't need to sign Plainsong because they already had Iain on their books and he owed them one more album under his present contract. This effectively meant Iain and his management could not look for a contract with Plainsong. Iain put forward an idea. His advance for a third album was £75,000. He made an offer to Vertigo that he would deliver a new album for £5,000 if they would release him immediately from his contract. Basically, Iain was offering to buy himself out of his own contract for £70,000. Vertigo agreed and freed Iain to shop around for a new deal.

Iain Matthews: I was deeply committed to the Plainsong project. It cost me a lot of money to buy myself out of the Vertigo contract, but it was the only way forward. The rehearsals at The Cabin had gone well, tours were being organised and obviously we needed to sign to a new label to make a record. There was even talk early on about a tour to America. Ken and Alan had already been corresponding with Herb Spar of The Millard Agency in New York.

Sandy Roberton was on hand at The Cabin offering creative guidance in his role as producer. But Sandy's role was to focus on the business affairs of the music too.

Iain Matthews: The Cabin was close to the offices of the Gemini Agency. Sandy had connections there to Max Hole and his musical and business ideas kicked off a relationship with them from the start. They took our first publicity photographs on a freezing cold January day. We're all wearing warm coats for the shot.

Max Hole started his career in music as Student Union Entertainment Secretary at Canterbury University. He managed Spirogyra, an important band on the Canterbury music scene who were also studying at the university, and produced their first album *Old Boot Wine*, now regarded as a classic of the 'acid folk' genre. After university, Max set up Gemini with his friend Geoff Jukes. They built a formidable roster of acts that included Mungo Jerry, Steeleye Span and Arthur Brown.[5]

Sandy Roberton: I rented a part of my offices in Mayfair to a young management company run by Marcus Bicknell and Geoff Jukes. In 1970 I signed Spirogyra to September Productions. Their manager Max Hole joined forces with Geoff Jukes and Richard Thomas to start the Gemini Agency and GAMA Records. I introduced Max and Geoff to Plainsong to be their agents.

Gemini wasted no time in setting up Plainsong's first tour, a lengthy crawl of mainly English colleges and universities that would continue through to March.

In the midst of everything that was going on around

---

[5] Max went on to manage A&R for WEA and, as managing director of East West Records, he was closely involved with the career of Simply Red. He eventually became Senior Vice-President for marketing at Universal where he was responsible for the development and promotion of international acts like Amy Winehouse, U2, Shania Twain and Bryan Adams. *Billboard* magazine described him as 'a serious contender for title of most powerful label executive outside America'.

Plainsong, Vertigo was hoping to promote Iain's album *Tigers Will Survive*, focussing on Iain as a solo artist. They announced they were to release 'Da Doo Ron Ron' as a single. Much of the attention from the press was centered on the fact that Iain had kept the original gender intact. He sang it as The Crystals had sung it, 'Yeah my heart stood still, yeah his name was Bill, and when he walked me home...' Iain told his friend Karl Dallas at *Melody Maker* that he didn't mess about with the lyric because he respected the song. Dallas chided that respect was perhaps too solemn a word and concluded that the song was a 'very happy performance'. Danny Holloway in *NME* went a bit further and wrote an ironic piece that asked 'Is this the start of Gay Rock?' In another article by Lon Goddard for *Record Mirror*, the writer mentioned that some American radio stations had banned the song. 'Bunch of pricks,' exclaimed Iain, before telling Goddard that he had no sympathy for people who tried to put something else into the song.

Ken and Alan, who were contracted to represent Iain rather than Plainsong, set to work and secured a spot on *Top of the Pops* for 'Da Doo Ron Ron'. Iain was adamant that he wouldn't do it.

Iain Matthews: As soon as I heard the words *Top of the Pops* I saw the writing on the wall and panicked. I thought, 'What if it does well and that whole Matthews Southern Comfort scenario repeats itself?' I really couldn't cope with the thought of that happening. What I did want, and had tried many times to explain to my managers, was longevity. I wanted to be taken seriously as a singer and more importantly as a songwriter, not some kind of toy that is wound up and trundled onto a stage to mime on the telly. Howard and Blaikley were of the opinion that I was sabotaging my career. I'm not sure that was exactly their concern, but I was definitely obstructing the flow of cash in their direction.

It's clear that Iain's record label Vertigo had lost interest in him after he declared a commitment to Plainsong by forfeiting his advance on the yet-to-be-made third album. And that his managers were struggling to promote him in a way appropriate to the new band and its young management and agency.

Later in the year, Iain gave an interview to Jerry Floyd for the November issue of *Let It Rock*. He reiterated his dislike for 'the hit single thing'. He also went on to say that following the release of *Tigers Will Survive* virtually no publicity was done for it and 'after five weeks they withdrew it from the shops'.

Iain must have felt that radio sessions were a more appropriate promotional vehicle for serious singer-songwriters. On Monday 24th January 1972, Plainsong walked into the Playhouse Theatre in Northumberland Avenue to record a BBC Radio 1 session for John Peel. It was their first official public engagement as a band. They performed Iain's song 'Tigers Will Survive', a song written by George Frayne of Commander Cody called 'Seeds and Stems (Again)', a Paul Siebel song from the *Woodsmoke and Oranges* album, 'Any Day Woman', and a song by Gene Clark, 'For a Spanish Guitar'. The selections were a statement of intent.

The radio show was broadcast on 1st February, by which time Plainsong had begun their first set of live concerts. Gemini had put together a run of shows scheduled to start on 29th January at Leeds University. In advance of this tour, the band performed a few warm-up shows.

Andy Roberts: We played a few impromptu gigs around London. Les Cousins was a basement club on Greek Street in Soho run by a guy called Andy Matheou whose parents ran the Dionysus Greek restaurant upstairs. Everybody on the folk scene played there – John Martyn, Bridget St John, Ralph McTell and the Americans Jackson C Frank, Paul Simon, Arlo Guthrie and Julie Felix played there too. Plainsong liked the intimate atmosphere. You didn't need a PA you just played.

Iain Matthews: I have a fuzzy memory of being on stage at Les Cousins. We must have been finding our feet and trying out the ideas we had rehearsed at The Cabin.

On 28th January, Plainsong played a warm-up concert at a Youth Club in Colchester. They were paid the princely sum of £10. The artist David Suff was there that evening.

David Suff: During my lunchtime breaks at school and on Saturdays I worked in a record shop called Howard Leach Records. The shop was run by Howard Leach himself, who was a classical music buff. There was a big classical and jazz section, but the shop sold music across the board. The customers were mainly students who listened to John Peel. On Saturdays Howard used to leave me in charge so I'd choose the kind of music I liked and pumped up the volume. Zappa's latest albums always got an airing and when Robert Palmer's *Sneakin' Sally Through the Alley* came out I sold 25 copies in one afternoon just by playing it on the shop's record player. This was also a time when the hip record companies like Island and Elektra would send people round to do window displays and merchandising. I met their reps regularly. It may have been from one of the reps or a customer that I heard Plainsong were to do a concert at Colchester Youth Club. The Youth Club was down a side street in the town centre. It wasn't the sort of place where gigs happened normally. I saw George Melly with John Chilton's Feetwarmers there with my girlfriend Jean, but most gigs in Colchester took place at the Corn Exchange or the university. Plainsong played to an audience of the kind of people who came into the record shop.

Plainsong's set at their first billed gig comprised a mixture of covers of recent songs the band liked, Iain's originals and some material that Iain and Andy had performed on the previous year's American tour with Richard Thompson. A setlist in Andy's handwriting reveals that they played 'Radio Lady'; 'Seeds and Stems', a song that first appeared on Commander Cody's *Lost in the Ozone* album the previous year; 'Tigers Will Survive'; 'For a Spanish Guitar' from Gene Clark's *White Light* album, also released in 1971; 'Never Ending'; 'Raider', the Jerry Yester and Judy Henske song; 'The Only Dancer'; 'Souling Song'; 'Please Be My Friend'; and an encore of 'Da Doo Ron Ron'.

The first official Plainsong concert was on 29th January at Leeds University, the start of a wide-ranging tour, taking in Liverpool, Cardiff, Bristol and Plymouth. The local student magazine previewed the Leeds gig.

> In these days of 'superstars' on the campus circuit you might be forgiven for asking what the hell 'Univents' are doing presenting Plainsong, a new and untried band, at tomorrow's hop. However, do not let the absence of publicity blind you to the fact that this act is potentially one of the best on the soft rock scene. The band consists of little known but very good musicians: Bob Ronga (bass) and Dave Richards (piano) together with Ian Matthews and Andy Roberts (guitars). Ian Matthews sang with Fairport Convention in the days before electric fiddling began to make its mark on their music. Andy Roberts first made an impression as a member of the Liverpool Scene, who in their early days were one of the more interesting groups, with their combination of poetry, songs and fine instrumental playing. Don't miss this band, you may regret it.

It transpired that a good number of the student population of Leeds didn't want to miss it. Iain was later to tell the music press that Leeds University was their best audience. The set was similar to the previous night at Colchester with the addition of 'And Me', Paul Siebel's 'Any Day Woman', and 'Hearts'. A record of their payment at Leeds reports that the fee was £150 (cash on the night).

The second show of the tour on 1st February was at Kent University in Canterbury, the night that the John Peel session was broadcast. Peter Kay, who was then a student in his second year, recalls the event.

Peter Kay: I was a peripheral member of the Student Entertainments Committee, which meant I moved tables and chairs in the dining room to the sides of the dining halls to make way for audiences and replaced them afterwards. Kent then was a campus university formed of four colleges, each with its own large dining hall where concerts were held: Darwin, Rutherford,

U.K.C. STUDENTS UNION PRESENTS

"PLAINSONG"

Featuring IAN MATTHEWS & ANDY ROBERTS

with

"GARRY FARR"

in THE DINING HALL
DARWIN COLLEGE
UNIVERSITY OF KENT
AT CANTERBURY
TUESDAY 1ST FEB.

TICKETS 40p AVAILABLE FROM USUAL S.U.S. SOURCES. BEGINS 8 p.m.

Keynes and Eliot. The Plainsong concert was in the Darwin dining hall. The social secretary was Max, a nice chap with a good understanding of the music business even at that early stage. There was plenty of good music at the time with lots of folk and folk rock. Al Stewart was a regular visitor and concerts by Fairport Convention, Sandy Denny, The Strawbs, Richie Havens and Martin Carthy spring to mind. Ian Telfer, Alan Prosser and Cathy Lesurf were students and regular performers. Spirogyra were more-or-less the university band. All of which should have suggested a decent turnout for Plainsong, but so few tickets were sold, even at just forty pence, that it was decided to make it a free concert. Presumably the only alternative would have been to cancel. I have vague memories of the band sitting in a row, or perhaps a semi-circle, just in front of the audience. My main interest would have been to catch Iain Matthews, who I had seen back home in Sheffield with Matthews Southern Comfort and, to a lesser extent, Andy Roberts who I once saw with The Liverpool Scene. It was a laidback performance in front of a small audience, 100 maybe 150 people, a lot of whom got in for free. I must have met Iain either before or after the performance because my copy of *If You Saw Thro' My Eyes*, which I obviously took along with me, is autographed by him.

Iain Matthews: Our support at Canterbury that night was Gary Farr. He was a sweet guy, intensely musical. I always expected him to make it. Gary had been around the same circuit as me for a number of years. He was a part of the fabric. I believe he played the Isle of Wight Festival when I was there with Fairport as far back as 1968.

Gary Farr was the youngest son of the heavyweight boxer Tommy Farr. In 1937 at New York's Yankee Stadium Tommy fought reigning champion Joe Louis for the world title. The fight ended with a points decision and was described as Joe Louis's toughest fight. Gary's older brother was Rikki Farr, who famously co-produced the 1968, 1969 and 1970 Isle of Wight festivals with Ray Foulk and plays a central role in the film director Murray Lerner's feature length documentary *Message to Love*.

On 4th February, Vertigo released 'Da Doo Ron Ron' to the shops as a 45rpm single. It came out simultaneously in the UK and The Netherlands with Iain's composition 'Never Again' on the B-side. The record company took out a quarter-page advertisement in the *NME* for *Tigers Will Survive*. The advert featured a close up photograph of Iain's face and the slogan 'You won't forget it! It really is a hit!' There were quotes from *Cash Box* – 'One of the genuine troubadours of our day' – and *Billboard* – 'Ian Matthews just keeps getting better all the time...' In the early hours of the following morning, 3.30am to be precise, Iain's wife Chris gave birth at University College Hospital. Iain was not allowed to be present in the delivery room. He was told that the hospital had a requirement that prior notice must be given before fathers were allowed to be present at the birth. Iain sat on a chair in a waiting room.

Iain Matthews: At some point I must have fallen asleep and the next thing I knew there was a gentle tapping on my shoulder. 'Congratulations Mr Matthews,' said the nurse, 'your wife has given birth to a beautiful baby girl. They are both well and resting. You should go home and get some sleep. Come back tomorrow morning and you can visit them.' Reluctantly I left. It was already tomorrow. I couldn't find sleep when I got home and by 10am I was back at UCH to see Chris and for the first time my little girl, with the heady realisation that I was now a father.

On the same day, Plainsong were to play at Croydon Technical College supported by the band Uncle Dog. Iain must have found a little sleep in the afternoon, because by the evening he was on stage at Croydon. Karl Dallas reviewed the concert for *Melody Maker*.

> At last, Ian Matthews has found the band he has been looking for all this time. I mean no disrespect to his colleagues of Southern Comfort when I say that, at his first

gig on Saturday night at Croydon Tech of the new band he has formed with Andy Roberts, I suddenly realised what he has been striving for. What he has got together now is, quite simply and without any hype, a supergroup. The band is acoustic in its emphasis, even when Bob Ronga plays electric guitar so tastily. But both he and bassist Dave Richards are no mean practitioners on the acoustic guitar. Vocally, the band is very strong, for not only are Ian and Andy both solo singers in their own right, but the other two musicians join them to give their four-part harmonies a punch. Their programming could be improved, I think, and the addition of one or two real stompers would have given their set a climax to work towards. As it was, though, each individual song was perfection.

If Iain was tired after a sleepless night and the excitement of a new baby, it didn't appear to show that night in Croydon. Fortunately for Iain there would now be a break from touring. It would be two weeks until the next gig. That meant two weeks at home with wife Chris and the new baby, apart from one radio recording session. For the rest of the year there would be little time at home and no respite from the rounds of rehearsing, recording, broadcasting and touring.

7. Against the Prevailing Wind

At the beginning of February, Andy received a surprise phone call from someone who he hadn't heard from since they'd hung out in Los Angeles. Glenn Frey's Eagles were now fully fledged and perfecting their laid-back California easy sounds recording their debut album in South West London.

Andy Roberts: Glenn Frey phoned me and said, 'Hey man we're in London, at Olympic.' I went down there and I hung around with them. I sat in the control room with Glyn Johns and listened to that album as it was being recorded. The band were living in a flat at Maida Vale. Glyn worked them hard. They did ten days straight and then he let them have a day off. I asked them what they wanted to do. Out of the blue Don Henley said, 'Do you know Vivian Stanshall?' I said, 'Of course I know him, he's one of my best mates, but how come you know him?' They told me that they had seen the Bonzo Dog Doo-Dah Band play at The Fillmore West and they loved it. Then like little lads they said, 'Can we meet him?' I arranged with Viv to take them over there, of course he hadn't a clue who they were. At the time I had a mini van and I'd filled the back with foam rubber for passengers to sit on. Randy decided he wanted to stay in and wash his hair or something, but Bernie, Henley and Frey sat on my rubber foam and I drove them over to Viv's place. Viv loved to have complete strangers as guests for the comic moments that might ensue. We smoked some African grass and played table tennis. Completely ripped on the grass, we decided to walk up the road to East Finchley for a curry. Halfway through the meal Viv started to hold his chest and wheeze. He said to me 'Do you think you could go and fetch my pills please dear boy?' I knew he was going to wind up the three Americans, so I played along and came back with a pack of aspirin or something. I don't know what he said or did to them, but when I drove them back to Maida Vale they were in shell shock.

The visit of the Eagles was a nice diversion, but the business of Plainsong pressed on. On 15th February they were in the BBC studios at Maida Vale to record a radio session for Bob Harris's *Sounds of the 70s*. They performed Iain's 'That's All it Could Amount To' plus a song by Chris Hillman, 'Time Between'.

The touring carried on at pace. A review of an early live show, likely to be Westfield College on 18th February, appeared in *The Birmingham Post* courtesy of Pete Carr.

> The hall was half full of apathetic students who chatted through the opening songs and were only later persuaded to attention and enthusiasm by the quality of the music. That was weird because the separate reputations built by Ian and Andy would guarantee them a good hearing from a packed house if they cared simply to put up their own names on the posters. They don't do that simply because with Plainsong they are into something entirely new and they want it to be treated as such.

The following night the band was supposed to head up to York University's Central Hall to support The Kinks, who were promoting their critically praised *Muswell Hillbillies* album. This gig was cancelled, or at least Plainsong's part in it was. The tour continued through Liverpool, Cardiff, Bristol and arrived at Southampton University on 4th March. Three days later Plainsong made their TV debut.

The Old Grey Whistle Test had recently taken over the slot previously filled by *Disco 2*. Broadcast on the higher-minded BBC2, it was a show that shunned chart music to concentrate on albums; a serious music programme for the counterculture presented by the editor of *Melody Maker*, Richard Williams. Plainsong made their first appearance on the show on 7th March and chose to perform two songs they had been performing on tour; 'Raider' and Iain's song 'Call the Tune'.

The tour continued through Penzance, Plymouth, Loughborough

and Alcester, arriving at Hampstead Country Club on 15th March after a brief detour to The Netherlands. The business of Iain's 'Da Doo Ron Ron' single rumbled on and, mindful of Iain's point-blank refusal to perform it on *Top of the Pops*, sleight of hand was used to get Iain and the band onto a Dutch TV show, as Dave Richards revealed in an interview with *Let It Rock*.

David Richards: They shipped us out to Holland for a live radio show. But when we got there, instead of radio it turned out to be a mimed TV show called *Ready Eddie Go*, which is even worse than *Top of the Pops*. There were all these twelve-year-old girls sitting on the stage and we had to mime 'Da Doo Ron Ron'.

The show was actually called *Eddy, Ready, Go!* which ran on Dutch TV between 1970 and 1973. It was presented by Eddy Becker, a former Radio Veronica DJ. Plainsong appeared on the show on 15th March alongside The Les Humphries Singers. David's claim that it was worse than *Top of the Pops* is borne out by a clip from an episode of the show broadcast a month previously of the Dutch husband and wife accordion duo De Kermisklanten, who played their latest single 'Arsène Lupin', a tune which wouldn't have been out of place had it been that year's Dutch entry to the Eurovision Song Contest.

The band flew straight back to London for their show at Hampstead Country Club, located down an alleyway just up Haverstock Hill from Belsize Park Underground station. Richard Lewis was in attendance that night.

Richard Lewis: The club was quite small and basic and a bit shabby. There was a small stage and to the right of that there was a bar which sometimes meant that you heard more bar gossip than the quieter acts on stage. People usually quietened down when asked to but it was not a great layout from an artist's point of view. There were basic rows of seats which filled up quickly. I went to see Plainsong because I had followed Iain Matthews since his days in Fairport Convention. With me the lyrics always come first ever since I heard Dylan. When Fairport started they performed lots of songs by the early singer-songwriters such as Joni Mitchell, Eric Andersen, Leonard Cohen and Dylan. With Plainsong it was both the songs that they chose and the harmonies that I loved, and in Iain and Andy they had great songwriters.

Richard wrote down the set as it unfolded that night into his notebook. Iain's song 'Call the Tune' opened a set that also included Siebel's 'Any Day Woman', a Glen Sherley song called 'F.B.I. Top Ten', a version of 'Raider' with Iain on tambourine, and an a cappella reading of the traditional song 'Lowlands Away', a sea shanty associated with the folk revivalists Shirley Collins and Anne Briggs.

Stuart Lyon worked as a producer, a promoter and manager at Hampstead Country Club.

Stuart Lyon: Hampstead Country Club used to be a jazz venue. I had a friend who lived on Haverstock Hill and I went with him to see the great Jamaican alto sax player Joe Harriot. That was back in 1967. I said to my friend that night, 'We could do better than this.' The owner said I could rent it for £10 a night. I was thinking about a hip name to give to my nights when I realised that Hampstead Country Club was already a hip name, so I let it be. The place sat 150 people comfortably, but I could squeeze 200 in. I had no hesitation in promoting Plainsong at the club. I knew Iain's music. In 1970 I had an agreement with Jeff Dexter who ran the Implosion nights at the Roundhouse to promote my own event there. We called it 'Spring Festival' and with a fifty-two quid promotions budget, we put on Arthur Lee's band Love, Matthews Southern Comfort and a band I managed called Jody Grind led by the Hammond C3 player Tim Hinkley. Arthur Brown was supposed to be there as well but he turned up late so I told him to fuck off.

Stuart's history of promoting the club gives good context for the live music scene at the time and the culture that Plainsong found themselves amongst.

Stuart Lyon: The first band I booked was Dick Morrissey's Soul Unit. They broke up before I could get them there. Spooky Tooth stepped in and they were the first band I promoted on 22nd May 1968. By July I promoted the first of many visits by Fairport Convention and later that year I had Pink Floyd, Sly and The Family Stone and David Bowie, who at the time was in a folk-rock group with his girlfriend Hermione Farthingale called Feathers. It seemed that everybody who was anybody wanted to come. It wasn't too hard to get these acts, I had a good booking agent and to be fair the club did have a reputation. Jimi Hendrix had played there within a couple of months of his arrival in London. We crammed 400 in when Elton John came. I can vividly remember getting the DJ to make an announcement asking the people to make room for more. I also promoted rock'n'roll nights. I had Gene Vincent there and Billy Fury who was bloody good. I stayed with the Country Club until 1972. They were good years. The musicians loved to hang out there; Keith Moon was a regular and Fairport Convention would come because they loved playing there. They might have played the Albert Hall a few nights before, but they would come and play for me for two hundred pounds.

Richard Lewis saw Fairport at Hampstead a fair few times. He has links to the origins of the band. He grew up in Muswell Hill and the Fairport house was on the corner of the next street. His family doctor was Dr Nicol who was the father of Simon Nicol, Fairport's guitarist.

Richard Lewis: Simon became good friends with my younger brother Danny and also Andy Brown who lived opposite us. Simon, Andy and lots of others were often at my house as my parents were very relaxed and understanding. I became good friends with Simon and then Ashley Hutchings. I knew Richard a bit but never really got to know Iain or Sandy although I followed all of their careers. Fairport actually decided upon their name at my house, when they played at a party here in April 1967 while my parents were away in Rome for the Easter holidays.

Richard has interesting stories of his own to tell about the cultural scene of the time.

Richard Lewis: Two weeks after the Fairport Convention party, I went to the *14 Hour Technicolour Dream* up the road at Ally Pally and took part in Yoko Ono's early concept art performances in which members of the audience took turns with a pair of scissors to cut off pieces of a girl's dress until she was just left in her underwear.

One of the centres of the counterculture in England was in Kensington Church Walk, an alleyway that cuts through St Mary Abbots Gardens. This was Turret Bookshop run by Bernard Stone, the Nottingham-born son of Jewish refugees from Odessa. Stone was a publisher and poet as well as bookseller; more than that he was a catalyst for friendships amongst the young upcoming writers, artists and poets, who used his shop to launch poetry books and for readings. Stone entertained royally and would often lay on wine in the shop, attracting a boozy as well as bohemian crowd, amongst them Lawrence Durrell, Alan Sillitoe, Michael Horowitz, Christopher Logue and Alexander Trocchi. Another regular was Andy Roberts.

Andy Roberts: Adrian Henri introduced me to Bernard Stone. Turret Bookshop became my hang out in London on Saturdays. It was more like a salon than a bookshop and the wine was always fine. Reginald Bosanquet the newsreader was a regular there and he was no stranger to a good glass of red. Frank Dickens who drew the Bristow cartoon for the *Evening Standard* was another and Ralph Steadman. I was very fond of Bernard and his assistant Eleanor, they were always decent and smiling. They were also brilliant, convivial and dedicated to the literary arts. Bernard helped many a poet and published their work in exquisite limited editions on handmade paper. There were shelves of rare books and first editions and one shelf that was a bit of an anomaly, as it contained books about aviation. When I asked about it I was told that Eleanor's boyfriend was into flying and the books were being sold on his behalf. I looked at that shelf one day and I bought a copy of a book by Fred Goerner called *The Search for Amelia Earhart*. I don't know what intrigued me enough to buy it. Perhaps it was because I liked the Amelia song that I heard on the album by Laramie that I took from the cupboard at the *Cash Box* offices. I read it and was completely swept up by the story. I passed it on to Iain and he loved it too.

Goerner's book flew against the prevailing wind and questioned the official story of what happened to Amelia Earhart and her co-pilot Frederick Noonan. The accepted wisdom was that in July of 1937, during an attempt to fly around the world, the plane ran out of fuel whilst searching for Howland Island, their stepping stone on the way to Hawaii. The plane then crashed and Amelia and Noonan were lost at sea. Goerner, a CBS news reporter of long experience, posited a very different theory after years of research. He had it that Amelia landed either by accident or design in Japanese held territory and had been taken prisoner to be interrogated as a spy. He claimed that she died in captivity and was buried on the island of Saipan where the Japanese had a military headquarters. He also stated that the Americans knew about Amelia's capture and that the US government withheld the true story to avoid political embarrassment and a conflict with the Japanese in the Pacific for which they were ill-prepared.

Andy Roberts: It wasn't long after we started gigging that I discovered the Amelia book and we found one of the ways to connect to the audience was to tell them stories from the book. Basically we were trying out a story within a performance on stage.

The first Plainsong tour ended at the Roundhouse on 19th March, a Sunday, the evening when the Roundhouse held its 'Implosion' events, when the air inside the old railway engine shed in Chalk Farm moved to the haze of cannabis smoke and a flickering light show. No doubt when they awoke the next morning they were glad of a lie-in. Since the beginning of the New Year they had played TV shows, recorded radio sessions, written and rehearsed new material and played to college audiences over a period of seven weeks. On top of that Iain had promoted his fifth album in less than two years, his wife Chris had given birth to a new baby and they'd moved house for the fourth time. An opportunity arose to buy a three-storey Victorian house near the railway lines in Gospel Oak.

Iain Matthews: After we had sold our flat in Highgate there was no extra cost for a much bigger space. It was the first place Chris and I could really call home and it was only twenty minutes into West London by train.

The poet John Betjemen was born in Gospel Oak and in later times when he moved on he poked fun at it, 'Here from my eyrie, as the sun went down, I heard the old North London puff and shunt, Glad that I did not live in Gospel Oak.' Iain liked it there.

8. A Change of Direction

Plainsong had less than a week at home after completing their first tour. On 24th March they opened a Dutch tour with a show at Demos in Eindhoven. Demos is a democratic student association focused on the equal status of its members. They operated out of a building called The Bunker. The following night the group played the Paradiso club in Amsterdam on a bill with Matching Mole, the band Robert Wyatt had formed after leaving Soft Machine. A newspaper review in *Het Vrije Volk* reported that the usually indifferent Paradiso audience rewarded the group's performance with demands for two encores. After gigs in Assen and Rotterdam, the tour progressed through Tilburg, Nijmegen, Leeuwarden, Goes, Winterswijk, Kerkhoflaan and Bergen, ending on 3rd April at The Ark in Maassluis.

The tour had been an expensive one to put on. The group were travelling by aeroplane or hiring expensive cars.

Andy Roberts: I can distinctly remember boarding a Fokker Friendship at Schipol for a domestic flight to Eindhoven. It was one of those flights where just as the safety belt light had gone off, it's back on again; it was a flight mainly used to take executives from Amsterdam to the Philips electronic factory.

There was also the not-so-small matter of insuring the equipment they took with them. A carnet from the time lists some of the instruments they took to Holland and how much they were insured for. Iain's Martin D-18 and D-28 guitars were insured for £585, Andy took a Fender Telecaster and a Gibson Dove, both insured for a similar amount, and David's Gibson J45 and Bobby's Gibson Heritage 12 string were insured for £200 apiece.

It was becoming clear that Iain's managers Ken and Alan were no longer calling the tune. They were still taking a commission on both the band's earnings and separately on Iain's but their services were less and less required.

Iain Matthews: Between the four of us in the band, along with Sandy Roberton our producer and unofficial advisor, plus Gemini, our booking agency, there was very little for them to do and I was still handing over twenty-five percent of my earnings to them. More to the point, the rest of Plainsong had no interest in being managed by them. Ken and Alan were old-school, show-business types who were mainly motivated by money. I don't think the rest of the band liked them, though it was clear they wanted to cling on to me. They wanted me to live the music high life, but it was costing me. I realised that when we got back from Holland with nothing to show, despite well-paid concerts.

Andy Roberts: Ken and Alan had organised that tour. We had been taking flights everywhere and hired a huge saloon car, an Opel Senator. We all met up at Howard and Blaikley's house a few days after we got back. We sat in the basement where they had their office. They showed us the accounting and it was clear the tour had made a big loss. We had played sell-out shows for good money and saw none of it. I don't know to this day who underwrote it. I came away thinking 'What's the point of doing all of that work to earn nothing?' Howard and Blaikley were a massive drag on our ankles. They were good at what they did; their modus operandi was to find pretty boy acts and push them out to massive exposure. Iain was their latest in a line that had started with Peter Frampton, but they didn't understand that Iain was a lot more than a pretty face.[6]

Iain Matthews: I believe that Ken and Alan didn't know what to do with me after Matthews Southern Comfort. I remember going to their house and seeing two silver discs on the wall for 'Woodstock'. I happened to say 'Shouldn't they be mine?' They

---

[6] Frampton was the guitar player with The Herd who had a hit in 1968 with one of Howard's songs 'I Don't Want Our Loving To Die'. In that same year Frampton was dubbed 'Face of the Year' by the teenage magazine *Rave*.

reluctantly gave me one. When Vertigo released 'Da Doo Ron Ron' as a solo single and they wanted me to go on *Top of the Pops*, and sent me to Holland to do a similar show with Plainsong miming, they had lost the plot really. We had a meeting and reached an agreement for me to buy them out. I think Ken and Alan already knew that once I made my mind up to do, or not do something, it was pointless fighting me on it. I wouldn't say they were resentful, but they were probably resigned to it.

Sandy Roberton: I went to see Ken Howard and Alan Blaikley. They lived in a beautiful house in Hampstead. I believe they remembered me from back in the middle of the 1960s when they had been regulars at Tom Springfield's house parties along with Dusty, Kiki Dee and Madeline Bell. I negotiated the deal that would free Iain from their management. I thought they were really nice people, and they had enjoyed so much success in the pop world as writers and producers, but I didn't think that working with Iain was a good fit. By the same token I don't think they were broken-hearted to stop working with Iain. I believe we paid £8,000 to get Iain out of the deal. It was normal to have a sunset clause and Howard and Blaikley got a ten percent override on the live work for a period of time.

Iain Matthews: Howard and Blaikley were taking twenty-five percent of everything I earned, Sandy took ten percent from Andy. I don't know how that worked within Plainsong.

Andy Roberts: It made sense to buy Iain out of the deal he had with Howard and Blaikley. To Ken and Alan it was just show business and that is the way they operated. Whether we liked it or not we were being drawn into that world and we weren't comfortable. Also, by that time Harry Isles was doing more and more of our everyday organising, Sandy was our acting manager and Gemini our agents.

Iain Matthews: Gemini were far too underground and unproven for Ken and Alan.

With Ken and Alan out of the picture and Gemini organising concert appearances, the other pieces of the new jigsaw started to fall into place. Harry Isles took charge of the day-to-day business. He was a stickler. Every Friday he produced schedules for the week ahead. These schedules detail dates, venues, times, payments and any other information required to get the band from A to B. They start on 28th April 1972 and run all the way through to Christmas week. They give us a complete behind the scenes timeline of a touring and recording band throughout a year in the life.

Sandy wasted no time in promoting the business affairs of the band. He approached Warner Elektra Atlantic with a view to them signing Plainsong to the Elektra label. The label manager in England was Jonathan Clyde.

Jonathan Clyde: I was just twenty-three at the time. I didn't really know what the fuck I was doing. I'd worked for Decca, but I didn't like it there. After the Rolling Stones left it became the most unhip of labels. Somebody from Warner offered me a job in promotions. I wasn't a 'knock down the door' type of promotions man. To be fair I didn't know diddly-squat about the business side of music then. I was one of a number of idealistic enthusiasts, none of whom had any training. I woke up in the morning, put some records on and that's how I went to work. Music is what we lived for. I trusted my instincts and tried to do what I thought was right and fair. Then I became a label manager and suddenly I was dealing with all of the big acts coming from America. Warner, Elektra and Atlantic were part of the same group, but they were each established labels who were still competing with one another. All of the bands and artists on each of the labels wanted to come to England, sometimes all at once, and it was left to us to choose the records. We were sent test pressings. The Grateful Dead would come and when they left Carly Simon would come and when she left James Taylor would come. Then after that Mo Ostin would come over from Warners and Ahmet Ertegun from Atlantic. They were giants of the music business with enormous influence. It was up to me to make day-to-day decisions, though I was in touch with the US every day. When it came to the Elektra label I deferred to Jac Holzman. In the middle of all this, Plainsong came to us. I knew Jac would like them. I liked both Iain and Andy, though they were like chalk and cheese. Andy was spontaneous and funny as well as creative. Iain was more introspective, even melancholic. I knew his music from Matthews Southern Comfort. I decided it would be great to sign them. I do believe though that Jac's interest in Plainsong was very much an interest in Iain. That was Jac and Jac was Jac. He was very good to me personally, though in meetings he could be prickly and restless and I sometimes felt uncomfortable. That said, I had nothing but admiration for what Jac did, Elektra seemed to be everybody's favourite label.

At some point in April, Plainsong performed three consecutive nights at The Music Workshop at The Scotch of St James nightclub in London's West End. Dave Richards told *Let It Rock* magazine that Jonathan Clyde came down to take a look at the band on one of the nights, and things turned a little bit ugly.

David Richards: It was rather disastrous when some drunk geezer came staggering down the stairs, knocking half of one side of the PA. Sandy Roberton came over to pick up the speakers and shift the guy away. The drunk got awfully stroppy, so Bobby put his guitar down on the stage while we were in the middle of a number and went across and knocked the drunk's head against the wall a few times. And then we continued with the set. Despite the theatrics, Elektra signed us.

Andy Roberts: For a brief moment there was a shit load of money flying about. I knew that Elektra weren't buying into me, my constituency was poetry and theatre. The other two, David and Bobby, were great musicians but unknown, so the money was there because Elektra were buying into Iain Matthews, the one with the proven hit-making potential. It was obvious that Iain was going to be the dominant character and lead artist. Sandy was the business operator who was going to be the steady hand on our

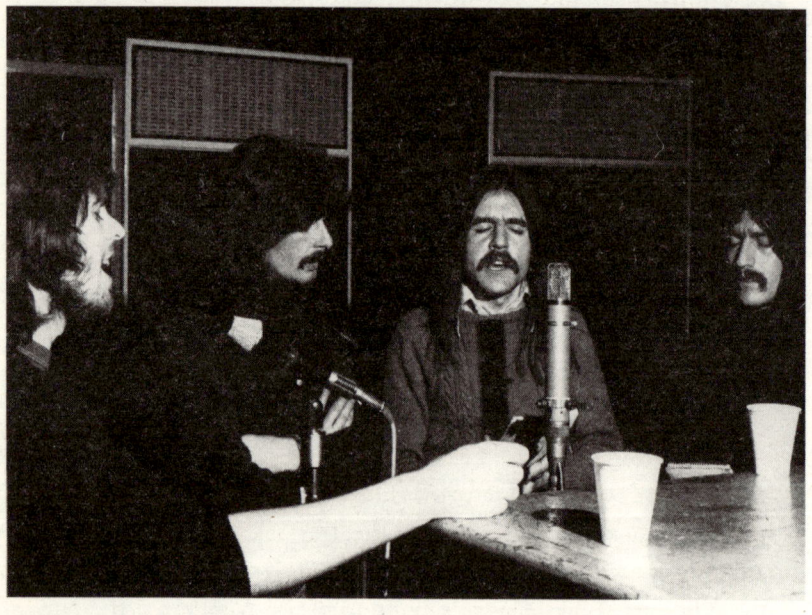

Radio sessions.

tiller and I was happy to feel rescued after the roller coaster ride I had been on over the previous couple of years.

Jac Holzman: I thought the music was perfect for Elektra, so I proceeded.

Sandy Roberton: I negotiated the recording contract with Jonathan Clyde, the Elektra label manager, and Ian Ralfini, the managing director of WEA records. I didn't play any music for them in advance. At this stage I loved Andy, Iain and Plainsong and I think I just did managerial duties to assist and help to get albums made and released. I do believe though that I had a management agreement with Andy.

The radio sessions and the touring continued at pace. On 24th April, Plainsong walked in to the BBC studios at Kensington House, Shepherd's Bush to record a session for John Peel. The five songs they chose to perform were ones that were firmly tethered to the live show repertoire: 'Truck Driving Man', 'Amelia Earhart's Last Flight', 'True Story of Amelia Earhart', 'Yo Yo Man' and 'I'll Fly Away'. Before 'Amelia Earhart's Last Flight', Andy did a spoken word story that he had been doing for the live shows.

> On 1st July 1937, Amelia Earhart, the female Lindbergh, crashed her Lockheed Electra plane somewhere in the Pacific Ocean whilst attempting the first ever round the world flight. The US Navy searched for some weeks, but no trace was found of Earhart, Fred Noonan her navigator, or her plane. At the time of the flight, many of the Pacific islands held by the Japanese were the subject of a military build-up that led finally to the attack on Pearl Harbour four years later. In recent years a great amount of evidence has been unearthed by Fred Goerner, a San Francisco journalist, which points to the real reason for her total disappearance. Her plane was in fact a very sophisticated and powerful machine equipped to spy on the Japanese islands and photograph them for US intelligence purposes. When bad weather brought Amelia and Fred Noonan

The band and Harry Isles (bottom right) en route to The Netherlands.

down in Japanese held territory they were captured by the Japanese and imprisoned. Amelia died of dysentery and Noonan was beheaded. The true story is that the American government knew of their fate, but they simply abandoned their own national heroes to avoid their own political embarrassment and to keep the peace in the Pacific for as long as possible.

Andy then sang 'Just a ship out on the ocean, just a speck against the sky, Amelia Earhart flying out that day, with her partner Captain Noonan on the first day of July, she fell into the ocean far away...' before his bandmates join in with exquisite harmonies, 'and there's a beautiful, beautiful field far away in a land that is fair, happy landings to you Amelia Earhart, farewell first lady of the air'.

The day after the BBC recording Plainsong travelled to Amsterdam to play at the Paradiso.

Andy Roberts: We always stayed at Hotel d'Herberg, on Geldersekade in Amsterdam. They had a dormitory room. It was basic and the 5 or 6 beds were old-fashioned, steel-framed ones. Iain used to have his own room, but all the rest of us plus Harry Isles slept in the big room. The café downstairs was a great place, with a billiard table that had no pockets. They did a fabulous steak fried in garlic, I ate that every night and the joint was jumping till the early hours. That's where a punter, probably attracted by the English accents, taught us a dice game called '5000'. We developed a huge passion for this and bought a baize-lined bowl so we could play in the van on the way to gigs. Iain and I had a good history of dice playing from our early backgammon games. The Hotel d'Herberg was on the edge of the Red Light District so it was the springboard for lovely, late-night strolls around the neighbourhood. I don't think any of us succumbed to the obvious attractions, though I can't speak for Bobby, but we all drank in the ambience. The availability and relaxed attitude to smoking drugs in Amsterdam was a joy for at least three of the members of Plainsong.

Harry Isles: The dormitory at that place reminded me of my days in the RAF during National Service. The Paradiso was the first place I had seen that had a bar for the serving of beer and another counter where you could buy marijuana.

Andy Roberts: After the gig at the Paradiso we were invited to a cafe on Prinsengracht called Folk Fairport. It wasn't a booked gig but we played there after our main evening show as a favour to the club owner who, as the name suggests, was a big fan of Fairport Convention. It didn't have a PA, and we played purely acoustically, but it turned out to be a great little gig. I clearly remember David singing the lead on 'The Poor Ditching Boy'. We were all wearing clogs. We were obsessed with clogs that we bought in shoe shops over there.

Iain Matthews: The Folk Fairport show came from a visit we had at the Paradiso. The guy who ran it came to the show and asked us if we'd consider playing for his opening night and we agreed. We were all night owls at that time and it seemed like a good idea.

Someone took a tape recorder into Folk Fairport that night. The tape gives a real insight not just into the quality of the musicianship and the close harmonies, but also the band dynamic. Whoever was in charge of taping missed the announcements, but it appears that the man who made the introductions had referred to the band as Iain Matthews's group because the first thing we hear is David Richards firmly stating, 'We're called Plainsong, that's the name of the band, Plainsong, and we're not Iain Matthews's band either.' Dave is audibly annoyed that the band are not being given their proper dues.

Once the music starts the mood switches to a loose, knockabout session in a small, smokey Amsterdam café filled with refreshed music lovers and much tuning of instruments. There are jokes about alcohol and cigarettes and David practises his Monty Pythonesque voices. The band perform versions of songs from their stage repertoire, an a cappella 'Souling Song', a heartfelt 'Louise', and strong versions of 'Raider' and 'Bold Marauder' accompanied by effective rhythmic percussion from the clogs they were all wearing. The humour continues with a *Goon Show* version of 'Tulips from Amsterdam', a wild and almost surreal attempt to connect with the audience. With the crowd laughing along, Iain suggests, 'I wish we had taken you over to the Paradiso tonight.' We hear an otherwise shy Bobby Ronga say, 'Yeah. I think when we went into that place it's like everyone was asleep.' Iain adds, 'It's like they've got glass hands.'

Just a few days after returning from Amsterdam, Plainsong played at the London School of Economics on a bill that included Camel, Keith Christmas, Third Ear Band and old mate Sandy Denny. This was followed by a concert at Reading University. A day later on 30th April, Plainsong, accompanied by support act Gary Farr, set off for Bordeaux where they played the Théâtre de l'Alhambra, a 1,500 seat venue. The following day, May Day, the group moved on to Paris to play the Théâtre Bobino in Montparnasse. This was the theatre of Brel, Moustaki, Trenet, Aznavour and Brassens, the place where Juliette Gréco recorded a fine live album.

Iain Matthews: We flew from Biggin Hill in a small propeller plane and we flew back home again.

The band weren't home long. Following a gig in Cambridge on 2nd May, they set off for a short tour of Scottish universities. They played Aberdeen and St Andrews on the 5th and 6th, and on 7th May, David Richards's 25th birthday, they were due to visit the Folk Club at Dundee, but it appears that gig was cancelled. The university shows continued back in England. On 12th May they played Liverpool University, Andy's alma mater, for a show gleefully attended by his old bandmate Adrian Henri, and the following night they were at Leicester. On 20th May, Plainsong played at Manchester University, supported by the singer-songwriter Keith Christmas. Peter Cowley, who two years previously had gone to the same venue to see Matthews Southern Comfort and come away disappointed when Iain failed to show, had a different experience this time.

David, Iain, Bobby and Sandy gathered at Andy's house to discuss the partnership agreement. Andy is taking the photos.

Peter Cowley: I arrived there early because I came straight from work. I wandered around the Union building and bumped into Iain, Andy, Dave and Bob who were pushing an upright piano. I started chatting to them. I think it was Andy who asked if I could give them a hand with the piano. It had to be carried up several flights of stairs to the room where the concert was to take place. I happily agreed as I considered it an honour to be asked to help such esteemed musicians. After a lot of grunting and groaning we managed to get the piano up the stairs. I was just walking away when Iain handed me a £5 note 'for my trouble'. I honestly didn't expect any payment and was delighted with the £5, which was a tidy sum in 1972. I had seen Joni Mitchell on her *Miles of Aisles* tour with L.A. Express supported by Jackson Browne at the Odeon only a few weeks before and the tickets for that were 75 pence.

By mid-May, negotiations with Elektra were complete, contracts prepared, and the band were ready to sign.

Sandy Roberton: The contract was secured with WEA Records Ltd, signed on 12th May 1972, and I was hired to produce the first album. Also on that day, the four members of Plainsong signed a document giving me a fifth of the advance and royalties of the album. The first term of the agreement was for two years and WEA had the option to extend the agreement for a further three one-year periods. During the initial period, Plainsong agreed to deliver three albums. WEA agreed to pay $50,000 dollars for each album delivered. The royalty was ten percent less a ten percent packaging deduction for phonograph records and twenty percent deduction for tape records. Outside of the UK the royalty was eight percent. There were some interesting clauses to this agreement. The seventh clause stated that if any member of the band made a solo album then WEA had the rights to that album. My feeling now was that Jac Holzman was already thinking and planning ahead. There was also a clause 16, which stated, 'The members of the group are jointly and severally bound by the terms and conditions of this agreement,' meaning if anything went wrong it was up to all of us to sort out responsibility. At the same time as Plainsong signed the WEA agreement they signed an agreement with me to say that I would be the 'sole' producer for the term of the WEA agreement and would not engage the services of another producer.

Andy Roberts: We had a series of meetings. The first one was in early May when we drew up a partnership agreement at my house. Nobody signed anything that day, but the principle was written down. A couple of days later we had another meeting to discuss the production agreement. Again we didn't sign anything, but we had a draft. On 11th May we all signed a partnership agreement and the following day we four and Sandy signed a production agreement. On that same day we signed our contract with Elektra. The signatory on behalf of the parent company WEA was Ian Ralfini. They told us we could have $20,000 as an advance on our royalties and a balance of $30,000 more on delivery and acceptance of the first album. There would be a further $50,000 on each of two subsequent albums. The music industry was awash with money at the time and you took them for what you could get. I wasn't under any illusions. The money was flying about because they were buying into Iain Matthews, for the same reason we were spending some of that money to get Iain out of his contract with Howard and Blaikley. The money we paid to get Iain out of that deal was worth it to get rid of Ken and Alan. In any case, we wouldn't have got a cent without Iain in the first place.

For Iain, the signing to Elektra was the squaring of a circle.

Iain Matthews: Starting in 1967, a long time before I knew how record companies functioned, Elektra was my go-to company. My credo was, if it was on Elektra, it had to be good. Almost all of the singer-songwriters that mattered in my life were on Elektra. Whenever I saw a new Elektra release, I bought it, sight unheard.

On Monday 22nd May, Plainsong crossed the English Channel to The Netherlands again, this time to the Pinkpop Festival. Pinkpop started in a small town called Geleen in the Dutch province of Limburg. Jo Peeters was one of the locals who saw Plainsong the day they opened the festival.

Jo Peeters: Limburg was not the most modern and progressive part of the country, the Catholic Church had a lot of influence over people's lives. Pinkpop was started in 1970 by some youth workers, mainly because nothing ever happened in Limburg that was interesting for young people. I was nineteen in 1972, I read our only music paper *Muziekkrant Oor*. The kids who went there were weekend hippies, trying to create a Woodstock feeling for ourselves. The festival attracted big names, the year Plainsong played they shared a bill with Mungo Jerry, Argent, Michael Chapman, The Incredible String Band and The Strawbs. The venue was called Burgemeester Damen Sportpark, a football field surrounded by a dirt racetrack for motors. On one side, there was a stand for spectators. On festival days the field and track were the place where the fans gathered and the stage, which was really just scaffolding, was built into the stand. It was divided into three parts: in one part, a band was playing, in another part a band was removing their equipment, and in another part a band was placing their equipment. All this was done from the front, so while a band was performing, forklifts were constantly passing by. If I remember well, Plainsong opened the festival on the left-hand stage. At that time, I very much liked folk music, and acoustic performances in general. And here were four men with just their guitars and voices. They impressed me from the first sentence they sang, 'Just a ship out on the ocean, just a speck against the sky, Amelia Earhart flying out that day.'

Plainsong were paid £450 for a one-hour set. The regional newspaper *Limburgs Dagblad* reported, 'Genoten werd er, en dat met volle teugen.' ('We enjoyed it to the fullest.')

Iain Matthews: We got the Pinkpop Festival early days. It is a huge prestigious festival these days. I believe we played the third one after Sandy introduced us to Gemini.

Gemini's Dutch booker was Frank van der Meijden. He booked tours and concerts in The Netherlands for Plainsong throughout the year.

Frank van der Meijden: One of my bands was CCC Incorporated, a folk band, a classic bunch of hippies, so I knew that scene. After that I moved on to manage Doe Maar who became very famous, so much so that they were known as The Dutch Beatles. I actually knew Iain Matthews before Plainsong. I had been the Dutch booker for Matthews Southern Comfort. I also loved both of Iain's solo albums. *If You Saw Thro' My Eyes* did really well here in Holland, it was one of my own personal favourite albums. I met Max Hole and Geoff Jukes from the Gemini Agency and I became the Dutch rep for all of their acts: Richard Thompson, Michael Chapman, Spirogyra and of course Plainsong. When they came on their first tour I managed it and went on the tour with them. I was very proud to be working with Iain. He was a real name.

Andy Roberts: Frank was a long-haired lad, even younger than us and we were only twenty-five. After our first loss-making trip to Holland when we flew everywhere, we usually went by ferry and van. We set out from Sheerness on the tip of Kent and landed at Flushing. It was the easiest, cheapest and quickest way to go to Holland then. Frank would meet up with us when we landed and then hang around with us. It was probably Frank who showed us where to buy the best clogs.

The issue of how the band was billed had reared its ugly head once again at Pinkpop Festival; the posters listed them as 'Ian Matthews and Plainsong'. This hadn't been the first time that promoters used this title, or the last. Redcar Jazz Club billed them in this way in June, and David Suff distinctly recalled that their concert at Colchester back in January had been billed as 'Ian Matthews's new band Plainsong'.

The journalist Caroline Boucher broached the subject in an article for *Disc and Music Echo*.

It is a very corporate effort, but they have the usual problem of being tagged 'Ian Matthews and new backing boys' on gigs and appearances. 'If a promoter wants to get people to come to gigs he'll use the name of the person whose face is known,' says Dave Richards who admits to being pretty fed up with Ian always being singled out. 'But you can't go to Plainsong and come away with the impression that it's Ian Matthews's band, the other people in the band are too sure of their own identities to be backing musicians.' Ian says it hasn't been that easy for him to turn his outlook as solo singer into part of a band overnight. 'It's been a very hard process sinking into a band. It's really nice, but you have to remember that I have been more or less a solo singer for five or six years and it's hard to accept other people singing lead vocals.' For a group of people who don't have a reputation for staying in the same band long, they all look on Plainsong as pretty permanent. 'Permanent as long as we all understand each other and there's room to enjoy it,' says Dave. 'The only thing that keeps it together is an assured conviction of the worth of the music that's played.'

In another interview with Steve Peacock of *Sounds*, Andy and Iain were put up as spokesmen.

Andy Roberts: The point about this is, it's not a band in that it's not vans full of equipment schlepping up and down the M1 seven days a week, which any Andy Roberts creation would have to be simply because I can't command that much bread on my own. The thing about this is that rather than a band it's a sort of travelling concert, we only intend to do two or three gigs a week, and from the outset we can equip the thing and keep it on the road without having to work ourselves to death. We want a lot of time off partly so we can write and a lot so that we can rehearse and keep the thing going. It's better to be part of a rehearsed team of four singers and instrumentalists, I can do far more of the things I want to do. It was just a question of finding the right team.

Steve Peacock wondered how permanent they envisaged Plainsong being. Iain told him, 'At the moment it's permanent, this week it is. But that's all you can say.' Andy added, 'If it stays

On stage at Redcar Jazz Club.

on the road long enough to end up solvent I shall be happy. It'll be the first thing I have ever done that has.'

On Sunday 11th June, Plainsong headed to the north east of England in their clogs to perform at the legendary Redcar Jazz Club. The club was based at the Windsor Ballroom at the seafront Coatham Hotel on Newcomen Terrace. It had started in 1959 and moved to the 1,000 capacity ballroom in November 1960. At first only jazz was played live, but as the sixties progressed the club booked blues music – T-Bone Walker and Sonny Boy Williamson played there – and then rock music. The club managed to catch many acts and bands just before they made the big time. Saturday nights were dance nights with music provided by local bands and Sunday night was when the big acts came; Pink Floyd, T. Rex, Cream, Rod Stewart and Fleetwood Mac all played there. The Who played there for £350 just a month before being paid $6,250 for their performance at Woodstock.

Local club member Arthur Lancaster was in the audience.

Arthur Lancaster: The first time I went to Redcar Jazz Club I saw Stone the Crows. I went fairly regularly after that. I went on the train from Middlesbrough and got a bus back that was provided by the club. The strangest gig I saw there was Roxy Music who were on as support to a film about Jimi Hendrix live at Berkeley. It cost £75 to hire the film and Roxy Music were paid £50. That was on 4th June and the following Sunday Plainsong came. I knew Iain's music. I worked as a motor mechanic at the Post Office and somebody there lent me his *If You Saw Thro' My Eyes* album. I went straight out and bought my own copy and then I bought a couple of Matthews Southern Comfort albums. Their support was the folk group Prelude who came from Gateshead. They were still over a year away from their one big hit, an a cappella version of Neil Young's 'After The Gold Rush'. The show was pretty sparsely attended with probably only about a couple of hundred there, if that. I sat on a table at the back and could still get a clear view of the stage. There was plenty of tables out and most of the audience sat down although some always stood at the bar to the left of the stage or the smaller room to the right. Prelude were enjoyable that night, but I loved Plainsong. They did 'Call the Tune', 'Raider' and 'Amelia Earhart's Last Flight'. I seem to think they played 'Reno Nevada' as well. The harmonies were just brilliant.

In the 17th June edition of *Melody Maker* under the headline 'Plainsong Changing Course' Karl Dallas interviewed the band about new plans. Dallas had sat through another radio session that Plainsong had recorded for the BBC for Pete Drummond's *Sounds of the 70s* and wrote that Iain looked 'almost happy with the way things were going'. Iain said, 'I am getting close to what I've always wanted so I think it's time to take a new direction.' He was referring to the fact that Plainsong had announced they were looking for a drummer. 'He's got to be a guy who does more than just sit behind his drum kit. He ought to be able to play all sorts of things, hand-drums and so on, whatever's needed. What would be really great would be someone who could double up on drums and guitar, but that's going to be really hard to find.' Iain added, 'We'll keep a lot of our acoustic stuff but then we'll be able to work to a climax, which we've not been doing so far.' Karl Dallas wondered if it might be a bit early to change direction before the band had recorded its first album. Iain assured him that, 'It's not so much a change in direction as a development. We can use session drummers like Timi Donald while we're still looking for a regular drummer.'

9. In Search of Amelia Earhart

In early June, the members of Plainsong started rehearsals for the recording of their album at the Jubilee Studios in Covent Garden. On 8th June they walked into the old dairy that was now Sound Techniques studio in Old Church Street, Chelsea to start work on the album that would become *In Search of Amelia Earhart*.

The band returned on June 15th, 21st and 23rd and the album was then completed in six days in July on 18th, 20th, 24th, 26th, 27th and 30th. The studio was booked out for them between two in the afternoon and midnight on each of those days. It was a studio not unfamiliar to Iain, it was where he had gone in August 1967 with a collection of LPs under his arm to show his musical taste to a young Fairport Convention who were about to record their first single.

Sound Techniques studio was founded by the engineers John Wood and Geoff Frost in 1965. This was where Nick Drake and John Martyn recorded and where Pink Floyd made 'See Emily Play'. When Iain Matthews first recorded there, his engineer was John Wood and the producer was Joe Boyd. For Plainsong the engineer was Jerry Boys and the producer was Sandy Roberton.

Sandy Roberton: Sound Techniques was sort of like a huge gang of friends hanging out and making music. All the artists seemed to know each other and all the session musicians did as well.

Jerry Boys: We would usually start work at Sound Techniques around midday and continue through to midnight. Plainsong were serious musicians who really meant it. Iain especially was very good at recording. He was so fast and accurate with his vocals and in particular with his backing vocals. He was a real talent.

Top: Plainsong at Sound Techniques during the *Amelia* recording sessions.
Bottom: Sandy Roberton and Jerry Boys working the studio desk.

Andy Roberts: Those Dutch clogs we all favoured throughout 1972 had to be sidelined in a row in the studio. We had to take them off, because they took over anything we played if we still wore them.

Iain Matthews: We were a drummerless act when we played live, but we decided to have drums on the album. We chose our friend Timi Donald. Timi was firmly in our circle at the time. He played on Richard's *Henry the Human Fly* and on Sandy Denny's *Sandy* album as well as my *Tigers Will Survive*.

The band already had some well-crafted material that they had been playing live and on radio sessions. They had a bunch of songs that were about finding the light. The first song on the album, 'For the Second Time', is one of Iain's highly personal songs and is introduced by Andy on his Kriwaczek string organ.

Andy Roberts: I heard a man on the wireless demonstrating this instrument that he had invented. I couldn't understand how it was played as he described it, but it had an amazing sound. I made it my quest to track him down; not the easiest task, but luckily he had a very distinctive name, Paul Kriwaczek. He lived with his family in Hendon, and he invited me round. He had been a dentist, worked at the BBC, and was a doper. I left that meeting with the only prototype Kriwaczek string organ, in expectation of becoming the official demonstrator of this remarkable instrument. I got to grips with it, though I didn't really play it the way Paul had envisaged. I took it to sessions and used it on my own albums. The only time I ever played it onstage was at a Cat Stevens showcase at the Theatre Royal, Drury Lane, but it was in the studio that it became a huge asset. It sounded like nothing else – it was a proper stringed instrument with frets, and the sound was made by finger on string, but it had infinite sustain and was fantastically responsive to touch. In some ways it sounded like the trick The Beatles used of playing a guitar solo and then flipping the tape and playing it backwards, like on 'I'm Only Sleeping'. I had the only one of those instruments in existence. After one of Iain's solo recording sessions at Morgan Studios, Alun Davies arrived. Alun was playing guitar for a Cat Stevens record and I was showing him the string organ when Steve, as we called Cat Stevens in those days, arrived. He started playing a new song, and instinctively I picked up my acoustic and played along with him and Alun. Before I knew it, Robin Black had me mic'd up. It was a song called 'How Can I Tell You'. After some discussion I ended up playing on the track as it was recorded and added a solo on the string organ. Then I just packed up and left. The album came out with my Kriwaczek string organ solo on it. I wasn't credited. Some years later when the deluxe CD version came out Paul Samwell-Smith wrote in the sleeve notes that I played on it and I finally got my credit. The PPL or Public Performance Licensing who look after payments for people who play on records tell me that 'How Can I Tell You' is now my highest earning piece of music; higher than the 'Comfortably Numb' I did with Pink Floyd, higher even than 'Lily the Pink'. On 'For the Second Time', it was just an idea to lead Iain's song in with an enigmatic, random sounding string organ line, and then overdub a second one, having them resolve to a melodic phrase underpinned by David Richards's beautifully romantic piano part. Job done. It was a unique way of announcing a new band.

In the song a young man arrives at his house in the early hours of the morning to find all the lights on but nobody at home.

Iain Matthews: In early 1972, my daughter Darcy was not long since born. Her mother Chris and I were struggling, learning how to be parents. Women have an instinct for these things, but men need to learn how to be fathers. I wasn't – or more likely chose not to be – very good at it. I wasn't mentally prepared to be a father. Music was my life. Chris and I squabbled in our nest on Highgate Hill. One day we fell out and I went off to work with Plainsong somewhere. I came home late, maybe two in the morning. It was deathly quiet in the flat. I called softly but there was no answer. Chris had left a scribbled note on the table. She had taken Darcy to her mum's house. I imagined all kinds of outcomes and scared myself awake. Sleep wasn't on the cards, so I sat down and began to write. 'I came home to find the lights all burning bright...'

Andy Roberts: Iain was the writer for the band on that first record. I brought in some covers, but my role was to be as good a musical support to that fabulous voice as possible, while staying true to our aim of going places with vocal harmony that were distinctive, and not just the usual pop choruses, with voices stacked on the 3 and the 5. I think that was a big part of the record, overall, to get beyond those country harmonies where we could.

In preparation for the recording, Iain and Andy spent a lot of time listening to music together. The second song on the album is 'Yo Yo Man', a song by Rick Cunha that first appeared on a Mason Williams album called *Sharepickers* with Rick Cunha himself on vocal and Bill Cunningham playing the fiddle.

Iain Matthews: Andy brought in a copy of *Sharepickers*. The album hadn't been out long when we sat down and decided we were taken by '(I'm a) Yo-Yo Man' and we earmarked it as a song we might include. The song itself was about a time not that long before in our own youthful years when kids would be bundled off to the local cinema on a Saturday morning. Back in the 1950s I went to The Oxford Picture Theatre in Barton-upon-Humber to watch Gene Autry or Hopalong Cassidy riding the range. Occasionally, before the main feature a special guest was brought on stage to demonstrate a new fad. I once saw a yo-yo man twirling and flipping his wooden discs on a string into all sorts of wonderful distortions. By great coincidence, when I moved to America, I became friends with Rick Cunha. He told me that the yo-yo man had been to his local cinema in southern California as well.

Andy Roberts: In my case it was *Mickey Mouse Club* at the Harrow Dominion. In between Hoppy in *Bar 20 Rides Again*, or terrible stuff like *The Perils of Pauline*, there would occasionally be specialist presentations, and a guy with two yo-yos going at once was one of those. Iain and I were born only four days apart, so we share a lot of common experience of the rationed, recently devastated world we lived in back in the fifties. When we sat down to copy the lyric from the original, we made it 'icy cola'. I only found out years later that there was a soda called Royal Crown Cola. Yep, R. C. Cola! Musically, David brought a solid bass groove to the song, and Bobby played the wah-wah electric guitar, which pulled us away from a full country vibe.

One of the records that Iain introduced Andy to was Paul Siebel's *Woodsmoke and Oranges*, an album Iain adored.

Iain Matthews: My favourite record shop then was Musicland on the corner of Noel Street and Berwick Street in Soho. I was in there one chilly day in the winter of 1970 when I came across this cover featuring a drawing of a man cupping his chin in the palm of his hand. The familiar E for Elektra was in the top left-hand corner of the sleeve. I was intrigued, this was in the days when you took the album sleeve to the front of the store and asked for a listen of the record. I didn't bother asking to listen, I just bought it, how could it not be good? It was on the right label and had great graphics. I took that record back to Rosecroft Avenue and played it over and over. The writing was stunning and the singing was delivered in a tough, soaring style, yet it had enough tenderness to grab and hold my attention. It was wonderful song after wonderful song; 'Bride 1945', 'Any Day Woman', 'Then Came the Children' and the one that became my personal favourite, 'Louise', a song about a dead hooker. I played that song, in fact the whole record for Andy, and we knew we had found another gem for our album.

Andy Roberts: Paul Seibel was a heck of a writer. We just went for it in the studio on 'Louise', like Dillard & Clark, I felt. Bobby and I played the acoustics, country style, weaving through each other's lines. Easy and tuneful, with Iain wringing all that pathos from the sadness of the lyric. We really mined that album of Paul's. Years later, Ed Kelleher introduced me to Paul Seibel in a late-night drinking place in New York City. It was a bare room down in Greenwich Village, with a giant heap of beer cans in the middle. I think Paul said he was now a baker; at any rate he wasn't writing anymore.

Iain Matthews: The fourth track on the record was the first original work I brought to the table for album consideration. I wrote it in the barely glowing embers of Matthews Southern Comfort. It's about what could have been and, had I been able to summon up the chutzpah, what should have been.

> If you're gonna try, you gotta face the music
> If you wanna dance, you gotta call the tune
> If you're throwing high, I wanna see you use it
> If you're gonna make it, make it soon

It wasn't the first time I had dressed up a song about personal frustration in maternal clothing. It was another song about being misunderstood by a kid who didn't even understand himself. There were a few of those during my Matthews Southern Comfort period; 'What We Say', 'Scion', 'And Me' yet another. Probably more if I put my mind to it.

Andy Roberts: Iain's song 'Call the Tune' stood out as something very special. We knew it was good, we knew it had an indefinable something that we needed to find in the studio, but it just wasn't there immediately. We had the basic track with acoustic guitars and vocals, but we all knew that somehow we had missed the DNA of the song.

Iain Matthews: Once the basic track was recorded we had a problem couching this song. Beyond its skeleton it just would not sit. We worked on it for the entire day, trying out a number of different approaches but by teatime frustrations were on the boil. Andy said he had an idea, but wanted to be left alone with just

Sandy and our engineer Jerry. He was polite about it, but I think what he was really saying was, 'Look, can you all please fuck off while I try and rescue this.'

Andy Roberts: Iain remembers me easing all the others out of the session so I could work on the track alone. Maybe, but I rather think I took a monitor mix home, of this song and of 'Even the Guiding Light', which had a similar problem, and worked on them by myself. Then I made a date with Sandy, a day or two later, to go into Sound Techniques with just the two of us and Jerry Boys to wrestle those two songs into existence. It was a late start session, for sure, and we went deep into the small hours, maybe four in the morning before I knew it was done. I just followed my nose, tracking as we went, but I had found something very satisfying in the tonality of the chords Iain had written that just brought out what I thought was an anthemic, slightly churchy feel. With Sandy's encouragement I knew we had a good direction going. I just hoped Iain would buy into it. After all, it was his song, and it had been his feeling that it wasn't yet right that had led to discord and insecurity while we did the basic track.

Iain Matthews: When we came back to the studio I was full of trepidation. Sandy pressed play and what came out of the speakers was magical, pure Andy. Double- and triple-tracked electric guitar parts piled on top of one another, forming a glissando, a waterfall of sonic bliss. I believe what I heard that afternoon was exactly what was heard on the record.

Andy Roberts: I had always loved ballads, and lush romantic ones, too. I liked Marc Benno's 'Icicle Star Tree' on the first Asylum Choir record, or 'Quicksilver Girl' on Steve Miller's album *Sailor*. This wasn't quite like those, but that sort of musicality hung over this arrangement. Tremolo guitar is always a nice way to go. The problem was only in getting the track to fit right, in elevating the guitars from just another mass of strings into something structured and elegant. The vocal harmonies always sounded great, and Iain's lead vocal was as stellar as always. It just needed a track that was as good as the song. Then I found the highline harmonies, layered them in behind, and it opened up. These things happen. I remember being hugely relieved when Iain liked what we had done.

'Diesel on My Tail' was written by Jim Fagan, a hillbilly songwriter raised in Coalfield, Tennessee who wrote hundreds of tunes about love, loss and working-class life. It was first recorded by the bluegrass brothers Jim & Jesse McReynolds and their band The Virginia Boys in 1967, on an album that took its title from the song.

Iain Matthews: By the time we got to the studio we had a wide range of influences, everyone from Judy Collins, Joni, Tim Buckley to Richard Fariña and Jim Kweskin's Jug Band to the old Appalachian stuff that I loved. Part of the attraction of collecting all that music and learning the songs we liked was that we could bring something new to the folk scene in England. Fairport and Steeleye Span were digging back into the tradition here, we were digging back to the stuff that had gone from here to America and we were bringing it all back home again. It was Andy who brought 'Diesel on My Tail' to us. It's a great little ditty about a VW bug being bullied along the highway by an impatient semi-truck driver. We had Martin Jenkins in the studio for this one. I knew Martin from the days when he was in Dando Shaft. They were managed by Howard and Blaikley as well. Martin added the mandocello.

Andy Roberts: *The Sunday Times* newspaper put out a double-album collection of country music. I borrowed it from a friend and put it onto a cassette. It was a huge education for me. I had always distrusted country music during my time in Liverpool. Real men leant towards soul music, black grooves, not that squeaky clean Nashville stuff. Okay, Ray Charles had shown us all the greatness of Nashville writing on *Modern Sounds in Country and Western Music*, but Ray had been a genius for so long already that it hardly counted. So when I started understanding what country contained, as a style of music, it was a revelation. I hadn't realised that The Everly Brothers, Buddy Holly, Elvis, for Chrissakes, were all deep country at heart. *The Sunday Times* compilation had interesting selections on it. 'Skip A Rope' by The Harden Trio, Tammy Wynette singing 'Ode To Billie Joe' and then this track, by Jim & Jesse McReynolds, which was pure bluegrass. At that time I hadn't heard of The Louvin Brothers, or The Blue Sky Boys, The Stanley Brothers, or any of those wonderful harmony acts. I just loved the sound of Jim & Jesse, and the content of the lyric drew me back to 'Beep Beep' by The Playmates, which I recalled from *Children's Favourites* on the Light Programme with Uncle Mac. The song stuck in my mind, and when I threw it into a rehearsal with Plainsong it lit a fire and was in the set. When we recorded it, it sounded a bit lame until Martin Jenkins came in and rescued the track with his mandocello. The country strand in Plainsong was all my fault, I think. Some of it worked fine back then, but some was an embarrassment. We rehearsed Gram Parsons's 'Luxury Liner' from the International Submarine Band record. Another of my *Cash Box* cupboard records, the first and only album by Glen Sherley had given us 'F.B.I. Top Ten'. We just threw out the net, and occasionally caught a big un.

'Amelia Earhart's Last Flight' was another song that came out of the cupboard of unwanted review copies at the *Cash Box* offices in New York, on an album by Laramie.

Andy Roberts: We had this song in our stage repertoire early on. The song has a gorgeous, spiritual chorus. It became a huge favourite of Viv Stanshall's. I lent him this one, and the Glen Sherley album, and he loved them both, uncritically. My copy of the Laramie album has a sticker on it that Viv put there, which states 'The Sheets Are Alive To The Sound Of Keynsham'.

'Amelia Earhart's Last Flight' was one of many topical songs inspired by news stories written by Red River Dave McEnery. Dave had a long career in entertainment after starting out as a yodeller and lasso trick performer at rodeos in Texas. He wrote his

Amelia song not too long after she went missing. He performed it on a very early television broadcast from the New York World's Fair in April 1939. It is believed to be the first song ever performed on commercial television.

Andy Roberts: After the album was out, a guy came up to me at a gig in Manchester and handed me a record. It was an album by Red River Dave McEnery, and 'Amelia Earhart's Last Flight' was on it. It had a verse we hadn't recorded because it was missing from the Laramie version. I always regretted not having the 3rd verse to hand when we made the track. Red River Dave was a radio cowboy singer who had written this tune within months of Earhart disappearing. It is an on-the-spot documentary song; that's what makes it so compelling.

Iain Matthews: The only problem with it was that it had a romanticised theme that chimed with the official American government version of events. I came up with 'True Story of Amelia Earhart' because after devouring Goerner's book I realised that Red River Dave's song was little more than a hokey folk tale. I had to write something with a little more meat on its bones.

Andy Roberts: Iain wrote his response to Red River Dave's song and a seed grew into a tree. Iain nailed it. He put the Fred Goerner book into a nutshell. The genius of this is that, although we had all read the book and thought it had a point to make, there was no way to get it across to an audience without boring them stupid for 10 minutes. That's not Iain's style, so he set out to tell the tale in 16 lines, or whatever it is, and it's all there. The tragedy laid bare, just set out for easy consumption, but with a killer chorus and an immediate connection that is inescapable. The song has a lovely solid acoustic rhythm from Bobby, leaving me to embroider with the tremolo Telecaster and a wah-wah pedal. This song demonstrates perfectly the Plainsong way with harmony. When we first got together it was immediately apparent that Iain's voice was in a higher register than mine, so I couldn't perform the traditional part of singing a third above his lead vocal.

David could handle the highline so I fell into the habit of finding a harmony part a fourth below his.

Plainsong recorded 'True Story of Amelia Earhart' thirty-five years to the month that Amelia went missing. In her attempt to fly around the world she had set off from Oakland, California on 20th May. She crossed America, headed south to Brazil and then crossed the Atlantic to land in Senegal by 7th June. She then crossed Africa and made the first non-stop journey over the Red Sea to India where she landed in Karachi, then a part of British India. She reached Darwin, Australia on 28th June after flying over Burma, Siam, Singapore and The Dutch East Indies. On 29th June she was in Lae, New Guinea preparing for the last section of the round-the-globe trip. The plan was to fly to Honolulu, Hawaii with a refuelling stop on the isolated Howland Island in the middle of the Pacific Ocean, before returning to Oakland, California. Howland Island is unique in that it is in a time zone of its own called 'Anywhere on Earth' time, meaning it is the last place on earth where a date exists before a new date begins. On 2nd July 1937, Amelia Earhart's plane hovered somewhere between the light, the dark, yesterday, today and tomorrow trying to find her refuelling spot in the vastness of the Pacific Ocean. She thought she had overshot Howland Island and turned to try again. Her fuel was running low. Amelia flew into yesterday and disappeared. The rest is a mystery still unsolved. The official reports tell us that her plane crashed into the waves, Fred Goerner's book tells a different tale and since then hundreds of countertheories have been posited, most of them false alarms.

> You take it or you leave it but I'm telling anyhow
> There's a story you should know
> Amelia was a hero in all of your hearts
> And that's all they want you to know
>
> She landed in the headlines on the first day of July
> When Electra hit the ocean bed
> And flying fifteen-hundred miles from her allotted course
> Was not what all the newsstands said

She left with Captain Noonan, her navigating force
From New Guinea to the Howland Isles
With thirty minutes fuel left, no landfall came the cry
And all of us believed them for a while

Oh Amelia it's true
You're the lady of the air
This I'm not disputing anyhow
But if what Mr Goerner said was only half the truth
Then Amelia

For thirty days the Lexington and others searched the sea
Before pronouncing Earhart lost
It all was going smoothly and the senators relaxed
Amelia and Noonan paid the cost

Then a CBS man Goerner was confused by all the facts
He said there's someone telling lies
Amelia's plane was not the one they detailed in the news
The fuel tanks alone were twice that size

Oh Amelia it's true
You're the lady of the air
This I'm not disputing anyhow
But if what Mr Goerner said was only half the truth
Then Amelia

Jesús Salas, one of many, he had no call to lie
He was working in the harbour that day
And Saipan was a wartime stronghold of the Japanese
And Jesús saw the fliers land away

So who's to point the finger more so
Who's to say what's right
Me, I just wanted you to hear
How brave Amelia Earhart, first lady of the air
And Frederick Noonan ended their careers

Oh Amelia it's true
You're the lady of the air
This I'm not disputing anyhow
But if what Mr Goerner said was only half the truth
Then Amelia
Oh Amelia

Iain Matthews: We added my song to the live repertoire and, combined with the stories we told about Amelia and her exploits, we were beginning to have a concept. In fact a lot of the reviewers talked about *In Search of Amelia Earhart* as a concept album. I don't think we did too much to discourage them and of course we had one more flight song.

'I'll Fly Away', written as a gospel tune by Albert E. Brumley in 1929, was inspired by a secular hillbilly ballad called 'The Prisoner's Song'. Brumley himself told the story that one day he was picking cotton in his father's fields when he found himself singing a fragment of a song, 'If I had wings of an angel, over these prison walls I would fly.' He thought he could turn this fragment into a hymn. 'I'll Fly Away' was first recorded by the Selah Jubilee Singers and by The Kossoy Sisters on their album *Bowling Green*. The latter version was used many years later in the Coen brothers' film *O Brother, Where Art Thou?* Iain knew the song from his obsessive collecting of Elektra records.

Iain Matthews: I blame The Dillards for my love of mountain music. I heard 'I'll Fly Away' on their album *Wheatstraw Suite*, it was the first track, thirty-seven seconds of harmonised a cappella. In many ways this song epitomises a lot of what I hoped to achieve when I agreed to be a part of Plainsong. Appalachian-styled, modal-based country music was what I was working towards. As time went by the band moved further and further away from that model.

Andy Roberts: Plainsong inherited Iain's and my own love of a cappella music, which we had plundered on his 'Da Doo Ron Ron' single, back in his solo period. Unaccompanied vocal music is an absolute joy, and Albert E. Brumley's gospel songs are as good as you can get for it. I had been totally knocked out by John Hartford's record *Aereo-Plain*. It seemed to represent the perfect meeting of old-school bluegrass and stoner hipness, with terrific lyric writing and uncompromising instrumental brilliance. The perfect mix of old and new. I love the exuberance of this song. Voices and a single Appalachian dulcimer seem to embody the optimism of the first half of that year. I had got the dulcimer from a builder in LA during our tour in 1971. I didn't know how to play one, never had tried, though Richard Thompson was playing a rental one on a couple of songs in the set. I just loved the look of the instrument, and that stringy sound, bringing no weight to the track at all. I have owned many guitars – acoustic, electric, bass, baritone. I've only ever owned one dulcimer, and it's the one I play here.

In more recent years when Iain has introduced 'Even the Guiding Light' on stage he says, 'In 1967, Richard Thompson wrote a song called "Meet on the Ledge" and in 1972 I finally got round to writing a response to it.' That's highly likely to be a retrospective story.

Iain Matthews: At the time I didn't really consider what I was writing the song about, I just let it out. I think the real story about this song goes back to me being twitchy about what journalists and managers said to me. The least little thing could set me off. If ever I felt slighted I would sulk or roll out the arrogance and then get it out of my system by writing a song. I believe this song is one of those. I suppose I got some decent songs out of being such a fuck-up. We did two different versions of this song. Andy sings a folky, picking version and the one I did, I like to think, is more like The Byrds.

Andy Roberts: This was the other track that I worked on with Sandy, along with 'Call the Tune'. I always felt that there should be one track that rocked, that had a dirty edge like the songs I had idolised back in the early sixties, when my world was defined by the blues: country blues, Chicago blues, blues with a groove. Obviously Plainsong wasn't a blues band, and in many ways it stood square against the music of my youth with its rough edges, but I wanted this track to have an attitude. I remember my first instinct being that Byrds sound from the mid-sixties, when they combined folk tunes with harmony and 12-string jangle. The other thing in my mind was Robbie Robertson's tone on 'Caledonia Mission', from the *Big Pink* album. Sweet, but spikey.

We weren't an electric band, but this was to be the electric track on the record. I had a Telecaster guitar and a Tremolux amp, and they are both right there, with no sweetening. All I did was double the guitar lines between the verses to give it that 12-string sound. I was pretty sure that Iain wouldn't like what we'd done on this one, and I was relieved when he let it go without a problem.

'Side Roads' is another highly personal song written by Iain.

Iain Matthews: My relationship with Chris was slipping away. I was struggling to know how to retrieve it, not knowing what it was that I was trying to save. I reflected, doubted and wondered whether us getting together should have happened in the first place. I blamed myself for missing all sorts of clues, 'If I'd been noticing side roads, following signs...' I started to think that a fresh start somewhere might be the answer, a place in the sunshine where we could leave all the shit behind and have a trouble-free relationship. I didn't consider that emotional shit travels with you wherever you go. Andy did what he always does best and blended the Kriwaczek string organ with the acoustic guitar to beautiful affect. I don't know what Bobby added. He must be on there. I can only imagine that he and Andy must have picked so well together that it's practically unnoticeable that there are two guitars.

Andy Roberts: That's Bobby on the heavily compressed lead acoustic. It's a great sound. What a beautiful song, with a great vocal performance from Iain. I just played the arpeggiated rhythm acoustic, and blended in the Kriwaczek string organ.

The last track 'Raider' was in Plainsong's repertoire very early. It was one of the songs they performed on their first *Old Grey Whistle Test* appearance at the beginning of March.

Iain Matthews: There is an ongoing debate about who brought this song into the fold. My money is on Andy. It's got his musical taste stamped all over it. I don't think Bobby brought anything to the studio and neither did David. He was a Deadhead. He brought two Grateful Dead songs, one called 'Ripple' and another called 'Friend of the Devil' into our live set, but he didn't bring anything for the album. I loved the way Andy made this song his own with the modal tuned picking he was always incredibly good at. In the foggy reaches I seem to recall that it was a toss-up between this song and another from Yester and Henske's *Farewell Aldebaran* album. There was another song on there called 'Snowblind' that we really liked. In the end I think we had a democratic vote and chose 'Raider'. Our friend Martin Jenkins played the fiddle on this one.

Andy Roberts: Not so many years ago, Iain gave me a gift, a copy of the Jerry Yester and Judy Henske record that we took this song from. It is signed to me by them both. *Farewell Aldebaran* is one of the greatest records ever made. This song is unbelievable, it has a sound, I think it's a hammer dulcimer, that just takes it someplace magical. I arranged it using Davy Graham's invented tuning, DADGAD, and it worked a treat. Then I plundered the catalogue of guitar pieces I have done over the years in collaboration with poets. This one was called 'Peter Pan Man' by Adrian Henri, my great friend and guru. The intro to that work opens 'Raider', and then the main theme appears in a different time signature as an instrumental melody in the middle of the song, before the extended solo, with Martin Jenkins's fiddle in the blend. I like the sense of continuation, that something I had done before Plainsong existed could be developed and incorporated seamlessly into new work. When we appeared on *The Old Grey Whistle Test*, we pre-recorded backing tracks for 'Call the Tune' and 'Raider' with Dave Mattacks on drums and sung the vocal live over the top of them when being filmed. We brought those backing tracks into Sound Techniques when recording the album and overdubbed them, hence on 'Raider' there is the steadiness of Dave Mattacks's drumming, pinning it all together. The line 'Oh, you're dreaming me!' seems to sum up the year we spent, reaching out for that place we couldn't describe, but we all felt at the time.

Sandy Roberton recalled that the recording experience was smooth sailing.

Sandy Roberton: I was probably closest to Andy as we had worked together for nearly five years by the time we went into the studio to make *Amelia*. We had recorded a number of albums and had a great working relationship. I had also worked with Dave Richards before with P.C. Kent and we had a warm friendly vibe together. I didn't really know Bob Ronga but he was an easy going kind of guy. Iain was different. He had already been in Fairport, Matthews Southern Comfort and made solo albums so I was very respectful of him and probably handled him a little differently. There is a lot of psychology in producing records with bands, it's not just having musical talents. With someone like Iain you have to let them feel they are sort of in charge even though they're not. The only thing I didn't like was the credit I got: 'Produced by Sandy Roberton at an Olympic qualifying price.'

The credit was in reference to Sandy bringing the album in quickly with low recording costs so the band were able to make more money each on the back end, and the album's production was completed during the time of the Munich Olympics.

Sandy Roberton: The album was made on a fund deal. WEA paid Plainsong $20,000 on execution of the agreement in May 1972, followed by $30,000 on delivery of the album ($50,000 in total, which was £20,000). WEA had absolutely no involvement in making the album. There was an incentive to get the job done quickly, because whatever was left over was the band's fee. I called up the girl who handled the booking at Sound Techniques and booked a number of days. In this case it was around sixteen days. The total Sound Techniques bill was £3,401.00. There was also a bill from Morgan Studios for some work we did there for £197.25. The extra musicians were Timi Donald who was paid £90, Martin Jenkins £24 and Dave Mattacks £39. The total cost of the album was £3,751.25, a small sum in comparison to other budgets at the time. Which means the band and I must have earned £16,248.75. To record, overdub and mix an album in 16 days was very fast. I was dealing with a great band and great material and the band were rehearsed and on their game.

Andy Roberts: That is typical Sandy to be so precise with the figures for the recording. Of course, from that £16k balance we had to pay Howard and Blaikley eight grand to buy out Iain's contract, so the split wasn't so much. I had to cancel the Lamborghini.

The recordings were sent to Apple Studios on Savile Row on 4th August for mastering.

The beautiful record sleeve for *Amelia* was designed by Seabrook Graves Aslett, who had created a celebrated cover for The Faces' second album, *Long Player*. For that they used stiff plain printed cardboard to make a facsimile of an old shellac 78rpm record. They used the same stiff printed card on *Five-A-Side*, the debut album by Sheffield band Ace, utilising the form of an old-fashioned football card album.

Derek Aslett: Peter Graves and I were teachers at the London College of Printing. We set up our graphic design business because we saw a market for our ideas. We were a low-key design company, we stayed small and did well. Everyone in the office was a designer, we took on some very talented young people and won loads of awards. For a great few years, young idealistic people were running the industry. It didn't last of course because when the suits took over, as they always do, everything changed. We ended up with our own studios in Urban Street in Covent Garden, but to start with we had a space in the WEA offices on New Oxford Street where they could just walk down the corridor and commission artwork. We were in the right place and, because this was the late-sixties, the right place at the right time. We made a rule from the beginning that when we designed record sleeves we would deal directly with the record companies and not with the bands themselves. Our work was done mostly to budgets provided to us by WEA. We would then start with a blank sheet of paper and they gave us carte blanche to come up with what we wanted. Occasionally we would break our own rule.

In Search of Amelia Earhart gatefold LP sleeve.

The associates produced the cover for Ralph McTell's album *Not till Tomorrow*, the one in which he insisted he be photographed smoking a Gauloise. The design was done and was passed to the printers with space left to drop in the title. According to Ralph McTell himself, a phone call was made to his manager Jo Lustig's office and the printer asked Jo's secretary, 'Have you come up with a title for the album yet?' The answer she gave was 'Not till tomorrow.' By tomorrow it was too late to change.

Derek Aslett: In the case of the Plainsong *Amelia* sleeve, we were given a concept around Amelia Earhart and some images and stories to work with. I should imagine the art deco flourishes were ours, but the materials for the collage came from the band. A very good young designer from Southend called Rosie Coole laid out the cut-outs and assembled the collage. Rosie was blonde and very pretty. We liked to surround ourselves with beautiful young people. They were different times then. WEA also asked us to organise parties for them. We did that free of charge because we wanted to be at these parties. When Alice Cooper first came over we organised a circus and when they signed Rod Stewart and The Faces there was a memorable party in Kensington. Years after I had dinner with Ian Ralfini who ran WEA in London. We talked about those good old days. He told me, 'If your invoices had been five times the amount we would have paid them.' You sometimes wish you had known then what you know now, but we still had the joy of going to work.

10. Rock and Fucking Roll

According to some scribbled notes in Andy's archive, Plainsong were given time off to take a holiday from 7th-22nd August. This gave Bobby Ronga the opportunity for a honeymoon after marrying his girlfriend Gill in July.

Andy Roberts: I think Bobby was still having difficulties living and working in England. He realised that if he married a British woman it would solve a problem. It was slightly a marriage of convenience, but he was also in love with his lovely Welsh girl. They married in the registry office in Hampstead. I think Elektra put on a bit of hospitality.

There was to be no extended honeymoon for Bobby though, come September things were busy once again for Plainsong. Up to this point Harry Isles had been organising the band's equipment and tour requirements, as well as driving, with occasional help from Jeremy Ensor, a band associate who had once played in Principal Edwards Magic Theatre. He now decided he needed more regular help. Before he came into the music business, Harry had taught art at the Southport School of Arts and Crafts. He wrote to one of his former students, John Cornelius, who was then playing in a band called Pavilion, a group that eked out a living in the working men's clubs around Liverpool.

Harry Isles: Jeremy Ensor helped me out occasionally, but he wasn't really a roadie. He had been a musician and I believe he was related to the famous Belgian artist James Ensor, who had been a member of Les XX, a group of influential painters who had once invited exhibitions from Gauguin and Monet.

John Cornelius: The life model at Southport was Adrian Henri's wife Joyce. That's how Harry Isles came to know Liverpool Scene and then, because of Andy, Plainsong. One day my mother forwarded a letter from Harry. In the letter Harry brought me up to date with what he'd been doing since moving on from teaching. He told me that for the past few months he had been road managing Plainsong and that a generous advance from their record company Elektra meant that he was now allowed to employ a roadie. He offered me the job. I came clean and told him that I couldn't drive, I didn't know the first thing about amplifiers, I could barely change a plug, I had a gammy leg which made it awkward for me to carry things, and I was a lazy bastard. Harry said it didn't matter, 'You'll be stuck in the cab of a truck or a hotel for most of the day, but you will be paid £18 a week and all you need is a current passport.'

John was to start immediately and found temporary board and lodgings with Harry and his wife Anne.

John Cornelius: After dinner on the first night Harry played me a white label promo copy of the *Amelia* album. It wasn't my cup of tea. It wasn't rock'n'roll or the blues and didn't have the knock-your-teeth out lyrics of Dylan, Lennon or Cohen. You had to grow into it. Now I believe it to be one of the best debut albums ever, back then I wasn't sure. Nothing happened in the first week of my stay at Harry's place. One day he said 'It's pay day' and thrust three fivers into my hand; three pounds had gone straight to Anne for my board and lodging. I still hadn't seen the band, though I was told a Dutch tour was scheduled. After two weeks I met Plainsong at a church hall rehearsal room on the Old Kent Road. They were already there when Harry and I arrived. They were playing table tennis. They were obsessed with ping-pong and the table football game where you twist the handles and shout a lot. Eventually the table tennis came to an end and Harry introduced me. Andy recognised my face from the Liverpool days and was friendly enough. Dave Richards and Iain Matthews barely threw me a second glance. The one

I struck up a warm friendship with almost immediately was the New Yorker, Bobby Ronga. Bobby had flowing chestnut hair and looked like Charles the First. He had a twinkle in his eye and more often than not a glass of red wine in his mitt. He was a real up-for-it rock'n'roller. After a couple of hours sitting around reading *Melody Maker* and smoking, while the band cranked themselves up from ping-pong to Plainsong, it was decided that I should make a trip to Oxford Street to collect from Townsend Thoresen the carnets, tickets and documents required for the forthcoming Dutch tour. I was instructed to bring back hot dogs and burgers. I experienced London prices for the first time when I bought the hot dogs. They were 47½ pence. Decimalisation had just come in the previous year. I walked back into the rehearsal room and spluttered at Harry, 'Nine and six, nine and six for a fucking hot dog.' The band turned slowly to look at me as though mildly intrigued to note that their new roadie had gone barmy already.

John later discovered some of the benefits of working in the music business.

John Cornelius: We were in and out of Warner's building in Oxford Street all the time. We picked up bundles of free review copies of albums. 'Such is the life of a rock'n'roll parasite,' laughed Harry on one such occasion as we loaded piles of records into the back of the van.

John's first opportunity to load in Plainsong's equipment came at the upmarket Selsdon Park Hotel in the Surrey countryside south of London. On 1st September, Elektra held a European sales conference there and took the opportunity to introduce their latest signings to the invited media people and well-heeled hangers on.

John Cornelius: Harry warned me not to indulge in heavy drinking. This was a bit of a surprise because to me rock'n'roll and getting hammered was something I considered went hand in hand. The band had a suite of rooms upstairs. Bobby, who was wearing the name badge provided for the DJ Alan 'Fluff' Freeman, invited me up there to do a line of coke. I didn't know what one was and envisaged a row of Coca-Cola bottles on a mantelpiece. Just then Harry needed me to switch one of the big bass bin speakers round, so I was spared from whatever frivolity Bobby was about to embark upon. We ate a sumptuous multi-course meal followed by coffee and cognac. Nestling inside each table napkin was a large, realistic cardboard butterfly which, when propelled on an elastic band, shot up in the air with a satisfying farting noise and landed in the soup tureen.

After dinner, it was time for the entertainment. The French singer Véronique Sanson sat at the piano to play her song 'Amoureuse'; later to be a huge hit for Kiki Dee. Véronique was the darling of the new crop of WEA signings. She later moved to America and married Stephen Stills. Then along came Plainsong who were introduced as the first British band to be signed to a worldwide deal by Elektra. Jac Holzman in attendance that evening must have been pleased to see the band live for the first time.

Andy Roberts: It was the first time I was within spitting distance of Jac Holzman. I don't think he spoke to me. He knew who Iain was but I'm not sure he recognised the rest of us. We actually played really well together that night.

Cash Box magazine reported on the event for their American readers.

> Under the title 'New Magic in a Dusty World' Elektra launched a massive sales campaign. After a film showcasing Elektra acts including The Doors, Judy Collins and Plainsong, Jac Holzman president of Elektra and Ian Ralfini Managing Director of WEA (England) conducted an informal interview session and announced that Elektra's Fall merchandise in England would be aided by several tools; 'Chief of which is a specially low priced sampler,

3,000 leaflet dispensers for record dealers and window streamers.'

The low-priced sampler – also called *New Magic In A Dusty World* – featured on its cover a butterfly carrying the Elektra logo from a hole left by a dislodged brick in a wall. It included Plainsong's take on 'Yo Yo Man' and was released that autumn. The compilation was filled with big hitters and songs that became big hits. Mickey Newbury's 'American Trilogy' was one, Bread's 'Baby I'm-A Want You' another alongside Judy Collins's take on 'Amazing Grace' and tracks by Harry Chapin, The Doors and the now barely recalled psychedelic hard rockers, Goodthunder.

Jonathan Clyde: I didn't like those ghastly sales conferences, but I had to do them. I felt uncomfortable with the people looking at me sardonically and asking 'Are we going to be able to sell this stuff?' To be fair some of them were music fans, but many of them would have been happy to sell anything.

On 4th September, Plainsong set off for another tour of The Netherlands with Harry Isles driving and John Cornelius as roadie.

John Cornelius: 'The honeymoon is over,' Andy told us sniffily, 'Our days of looning about are over. We need to start treating this as a professional enterprise.' Bobby and I exchanged knowing glances. Neither of us could ever imagine a time when that band would walk on the grass, let alone throw a television out of a hotel window. On the way over to Holland, Bobby travelled down to Dover with me and Harry. The rest of the band took a different route. Bobby held up a banknote to examine the watermark and exclaimed in his New York accent, 'Hey there's a dude in there.' This became a standing joke throughout the tour. We started with a show in a slick new concert hall in Rotterdam. I sat in the sun on the terrace outside of our hotel in the afternoon. Iain said to me, 'Dear Mum' as he observed me chewing a pen over a postcard that was a picture of the flower market. I murmured out loud, 'Dear Mum, Love John.' Iain grinned, 'Yes that's about the extent of my postcard writing too.' That trivial exchange stays with me, only because the number of times Iain engaged with me or Harry in normal conversation can be counted on one hand. Iain was slight in build with dreamy elfin eyes and sleek brown hair. He usually had olive-coloured rings around his eyes due to lack of sleep. When it came to songs and singing he was inspired, but there were dark rumours in the camp about his lack of guitar playing skills, despite the fact that he owned a collection of very expensive guitars. He played the simplest inversions and strummed away unabashed. I once played The Beatles' 'I Feel Fine' in a back room somewhere. Iain came over bubbling and asked me to show him how to do it. I couldn't teach him because he couldn't do a barre chord at all.

The tour moved on to Amsterdam and the band stayed in their favourite guest house, Hotel d'Herberg.

John Cornelius: They went ahead and we trailed along a couple of hours behind with the gear. We negotiated the canal sides and humpback bridges and eventually arrived mid-afternoon in the heart of the Red Light District. Harry said to me, 'You've never been window shopping until you've been window shopping here.' The cobbled street was lined with girls in windows reading magazines or knitting. There was a theatre that announced in billboard letters, 'Real Fucking Show'. We walked into the bar of our hotel, in the middle of the reddest red light district in Europe, and the band were in the back room having discovered a football table. They were waxing enthusiastically about 'guilder in the slot' shower cubicles that had been installed since their last visit. Rock and fucking roll! Actually, in Amsterdam everything seemed to cost a guilder, whether it was a glass of Amstel lager, a bus ticket or a packet of Drum rolling tobacco. The band played at the famous Paradiso that night. It was an all-embracing alternative culture world where you could buy dope, pills, red wine and get off your face and then for health reasons eat homemade macrobiotic cake. The air was thick with marijuana smoke. It was that night where

I saw the most savage fight I've ever seen when two Marc Bolan clones tore into each other, trying to prise one another's eyeballs out their sockets and glass each other with broken wine glassses. After the concert we had dinner and everyone went off to play ping-pong. At midnight Bobby and I hit the streets. He normally drank red wine, but he was intrigued by my beer and whisky chasers so joined in with gusto. It then became like the novel by Albert Camus, *The Fall*, which consists entirely of a man in a bar in Amsterdam having his ear bent by another man telling him his gloomy life story. Bobby told me that he felt socially isolated in the band. He was getting pissed off because as a rocker he wanted to grab the business by the horns instead of prissily stepping round the edges with a feigned disdain for anything commercial. This made him feel cramped and undervalued. We sallied forth from one bar to another and Bobby lit a joint of the best Amsterdam hashish. And our conversation meandered on. We were thrown out of a brothel and a sex supermarket in fits of giggles. We caught sight of our reflection in the canal. 'Hey there's a dude in there.'

Bobby and John made it back to their lodgings just in time for a breakfast of black bread, rubbery cheese and strong coffee. The band then set off for Breda, the next town on the itinerary.

Andy Roberts: That night in Breda I was really ill on stage. I barely slept and the following day we had a long drive to Groningen in the north of Holland. I thought I was going to die. On the way we stopped for lunch and I couldn't even get out of the van. They brought me an ice-cold Coke and I sipped that. When we arrived at the hotel in Groningen, Harry called the doctor. I was carted off to hospital and told that I needed an operation to remove my appendix. They wouldn't start the operation until they had a guarantee that they would be paid; wouldn't give me so much as an aspirin. Eventually a call came through that Warner's would pick up the bill. As soon as that happened the nurse started to lather a shaving brush. The tour had to be cancelled.

Frank van der Meijden was once again the promoter for this Dutch tour.

Frank van der Meijden: Memories have faded, but I recall Plainsong were due to play at De Kolk theatre in Assen the following night. It was a five-hundred seat venue, we usually booked Plainsong into theatre venues and one or two student clubs. I found Andy in the brown suite of the hotel bathroom screaming in pain. My English vocabulary didn't stretch to the term acute appendicitis then, so due to being half-asleep and half-awake I wasn't sure what was going on. The hotel staff arranged for an ambulance. I saw Andy when I visited later in the day. He asked me to bring him a book. The only English language book I had with me was one I was reading on the tour, it was John Steinbeck's *The Pearl*, so I took him that. Then I drove home and started calling round the venues to cancel the tour. This was a drama in itself because everybody was looking forward to Plainsong. The worst nightmare for a music promoter is when we have to cancel a tour that has already started.

Andy Roberts: I stayed in hospital for six days and had no idea how I might get home. I phoned a guy called Michael Bootle from the British Council. During our summer break in August I had played at the Poetry International Festival with Adrian Henri and Michael had been to see us. He gave me his card and for some reason I had hung on to it. I'm pleased that I did because he was the only person I could think of to call. He said he would come and pick me up and drive me back to Amsterdam and put me on the plane next morning. I stayed at his place. Groningen was maybe a four-hour drive to Amsterdam then. I was still sore from my operation, but Michael suggested we should stop for lunch in a small town somewhere in Friesland. This is the most traditional of Dutch regions. The men in this small town were wearing pointed wooden clogs and the women wore white lace bonnets. It was a very different glimpse of The Netherlands to the one I had seen around the music venues and bars of Amsterdam.

While Andy was recovering from appendicitis, the other three members of Plainsong did a good-natured and revealing interview with Jerry Floyd for the November issue of *Let It Rock* magazine shortly after they returned from Holland. Bobby and Dave seized their opportunity to talk to the press with a certain amount of relish and told their back stories with great humour. Bobby recalled his days as a songwriter in New York.

Bobby Ronga: It was a big mistake. It was the classic Carole King trip – sitting in a room all day tapping out tunes. The guy would come in and say, 'We need a single for Joe Cocker... Blood Sweat and Tears, so give me one.' Or 'How many ideas did you get today?' It was like being on a chain gang. Most of the songs went into kiddies' TV programmes or ended up as background music for documentaries. Matt Monro recorded one of my songs – George Martin produced it. I can't recall the title and I don't want to. It was supposed to be a hit in Germany. It was really awful.[7]

While Bobby was reminiscing about his early musical experiences in the New York song factories, David Richards got stories off his chest about more recent events. He told the tale about the time in February when Plainsong were sent to mime to 'Da Doo Ron Ron' on Dutch TV, and recounted Bobby's violent intervention with a drunk in the audience at the gig at The Music Workshop when Jonathan Clyde had come to see them.

David Richards: After you've kicked around and seen what most record companies are like they are a real knockout. Jonathan Clyde – who's in charge of the Elektra label here – is under the same pressures as anyone else, yet he also knows what we're talking about. And we're still waiting for something suspicious

---

[7] The song Bobby wrote and Matt Monro recorded was called 'Lily M'Lady'. He was one of three writers to be credited. The others were Aaron Schroeder who wrote 'It's Now or Never' for Elvis, and George Goehring who penned 'Lipstick on Your Collar'. 'Lily M'Lady' was released as the B-side to the famous Matt Monro song 'On Days Like These' which plays over the opening scene of the film *The Italian Job*.

to show up! Under the contract, we will cut three albums in two years, with an option for another three years.

Iain talked up the importance of country music in the band.

Iain Matthews: I've been doing country songs for ages, but I always felt inhibited by the fact that I was English and into country music. But with this band, we're all into it and nobody is inhibited. We do quite a few country songs and even our own songs come out countrified. Andy's music has changed considerably during the last year. When I met him he was playing Spider John Koerner things – finger-picking blues – and now it's electric country. His heart throb at the moment is Roy Nichols who plays in Merle Haggard's band.

Iain and David went on to talk about how much they had enjoyed playing at the Folk Fairport cafe.

Iain Matthews: It's a really good little club, a rectangular room with breeze-block walls and benches. We had a gig at the Paradiso which was all right, but it isn't really the kind of place where we should play. The owner of Folk Fairport met us there and took us back to the club. We played without a PA, just two mics and a bass.

David Richards: We did the same kind of thing at Les Cousins in the early days of the band. It's really, really good and I think all of us would like to do it all the time but it's not possible in terms of economics.

On the subject of economics, Iain talked about the band's decision to dispense with managers.

Iain Matthews: It's cost us a lot of bread and a lot of frustrations to get out of contracts. We manage ourselves now. Managers are more trouble than they're worth and they're not worth much anyway. Do it yourself, get a good agency and record company, and scrutinize everything personally. Don't let anyone make decisions for you.

To round off his article, Jerry Floyd mentioned that Plainsong were preparing to hit the road to promote their new album, and that they were not interested in being a supergroup on *Top of the Pops* but simply wanted to reach as many people as possible to 'keep the pennies flowing in', in David's words.

Andy recovered in time to play at Canley College, Coventry on the 29th September. The following night they played at St Albans in the square in front of the City Hall. The billing issue continued. Even though the band had been working without a break since the beginning of the year, promoters were still not keen to bill them purely as 'Plainsong'. The advert for the St Albans gig proclaimed 'Plainsong (Ian Matthews, Andy Roberts, ex-Southern Comfort, Fairport)'.

On 1st October, they played Newcastle Polytechnic on the same night that Lindisfarne played one of their famous homecoming concerts at the City Hall. Plainsong's gig must have finished early because *Sounds* magazine reported that the whole of Plainsong and Simon Nicol were in the audience for the Lindisfarne gig, who came on late after a supporting gig from Genesis. Afterwards, they made their way to The Lambton Hotel in Chester-le-Street.

John Cornelius: When we got back to the hotel, Bobby was full of the excitement and exuberance of a Lindisfarne homecoming. We were given a cold table prepared by an elderly Geordie night porter in hotel uniform: cold ham and eggs, salad, pickles and sandwiches. The old geezer came to the table and asked 'Are you talking confidential like?' which meant 'Do you mind if I join you?' All of a sudden and for no apparent reason, some of the group started throwing sandwiches at one another and against the wall. I'd always complained about Plainsong being strait-laced and boring and now they were doing this. The old lad looked hurt and bewildered after the trouble he'd gone to. It wasn't even done in the reckless spirit of rock'n'roll. Nobody was drunk. Nobody had been snorting coke. They always seemed to get it wrong, even when they were behaving badly it looked awkward and insincere.

11. Weighed Down by a Concept

The *Amelia* album was released worldwide on Friday 6th October. On the night of release, Plainsong played a concert at Queen Elizabeth College in London, two days later they appeared at the Roundhouse, followed by a five day gap without a gig.

Iain Matthews: I was uncomfortable about the autumn dates. I had a feeling that our booking agency Gemini were giving up on us and the concerts were getting fewer and far between, which wasn't good considering we were out promoting a brand new album.

To bolster the efforts of Gemini, Plainsong became involved with 'Management Agency and Music', or M.A.M., a relatively new agency that had started out as a record label in 1970. It was founded by Gordon Mills who had been a successful songwriter; he co-wrote 'It's Not Unusual' for Tom Jones alongside Les Reed. M.A.M had Gilbert O'Sullivan and Lynsey de Paul on their books. In addition to augmenting the gigs booked by Gemini, they booked Plainsong onto two TV shows in October.

It's at this point the group became a five piece. With two TV shows booked in, an album to promote and a high profile showcase/launch gig coming up, it was felt they needed a drummer. The four were joined by Roger Swallow, who had been the original choice behind the kit for Matthews Southern Comfort back in the day.

Roger Swallow: My tenure with Matthews Southern Comfort didn't last long. Iain let me go, but we remained good friends and stayed in touch. In late summer 1972, the *Amelia* album had been completed and Iain invited me to be part of the Plainsong touring band.

Nick Lambert's photos at Palais de Danse, Nottingham.

Roger probably started his Plainsong career with two gigs in Nottingham and Bristol. He remembers the Bristol one, though not so much for the gig itself, and there's photographic evidence to suggest he appeared at Nottingham. Nick Lambert, a young law student at Nottingham University and keen photographer, took his camera along to see Plainsong at the Palais de Danse on 12th October.

Nick Lambert: I'd been a big fan of Iain Matthews since the Fairport days. I first heard them as an avid listener to John Peel. I then followed Iain through Matthews Southern Comfort and remember spending my newspaper-round money on the first album, and then I bought the two Vertigo solo albums. I visited Selecta-disc in Nottingham every week to spend my student grant. That's probably where I learned that they were to play. I looked forward to it with anticipation as I did with anything that was folk rock or Fairport related. I was teaching myself photography and black and white processing at the time. I didn't have a fancy camera but I took it along on the off chance. Plainsong presented quite a strong image, four men with acoustic guitars across the front of the stage. It's difficult to recall the performance after all these years, but I do have it in my head somewhere that they seemed weighed down by a concept.

The following night the band played at the Victoria Rooms in Bristol.

Roger Swallow: I have a memory of playing at Bristol, I think without much rehearsal. I don't remember much about the concert itself, but in the afternoon we all visited the *SS Great Britain* ship that had just been opened as a museum. I purchased a letter opener that had been fashioned out of a piece of the ship's decking and a yellow duster featuring an image of the ship. That year I had also taken possession of a magnificent vintage 1920s Abbot five-string banjo. I began using the duster as a dampener beneath the bridge inside the tone ring, where it remains today – unwashed for nigh on 50 years.

There was a few days spare for Roger to rehearse with the band before 17th October when Plainsong travelled to White City to record their second appearance on *The Old Grey Whistle Test*, this time presented by Bob Harris, who had been a big supporter of the band since the beginning. He introduced them by describing their new album as 'lovely'. They played 'Even the Guiding Light' from *Amelia* as their first allotted song, and for their second they chose Richard Fariña's 'Bold Marauder' which Harris introduced as 'one from their next LP as a matter of fact'. After the recording at the BBC they headed over to Kew Bridge for a gig at The Boathouse.

Three nights later, Plainsong were a part of a three-act Elektra showcase/album launch party at the Queen Elizabeth Hall, a nine-hundred seat venue that's part of London's South Bank Centre. Plainsong appeared on a bill with two other recently signed Elektra acts, Mickey Newbury and Harry Chapin. The record company produced an excellent press pack for the event, featuring biographies of the four band members, details of the album and a ten-page trawl through the life, career and disappearance of Amelia Earhart. Karl Dallas took his press pack, his seat and filed a review of the evening for *Melody Maker*.

> Harry Chapin's story songs made a considerable impact, notably 'Taxi', which was a hit for him in America, and the spine-chilling 'Sniper'. Newbury, for his part, flouted convention by establishing contact right away with his hit 'American Trilogy' instead of saving it up, say, for an encore. What can one say about Plainsong that hasn't been said before? Have there ever been four voices to blend so perfectly together, coupled with so much instrumental expertise? Most of their songs were from the recent album, but the real hit of the evening was the old Jimmie Rodgers number they did as an encore, in which they combined exactly the right proportions of sincerity and affectionate humour, even extending to a sweet ensemble yodel at the end of a lovely but insufficiently promoted and attended concert.

Roger Swallow: Iain and I sneaked out front to watch and admire Newbury. I may also have watched Chapin's set. I do remember him in the dressing room having a cello player; unusual at the time. I was also somewhat in awe of Harry as the son of Jim Chapin, the world-renowned drum instructor and master of hand and feet independence.

John Tobler, who at the time wrote previews for Elektra releases, was at the South Bank concert.

John Tobler: I recall Jonathan Clyde gave me a copy of the Fred Goerner book.

Elektra gave away a fair number of copies of the Goerner book to journalists after Eleanor at Turret Bookshop managed to supply two boxes full of pristine first-edition copies to the band. Jonathan Clyde also contacted Fred Goerner himself and sent a pre-release copy of the album to Goerner's office in Presidio Terrace, San Francisco asking for a comment. Goerner duly wrote back:

> Convey my regards and congratulations to Mr Ian Matthews. I found the album of uniformly high quality and the Amelia Earhart sections in particular to be unique, amusing and more than a little poignant. The title of my bestselling book was by the way THE SEARCH FOR AMELIA EARHART. It was published by Doubleday & Company in the United States and by Bodley Head Press Limited of London, England.

Also present at Queen Elizabeth Hall was Richard Lewis who had seen Plainsong in March at the Hampstead Country Club.

Richard Lewis: It was a grand affair, they gave out EPs to anyone who wanted one. On the A-side was Plainsong doing 'Amelia Earhart's Last Flight', with Mickey Newbury and Harry Chapin on the B-side. It came in a fold-out booklet with the stories of each artist.

Richard made a set list of the songs that night. They performed six of the eleven songs on the album, missing out Iain's compositions 'For the Second Time' and 'Side Roads' and adding Richard Fariña's 'House Un-American Blues Activity Dream' and Richard Thompson's 'Poor Ditching Boy', which Iain, Andy and Bobby had performed alongside Richard when they first played The Troubadour. This time, Andy played dulcimer and David took a rare lead vocal. Richard also noted that Roger Swallow played drums and that the encore was 'Miss the Mississippi', a song that was becoming a regular part of the live set.

There had been tension in the band about what material they should be playing and about who exactly was making the decisions. Some of the tension in the band was caused by Bobby Ronga's fondness for red wine.

Harry Isles: Iain was becoming temperamental. I can see him now pulling his lead out of his guitar and flinging it onto the floor because he wasn't happy with the sound. He was also not very nice towards Bobby by that time.

John Cornelius: Bobby was getting more and more isolated. They were deliberately snubbing him, even down to excluding him from the ping-pong and table football games. He invited me round to his flat at Kentish Town one night, with an idea to perhaps play some music and write some songs. Gill made a chilli with rice. Bobby had a few more flagons of red wine than was necessary and ended up blotto. This was playing right into the hands of the teetotal element in Plainsong who blamed Bobby's affection for the grape on all their ills.

With the album release and the prestigious showcase concert at Queen Elizabeth Hall, the autumn of 1972 should have been a happy time for Plainsong. It wasn't. On the day after the Queen Elizabeth Hall concert, Plainsong played at Cardiff University. Following the show, the roadies Harry and John stayed in Cardiff at The Central Hotel. The band travelled back to London together. Bobby Ronga was very drunk on red wine.

Iain Matthews: For reasons only known to himself, Bobby had started to drink heavily. On the way home from the concert in Wales things came to a head. We had travelled together in one car. Somewhere along the return journey Bobby called out from the back seat, 'Stop the car, I need to take a piss.' On a dark country road we pulled over. Bobby staggered through a gate into a nearby field.

Roger Swallow who was only just finding his feet behind the drum kit was in the car on the way back from Wales that night.

Roger Swallow: We stopped in the middle of nowhere on the way to the Severn Bridge. We were tired and it was very late with another few hours to go. I also stepped out of the car to pee but I didn't follow Bobby into the field. The mood wasn't great waiting for him and getting no reply to our yells.

Iain Matthews: We waited. Ten minutes slipped by and he hadn't come back. Considering his state, we decided to give him a while longer, but after twenty minutes we went into the field to look for him. He was nowhere to be found and after much discussion we had to decide what to do. Do we wait, do we search some more, do we report him lost or should we just leave him to it and go home? We eventually made the latter decision. It was late, we were tired and cranky, rightly or wrongly we just thought 'fuck him' and drove off. We got back to London feeling incredibly guilty about our decision and stopped at the house Bobby shared with his wife Gill to tell her. By this time it was almost three in the morning. We banged on the door until Gill came down to open it. We told her sheepishly that we had some bad news, we'd lost Bobby. 'What do you mean?' she giggled. 'Bobby's upstairs in bed. He's been home for more than an hour.' He had apparently taken a piss and in his drunken haze had lost his way out of the field and arrived back at the road around the corner from us. Confused as to why we would have left him and apparently angry too, he began hitchhiking home. By some huge stroke of fortune he had managed to get a lift from a passing car all the way back to London.

Roger Swallow: When Bobby's wife answered the door and told us he was in bed our jaws dropped – and the incredulity hasn't diminished over the years. How he beat us back is a complete mystery, maybe we stopped for something to eat but I don't think so.

Iain Matthews: As we drove away that morning we decided that Bobby was becoming too much of a liability and something had to be done.

Whatever had to be done would have to wait for now. The agents at M.A.M. had brokered a deal with the BBC for Plainsong to appear in a televised show in front of a live audience. This was part of a series called *In Concert*, and they were due to record it in just over a week's time, for which they'd need Bobby's services. The Plainsong diary reports that they rehearsed at The Fishmongers' Arms, the home of Wood Green Jazz Club, on the afternoons of Thursday 26th and Friday 27th, and at GCD studios in South West London on Sunday 29th in preparation for a trip to Shepherd's Bush on Monday 30th October for the recording.

John Cornelius: We turned up at some grey BBC studios. Afterwards Dave Richards complained to me that he had barely appeared on the TV monitors and that Iain had hogged the whole thing.

Andy Roberts: I didn't like the way they arranged the stage for that show and some of the camera angles were a bit off key. They put Roger Swallow's drums up on a raised platform and that didn't sit right either. It was done at the Shepherd's Bush Theatre and introduced by Noel Edmonds. Noel came into the dressing room, he plainly didn't know anything. He came up to me, stuck out his hand and said, 'Hello Iain, it's great to meet you at last.' I thought I would have a bit of fun, so winked at Iain and said, 'Good to meet you Noel have you met Andy?' and introduced him to Iain. He was a complete muffin and we milked it and took the piss for the rest of the session.

The concert was in the can, but a lot of water was about to flow beneath the bridge before it was eventually broadcast.

12. Everybody Had a Say in What Went Down

Whatever the mood within the band, it should have been encouraged by the reviews garnered by *Amelia*, both in the UK and the USA. The celebrated music journalist Charles Shaar Murray reviewed it for *NME*.

> *In Search of Amelia Earhart* is a concept album, and the days when the very mention of the phrase 'concept album' was enough to send any reasonably sensitive music journalist screaming for shelter are by no means long gone. All things notwithstanding, this is a startlingly fine album. Plainsong are more than just Ian Matthews's new band, or even Ian Matthews, Andy Roberts and two mates. It's these two aforementioned gents, plus Dave Richards and Bobby Ronga, and this, their first recorded work, is pretty remarkable. It's an extension of the country/rock harmony thing that got so stultifying a couple of years back, but so revitalised that it once again becomes a workable concept. There are in fact only two overtly Earhart songs on the album. The others are either new Matthews songs, with 'Call The Tune' particularly outstanding, or songs by such as Jerry Yester and Judy Henske and Paul Siebel. Add to that a production by Sandy Roberton and you have as good a potential classic as I've heard recently. This, the Steeleye album, *Ziggy Stardust* and the new Crows are probably the best bets for the classic 1972 albums.

Sounds magazine pushed the boat out. They asked Ray Hammond to review the album and they ran a feature in the same issue. Hammond said of the album:

> An album destined to crash its way through the crap and hassles of the music business to the ears of the people. Plainsong have produced an album that is delightfully low-key yet which is not irritatingly fragile. The approach is so subtle and understated that each hearing reveals more delights. The harmonies are unusual and superb,

the instrumental work tightly controlled and tasteful and Sandy Roberton's production must place him as one of the most sympathetic translators working in studios today.

Hammond interviewed Iain and David Richards, who sounded as harmonious as they did on the record.

Iain Matthews: None of us came into the band for the bread or for the prestige. We'd all had too many years in the business for that. We wanted to make the music we liked and we hoped other people would like it as well.

David Richards: The conception of Plainsong is us four playing acoustic guitars in a small room. At the other end of the room is the audience, that's the sort of communication we want to achieve.

Iain Matthews: In the music we play and the way we play it we are moving in the opposite direction to everyone else.

Karl Dallas in *Melody Maker* picked up on the subtlety of the album.

> A group that doesn't come and sock you in the eye, all decibels blaring, but kind of sneaks up and insinuates itself into your psyche almost before you have begun to notice it. By that time you are hooked on its gentle genius. Part of that genius is the fact that the considerable talent combining its forces in Plainsong is working collectively rather than individualistically, with each one contributing as much as the rest.

In America, Iain became the focus of attention. Gerrit Graham wrote:

> It's very democratic of him not to plaster his name all over the record, because Plainsong in fact amounts to another Ian Matthews album – he wrote most of the material, he does most of the singing and his musical sensibilities set the scene. This record is singularly free of the noisome

detritus that collects around such supposed wellsprings of originality as James Taylor and Rod Stewart. It's a record of deft eclecticism, paramount subtlety, immense charm, and wonderfully good music. A complete success; let's hope it augurs well for Ian and his band.

A 15-year-old Cameron Crowe reviewed the album for *San Diego Door*:

> *In Search of Amelia Earhart* is, and let us not mince words, the finest display of gentle, sometimes liltingly so, English folkiness and rockabilly to surface in a long while. Too long. While David Bowie is being wildly applauded for his choice of concepts musically explored in Ziggy Stardust… the rise and fall of a pop star, it is distressing to consider that Plainsong just might not gain the respect they deserve for choosing the topic of Amelia Earhart as a concept album. While the songs on the LP do not directly confront the issues of her mysterious disappearance as bluntly as, say, John Prine would if it were his project, the lyrics deal with the images and feelings that permeated the whole event of her flying around the world. Hopefully *In Search of Amelia Earhart* is representative of the brilliant recordings forthcoming from this band. Bravo.

The album went down well in Plainsong circles too. Geoff Jukes, one of the owners of Gemini agency, loved the album.

Geoff Jukes: I loved their music anyhow, but that album was a gem. It still is a gem.

Despite the great reviews, early reports of record sales were not good. The album was not selling. According to David Richards, Plainsong shied away from the hype and publicity in the wake of their album release. David spoke candidly to *Dark Star* magazine some six years after.

David Richards: The first album was out and, of course, we were really silly about promo. You know, we wouldn't do any promo, there was all this sort of low-key thing, publicity being a dirty word and all the rest of it. Nobody hustled. So, not surprisingly the album didn't do very much.

Jonathan Clyde: We did a lot of work to promote the album. We took out full-page adverts in the music press. It just didn't take off. We didn't mind, we were in it for the long haul. We really wanted the band to develop and we were prepared to take time. It was so disappointing that we didn't get that time.

Andy Roberts: I think there was good promo for the album. The record company did a lavish press kit with a big feature around the conspiracy surrounding Amelia Earhart's disappearance. We didn't schlep around talking to third string journalists while sipping tepid instant coffee, but we did some high profile gigs like the one at the Queen Elizabeth Hall. It's just that some good albums don't always get the buying public's recognition at the time, look at Gene Clark's *No Other* and the Nick Drake albums for that. I believe we did put in the hard graft, but we didn't get the rewards, you just don't always get what you want.

Iain Matthews: The record company worked hard on the publicity, but in retrospect I wish they hadn't concentrated so much on the idea of it being a concept album. I guess we went along with it at the time, but the whole Amelia thing did weigh us down and we never really found a way out of it.

When Iain wrote the opening track of the *Amelia* album, he couldn't have foreseen how prescient the lyrics would become, especially the plaintive line 'You know that thing that hits you, when you realise you've thrown it far too high'.

If the band themselves had been prepared to take time and be in it for the long haul like Jonathan Clyde at Elektra UK, then they might have seen the fruits of their labours. The promotional work, especially the TV shows, had the desired effect.

Keith Skinner became a dedicated fan of Plainsong after he saw them on *The Old Grey Whistle Test* in his front room up in the far northern English city of Carlisle.

Keith Skinner: I bought the album on the strength of their *Whistle Test* performance in October of 1972. I wasn't disappointed. In fact I copied the song sheet that came with the album about a dozen times in order to enjoy the LP with a wider audience. With our friends at the time, we held Plainsong parties at my girlfriend Pat's house in Keswick. The coal fire was lit, several bottles of beer and a few fine wines came into the equation. *Amelia* graced the stereo system and, in less than perfect harmony, every song on the LP was belted out with gusto from an appreciative audience. I know at least ten people who bought the album as a result of our late-night singsongs. They were a mixed bunch: Alan Welch was an English teacher from Liverpool, Sandie was a social worker in Workington, Mike Lawson was a barman at The Lakes Hotel, and Peter Carr played football for Carlisle United. The album wasn't well known at the time, at least not in Keswick, so I reckon we did our bit in promoting such a great collection of music. In fact when our friends Terry and Gill got married in 1976 I bought them the album as a wedding present, so I was still promoting it four years after.

The *In Concert* TV programme wasn't broadcast until February 1973. When it was, it had a profound affect on one young man who, from the moment he saw it, became a devoted fan. The young man was Barry Eaton, these days a major collector of all things Plainsong.

Barry Eaton: I was a month away from my sixteenth birthday and stayed up because it was school half-term. It was a half-hour programme that came on at ten to eleven. I think it was the singing that got to me first. The harmonies were so fine and then the playing though laid-back and relaxed was precise. From that night I followed the songwriting trail, mainly Iain and to a lesser extent Andy. With Plainsong though you had a prime example of something whole that is far greater than the sum of its parts. The interest sparked that night led me to buy the *Amelia* album and play it to anybody who I thought might be interested. I then collected with dedication anything I could lay my hands on that Plainsong put out. I even read the Goerner book. Over the years

I have also collected Plainsong rarities, radio and TV broadcasts, live shows that were taped by fans, and through that I have made friends all over the world. I wouldn't like to think how much money I have spent on following the band I saw on TV that night in February 1973. Plainsong is the type of band who inspires that kind of dedication.

For a band who had toured for most of the year without an album out, to start to fall to pieces just when they had one was bad timing indeed. The Plainsong diary entry for 1st November, just two days after the *In Concert* filming, records that Iain and Andy were in the studio and there was a concert at Bath University. Then its pages are blank for the next two weeks.

One reason for this gap is Iain's unfinished business with Vertigo. He still owed the label an album, and he had just £5000 to deliver it. Iain invited Andy to work with him on the record, but not Bobby, David or Roger. Instead he brought in old pals and seasoned session men Jerry Donahue on electric guitar, Pat Donaldson on bass, and Timi Donald on drums. Jerry Boys engineered and Sandy Roberton was in the producer's chair.

The album was recorded at Sound Techniques in just five days in November. For an album recorded in such haste and on a miniscule budget, it is a remarkable record. It contains just two Matthews originals; the opening track 'Knowing the Game' and 'Franklin Avenue', a song about a house in an unfashionable part of Nashville that Hank Williams once lived in. The other eight songs on the album are tastefully chosen covers of songs by a diverse collection of writers from Mickey Newbury to Tim Hardin to Jimmy Webb and Dan Penn, plus the by now obligatory song from the pen of Paul Siebel, 'Bride 1945'.

Iain spoke with David Wells in an interview for the sleeve notes of a CD reissue of the album in 2006.

Iain Matthews: I was partly saving my songs for Plainsong, but in equal part there was a shortlist of interpretations burning a hole in my head. I knew if I didn't do them now they might just fade into oblivion.

Iain did do them now and in some cases did them so well that there was no chance of them fading into oblivion. His version of Webb's 'Met Her on a Plane' is a classic and was released as a single with an added string arrangement by Harry Robinson. There is a stellar version of 'Do Right Woman', a song well known for the version by Aretha Franklin but learned by Iain from The Flying Burrito Brothers' first album *The Gilded Palace of Sin*.

Iain called the album *Journeys from Gospel Oak* as a reference to the journey he made from his home to Sound Techniques by tube each day he worked on it.

Iain Matthews: I lived near the main line but it was easy to jump on the tube at Camden Town, travel down to Sloane Square and then walk down the Kings Road or, alternatively, I got off at Embankment and went in the back way.

No doubt because Iain was now an Elektra artist, Vertigo decided not to release the album. They sold it on and it appeared a couple of years later on the Mooncrest label.

With the contractual obligation album done and dusted, Iain came back to face the music with Plainsong during the second week of November. Since the drunken escapade on the way home from Cardiff on 21st October, Iain had been concerned about Bobby Ronga's drinking being out of hand. Bobby was still a member of Plainsong when they recorded the *In Concert* television programme on 30th October. It may have been his last involvement with the band.

John Cornelius: After weeks of moaning and trying to decode what was wrong with the band, largely by Iain, it was decided that the problem was Bobby. The decision was made to sack him and David and Andy went along with the ride. Bobby was devastated. He had given up a lot to emigrate to England and he'd given his all. I believe Bobby was the only member of the band who actually relied on the thirty quid a week that the band paid themselves.

Sandy Roberton: I liked Bobby and I always got on well with him. The discussions about firing him were made by the rest of the band. I wasn't involved.

Iain Matthews: We all agreed that Bobby should be asked to leave. He was a drunk. A happy, sloppy drunk, not nasty at all, but a drunk nevertheless. We put him on a final warning, but I don't know if we ever told him that. In retrospect it's easy to say we should have addressed it better than we did, but at the time we didn't know what to do with him. We should certainly have been more compassionate.

Andy Roberts: Bobby was a lovely, bewildered bloke. He had lived at my parents' house when he first came to England. Then he had a place in Burghley Road, Kentish Town when he was with Gill. I can admit now that I sensed Bobby was about to be pushed under a bus. I didn't say anything. I was still trying to believe in it. And I really did believe in Plainsong. We were a consummate studio band. I wasn't initiating or steering anything like Iain was. I didn't have any grand plan, I don't think Iain did to be fair, we just worked off emotion. Iain could be moody though. When he couldn't quite articulate what he wanted the next week of gigs would be a fucking nightmare. For me it was all about improving, I wanted forward motion. I took a step back when Iain suggested we get rid of Bobby. I just thought it was the next step in the evolution of the band. The problem for Bobby was it was easy to see him as a junior partner. He had no real support network and he lived from what he took from the Plainsong table. I don't think we cut Bobby off without a penny, we would have made sure that he got some money until he found other work. I kept my head down and wished it would all go away. I just wanted to get back to the music. When it all started unravelling I was a spectator, a 'Yes' man, maybe even part of the mob that was going along with it. Bobby's departure hung over me. When the axe fell I avoided even seeing him. I have often looked back and thought that I wasn't a good enough friend to Bobby.

Roger Swallow: Bobby was a genuine but functional, for the most part, drinker. His cheap Spanish bota wineskin filled with who-knows-what was ever-present. I do not recall any aggression or any major single argument about this, though it must have been an issue as eventually I believe it played no small part in the band's demise. Why it would ultimately matter I do not know as Iain and Andy did not need any of us in particular. Logic suggests that Iain's patience had gone off again to where it would, or Andy and he had some now long dismissed disagreement. There is always a tale of woe and anger in the break up of every band. 'You fucking bastard, WHY ME?' or '...and your wife's a...', indiscretion and insecurity lurking in the backstory somewhere.

With Bobby gone, Iain led the discussion on dispensing with the services of Roger Swallow.

Andy Roberts: Iain was our barometer. He led on the decision making. He added Roger Swallow on drums, then dropped him after only a brief period. Within weeks Iain said, 'I don't like this, it's not working for me.' By then we were somewhat in freefall.

Roger Swallow: I wish I could recall the actual sequence that led to me moving on, but I have no recollection whatsoever of why or how I left or if indeed it all crumbled under its significant weight or lack thereof. I must have been asked to leave Plainsong by November or early December because I know that toward the end I was also playing or about to play with the newly-created Albion Band courtesy of Mr Hutchings and a combo of Richard and Linda Thompson and Simon Nicol; often with Shirley Collins and the magnificent Albion Morris Men cheering, frolicking and stick-banging alongside or in front of the band.

It's now beyond the recall of the surviving members of Plainsong to state definitively on what date Bobby and then Roger were moved out of the band. There are three contracts drawn up with the BBC for a *Sounds of the 70s* John Peel radio session that was due to be recorded on 27th November. The first contract dated 3rd

The Plainsong Three.

November shows that Bobby was still a band member. Another dated 13th November still includes him but a third and final contract dated 24th November omits Bobby's name. Contracts are usually drawn up before the date they are issued, so we can't read too much into that, but it's likely that Bobby was sacked in the early part of November, with Roger leaving shortly after.

Iain Matthews: We struggled on after Bobby left but, like the Carl Barnwell situation in Matthews Southern Comfort, it wasn't the same without him. The dynamic always changes when a member leaves and I felt incompetent as the lone rhythm guitar player. We speculated as to how we might replace him.

The discussions about who would replace Bobby led to Iain suggesting his inspiration, the New York singer-songwriter Paul Siebel, whose *Woodsmoke and Oranges* LP Iain adored.

Andy Roberts: I guess we thought it was a fanciful idea, but Iain has such a 'go get 'em' personality and he works very quickly at times.

Iain Matthews: I contacted Keith Sykes, a southern folkie who I had made friends with when I toured America with Andy, Richard and Bobby. I told him that I was coming to New York to find Paul Siebel and asked for his help, as he was part of the New York songwriter inner circle. I flew over to New York with Jonathan Clyde who was on business. Jonathan was booked into The Gramercy Hotel and I planned to stay at Keith's place. I arrived at Keith's to find that he lived in a very small room, in a walk up, in the village. The place smelled strongly of chlorine. Keith offered me a spot on the floor. I thought straightaway 'How can I get out of this?' There was a phone in the hall outside of the room, so I used it to call Jonathan at The Gramercy. I explained my predicament and he said I could come over to his room and sleep on the couch. I made some kind of excuse to Keith about an important meeting and hightailed it over to Jonathan's hotel. I slept on his couch and the next day, through Keith, I made contact with Siebel. He agreed to come over to Jonathan's hotel room that night to meet me. Jonathan went out for a business meeting over dinner. Paul came that evening with his guitar and played a couple of songs. It hadn't occurred to me to take a guitar with me, but I believe in his mind we were meeting to jam and see what happened. I remember thinking that his timing was all over the place and that as good as he was, I couldn't hear his voice fitting into Plainsong. I was pretty quick to make my mind up in those days and for me, it didn't work. I probably flew back home the next day. I reported back to the band, told them of my experience and we agreed to carry on as a trio.

Plainsong played as a trio at a gig in Chelmsford on 26th November. The following day they turned up at the BBC's Langham studio in Portland Place to record a session for John Peel. They recorded 'Nobody Eats at Linebaugh's Anymore', 'Old Man at the Mill/Charlie', 'Save Your Sorrows' and 'Home'.

13. Now We Are 3

On Monday 4th December 1972, Plainsong were back in Sound Techniques to start work on a new album. Andy recalls it was Sandy who whipped them back into the studio but Iain thinks it was David who suggested they should make another album. There was advance money sitting in the contract with Elektra, so it made sense for them to get to work.

Andy Roberts: The pressure was on and the thought was 'Let's get some money'. We were due another $50,000 out of a second album so we thought, let's make one and Elektra can't turn it down.

Sandy Roberton: The second album was done quickly so that there would be a pay day at the end of it.

John Cornelius: Sandy Roberton was producing again. There was always mirth at the mere mention of his name because Sandy Roberton also happened to be an anagram of No Andy Roberts. I have some good memories of the album being recorded, sitting in the control box drinking coffee and watching proceedings through the window. A band called Blackfoot Sue was in there before us one day, some young lads from Birmingham. They'd had a song called 'Standing in the Road' which had been a big summer hit and were trying for a follow-up. They were pleasant, eager and enthusiastic young lads, not at all like Plainsong, and I wished I was working for them instead. David was unhappy throughout the recording sessions. He made suggestions but they were summarily dismissed or ignored. It was clear that following the sacking of Bobby, David was next to be marginalised.

Iain Matthews: My recollections of the recording of this album are very hazy. I can only imagine that my focus was more on baby Darcy and holding together a fraying relationship. I know we made it quickly at Sound Techniques in Chelsea, maybe too soon after the *Amelia* album.

The band spent four days in the studio through to the Thursday evening of 7th December.

Iain Matthews: It was mostly a drum-free album, quite sparse and definitely more lo-fi than the first one. I just didn't think it was working for us as a trio.

Over the weekend of 9th and 10th December, Iain flew out to New York on Elektra expenses after receiving a phone call from Jac Holzman. In his memoir Iain recalled taking a test pressing of the finished album with him. He more than likely took a tape of the work in progress.

Iain Matthews: Jac picked me up at JFK and we drove upstate to his house. We were sitting down together to listen to it when he said, 'Before we play it, tell me what you think of it.' I didn't want to lie. 'To tell you the truth Jac, I'm not that crazy about it. It isn't as good as *Amelia* and that disappoints me.' 'If you don't like it, then I'm not interested in hearing it.' And that was that.

Over the weekend Iain was to learn the real reason for Jac Holzman bringing him from London to his home in upstate New York. Jac told him that he had formed a new label out west called Countryside Records, a joint venture with Michael Nesmith, late of The Monkees. He asked what Iain thought about flying to California to meet Michael and talk about the possibility of making a solo album. Iain thought it an exciting prospect and decided there and then to go.

Iain Matthews: I headed to Los Angeles to meet with Michael. I liked him instantly. He was funny, engaging and a zero-tolerance-for-bullshit sort of person. He seemed like someone who had been through the music-business mill and learned a few important lessons along the way. I felt that we made a solid musical connection and that I could work with him. We spent a few days sitting in his Countryside Ranch Studio discussing music and tastes and the logistics of such a project. It would mean me leaving my family to be in Los Angeles for an extended period of time.

Before he left, Michael asked Iain who he would like to play on the record.

Iain Matthews: This was beyond my wildest dreams and I gave Michael a list of players I had recently been listening to and admired. Leland Sklar, the bass player with Carole King; Danny Kortchmar, guitar player with James Taylor; Jimmy Gordon; Sneaky Pete; Larry Knechtel, keyboard player with The Wrecking Crew; Chris Ethridge, the Flying Burrito Brothers' bass player. The list went on and on. Michael said, 'Leave it with me. I'll make some calls and do my best to get them for you.'

Iain's mind must have been in turmoil on the flight back to London. He had family considerations. He was part-way through recording a second album with a band that had promised a lot and now he was being enticed to work as a solo artist on the other side of the world. Whatever was going through Iain's mind, and whatever decision he had made or not made, he didn't share it with the rest of the band. He fulfilled three booked gigs at Barnstaple, Penzance and Plymouth on 14th, 15th and 16th December and then went back to Sound Techniques on Monday 18th to complete three more days work on the second album.

The album they recorded was never released though it did appear as a white label promo and was assigned an Elektra catalogue number.

John Tobler: I was quite friendly with Jonathan Clyde, the Elektra label manager and he gave me a white label of what was called at the time *Plainsong 3*. I think the original idea was that I would write a short publicity piece which would be sent out with the album as a press release for reviewers, which I did for a number of Elektra releases. Then the album wasn't released. I still have the white label. I would occasionally play it to any interested people, though I never allowed anyone to copy it.

Recently, Iain found his own copy of the white label promo.

Iain Matthews: I found a reference disc with nothing written on the sleeve but 'Plainsong. K42136'. I hadn't listened to this album in a very long time, so when I pulled it from my archives it was with mixed emotions. I was anxious to hear it again, but that anxiety was tinged with the guilt of having pulled the plug on it. My memory of it was that it wasn't very good. There is, somewhere, artwork for the record. We'd called it *Now We Are 3* and gone so far as to hire a graphic artist to design the cover using an A. A. Milne, *Winnie-the-Pooh* type theme. I don't remember who did it, or what it looked like, but I do remember us approving the concept. My first impressions on hearing it for the first time in years was that it wasn't half bad. Pretty good in fact. As I listened a second and a third time, the inconsistencies of the album began to hit me. Sandy Roberton is a great producer, one of the best I've worked with, but this time I felt he'd somehow got it wrong. The record sounds small, with too much reverb, particularly on the vocals and mostly on mine. It feels to me, unfinished. We'd gone for a simpler, rootsier, acoustic sound and somehow missed the boat. It sounds hollow. I can only imagine that Sandy let the band have far too much input into the sound and at a certain point it became irretrievable. I don't know for sure, but it doesn't sound like a Sandy production. Andy, David and myself talked at the time about a simpler production approach than *Amelia* and that the album should be a combination of current stage songs and new compositions. I recall very little now of the song gathering and recording to be certain who suggested what, but in retrospect I would have dumped a couple. Definitely Merle Haggard's 'Swinging Doors' and either the Jimmie Rodgers classic 'Miss the Mississippi' or Bruce 'Utah' Phillips's 'The Goodnight-Loving Trail'. Having both on the same album made it too country. Instead of those, we should have added Paul Siebel's 'Any Day Woman' and the delightful Nils Lofgren song 'Take You to the Movies Tonight', both of which were in our live set.

It's clear that the band were pulling, or being pulled, in different directions during the making of the second album and struggled to focus in the way they had at the time they made *Amelia*.

Iain Matthews: 'Old Man at the Mill', the first track, was a real crowd pleaser from our stage show. I imagine we all gave this one the nod.

Andy Roberts: We got this from The Dillards. It's on their record *Copperfields*, and frankly there wasn't much they did that we weren't in love with. I didn't know much about bluegrass. I had Johnny Duncan's version of 'Last Train to San Fernando' on 78, which was a huge hit in the UK in 1957, but I never realised it came from the bluegrass tradition. We just called it skiffle, though of course skiffle came from a blend of blues and bluegrass. Once I got my dulcimer on the 1971 US tour, I felt an affinity with all that mountain music. I was learning about folk and country all the time because of my association with Iain, and through him with Richard Thompson, and all the electric folk crowd. Iain bought records by the armful, and anything he didn't want to keep, he passed on to me. This song is very old. It seems to be a blend of 'The Jolly Miller' and 'Leatherwing Bat'. Certainly the origins of the song go way further back than The Dillards, who claimed the copyright when they recorded it. I found a reference to it in a ballad index that mentions a version all the way back to 1719. That said, it was exactly The Dillards version that we lifted.

Iain Matthews: 'Urban Cowboy' was a song of Andy's, another from our live set. We all liked it, but if I could change anything,

I would have left out the pedal steel and softened the country feel.

Andy Roberts: I wrote 'Urban Cowboy' during the year that Plainsong was active, but it has its roots in that 1971 US tour, when I met Karen at the Poison Apple in Detroit. I spent a lot of the next few months calling her, trying to persuade her to leave her husband and come to England. Thank heavens she had the good sense to say no, otherwise a lot of innocent lives would have been ruined. In the meantime, I wrote a whole slew of songs about her. 'Make up your mind, and take that plane, you could be with him today' couldn't be clearer. Although the song presses all sorts of American cultural references, it is really a folk song, despite B.J. Cole's excellent pedal steel giving it a country quality. This was the first time I worked with Beej, in a relationship that has endured to the present time. He was really good news, particularly because he showed up with his then wife, Drusilla, who rolled very neat and powerful joints throughout the session! Beej contributed a lot to the album. Once it was clear that the second Plainsong album wasn't going to be released, I grabbed the track and used it unaltered on my solo album of which this was the title track.

Iain Matthews: 'The Fault' was one of mine. A curious song. After all these years I can no longer remember what it was about. It has relationship vibes to it. I was infatuated with Neil Young's writing at the time and was forever trying to emulate him. It did enable me to go out more on a musical limb. I admired what Neil Young did with the old song 'Oh Lonesome Me' on the *After the Gold Rush* LP.

Andy Roberts: I love 'The Fault'. The tonality is wonderful, and there's lovely lyrical piano from David, nicely understated on the bridge, and then Ray Warleigh wailing on alto sax. There is a desolate quality in the minor key, and the vocal harmonies are extraordinary. It's exactly what we always wanted Plainsong to do, which was to get away from the usual harmonies stacked on the 3 and the 5. For me this is one of several tracks that got lost in the wreckage we created for ourselves. This is the way we could have gone and would have, if we had been able to hold it together.

Iain Matthews: I think Andy and I have always had that country aspect in what we do. It seems to me that on the second album Andy chose to enhance it while I tried unsuccessfully to resist it. During our Plainsong year country was ever present, but for me 'Swinging Doors' was a step too far.

Andy Roberts: I don't know what I was thinking of when I chose 'Swinging Doors'. It was a total abdication of taste. It should never have made the cut when we were choosing the songs. I don't know how it sneaked in. There certainly wasn't any argument about it, it was recorded by agreement, though I think it was one of the last tracks we made, and as such it may have been included to make up the numbers. The major problem, to my ears today, is that the rhythm section, David on bass and Timi on drums, is too square to the beat. There is no feel to it. But there is a reason for all this. Iain gave me a copy of a Merle Haggard live recording called *Okie From Muskogee*. I was swept away by this record of Merle's; the writing, the singing, the humour, the audience reaction, and the guitar vocabulary of Roy Nichols of the Strangers, Merle's band. This whole country music genre is built on different scales to the ones I had grown up with, the pentatonic blues scale. This scale is major, with a sharp third and often a sharp seventh. Then, when you introduce a blue note, it creates tension. So I wasn't seeing straight, but I was learning, I just needed to explore the genre more.

Iain Matthews: 'Keep on Sailing' is more of my opaqueness. I think it's a good song and has, over the years, become a people's favourite. This, and in fact most of my songs on the album, I would later enhance, Californicate and use on my 1974 album *Some Days You Eat The Bear*. I had attempted a re-imagining of the song on *Valley Hi* and completely missed the target. I had enough confidence in the song to try and set the record straight.

Andy Roberts: We put 'Miss the Mississippi' into the set early on, and first recorded it for a Bob Harris radio session in July. I clearly remember that at our request it was recorded using an old ribbon mic we saw in Studio 2 at Aeolian Hall, in mono with all four of us around it, to get that old-timey feel. Producer Jeff Griffin just let us get on with it, bless him. Despite his cautions, Iain can clearly be heard nailing the yodels at the end, so I don't know why he declined to sing the full package when we finally did our studio version for the album. B.J. Cole is on dobro for this track. His instrument had been built for him by his dad, and it sounds pretty good here.

Iain Matthews: 'Miss the Mississippi' is a song written by Bill Halley and made famous by Jimmie Rodgers in 1932. Either Andy or I heard the Rodgers version and decided to include it in our stage set. I could neither abide by or had the chops to carry off the gorgeous yodelling parts, so we simple pretended they didn't exist.

The yodels do exist on an *In Concert* radio session Plainsong did for Bob Harris on Radio 1 which was transmitted on Saturday 16th December.

Iain Matthews: 'Home' is another song of both reflection and anticipation. Here I am wondering where to go and what comes next. The black sheep. The adventurer. I never could quite get that bridge right. I probably changed it three times.

Andy Roberts: 'Home' is another Matthews original that survived the fire sale to resurface as the basis of a new country version on his 1974 collection, *Some Days You Eat The Bear And Some Days The Bear Eats You,* drenched in Jeff Baxter's steel guitar. A deceptively simple piece with a killer melody, and one that I always enjoyed playing. It has a rolling pick that just sits under the fingers and is very satisfying to play.

Iain Matthews: Andy and I had a fascination with John Hartford's writing. We both owned and loved his more recent albums; 1971's *Aereo-Plain* and its 1972 follow-up, *Morning Bugle*. Both of our interpretations of his songs on this record came from those albums and both were stage songs. I chose 'First Girl I Loved'. We always talked about putting together a version of his 'Up on the Hill Where They Do the Boogie' but it somehow never made it off our to-do list.

Andy Roberts: It is a fabulous bit of writing, embodying all the wit at John Hartford's disposal, along with an effortlessly great tune and terrific changes. *Aereo-Plain* was a great hit with us, I can still quote from it endlessly even now. We must have discussed its evolution on the recording sessions, because the original monitor mix, which I took home, has my guitar parts underpinned by David's bass, whereas the final version is just my guitars with Harry Robinson's sweetly inventive string arrangement as the only additional feature. Harry was Sandy's suggestion, and I was surprised, though delighted with the end result. I figured we would have gone with Robert Kirby, a big friend of mine, who had crafted such a beautiful piece on 'I've Seen The Movie' on my *Nina and The Dream Tree* album. I know we were in a hurry to complete the record by the end, maybe Bob Kirby wasn't available, but anyway, I couldn't have bettered Sandy's choice. This track never got used again. It died with the demise of Plainsong.

Iain Matthews: 'Save You Sorrows' is another of my push and pull relationship songs. I love Andy's vibrato acoustic guitar. It brings just enough lightness to what could have been a big downer of a song. My admiration for Andy's playing is bottomless.

Andy Roberts: This is another of those tremolo acoustics which I love, with David's bass beneath. A couple of piano flourishes and a light dusting of Kriwaczek string organ right at the end. This is another track which appeared on Iain's *Valley Hi* album with the addition of a very prominent B-Bender Telecaster taking it way down the dusty trails.

Iain Matthews: John Hartford's tune 'Nobody Eats at Linebaugh's Anymore' is about what happened when the Grand Ole Opry moved out of its traditional home at the Ryman Auditorium to a purpose-built theme park called Opryland on the outskirts of Nashville. The move created all kinds of financial hardship for local businesses, including the downfall of this favourite performers' hangout and eatery. Downtown Nashville went in to a steady decline and became a haven for peep shows, pawn shops and rough pool halls. By the time I got to Nashville, Linebaugh's was long gone. But the Merchants Hotel, where Hank Williams, Patsy Cline and Johnny Cash stayed, was still functioning.

Andy Roberts: It could be argued that, since none of us had been to Nashville at that time, we had no investment in the truth of the story. But I felt we were carrying the weight of the country tradition to our fan base, and we genuinely felt indignation at the way that commercial concerns had destroyed the whole scene and neighbourhood around the Ryman. This is another dive into my country obsession. I think Beej's dobro is a good touch, and it is a fine song.

Iain Matthews: 'The Goodnight-Loving Trail' was a cattle trail forged by Charles Goodnight and Oliver Loving in the late 1800s. It ran Texas Longhorns from Fort Belknap in Texas, all the way up through Colorado to Wyoming. Utah Phillips was fascinated enough by this to write a song about it. I find the lyrics both emotional and poignant. Our friend Rab Noakes taught us the song when we played a show together in Scotland and later sang it with us on a Bob Harris live radio recording.

Andy Roberts: Rab Noakes is a hero. This song was my introduction to Utah Phillips, a true American original. Utah was a folklorist and storyteller, and had a huge left-wing sympathy, too. He was a latter-day Woody Guthrie. Steve Ashley played harp on this. I don't recall how we found Steve, but we must have met him on the road and been impressed. Steve is another one who is the real deal. A lovely bloke.

Utah Phillips was born in Cleveland, Ohio in 1935 and died in 2008. In his youth he travelled the west hobo-style, riding the rails. He was a passionate member of the Industrial Workers of the World, better known as The Wobblies. In the 1990s he made a comeback and recorded two fine albums with Ani DiFranco. Richly traditional in ethos, but overlaid with technical experimentation, they were recorded at the Congress House studio in Austin where the latter-day incarnation of Plainsong also made two albums in the 1990s.

Iain Matthews: I always found 'All Around My Grandmother's Floor' to be more psychedelic than folky. In a good way though. It came and went from the Plainsong repertoire but was always a consideration.

Andy Roberts: 'All Around My Grandmother's Floor' began as a poem by Mike Evans, who played saxophone with The Liverpool Scene. Mike was a terrific poet, and I don't think he conceived of this as a song lyric till I persuaded him that it should be. I wrote the music in 1968, and it was in The Liverpool Scene's debut set for John Peel's *Top Gear* show on 19th January 1969. I always believed in it as a song, and Sandy must have liked it as it got an outing on a 1970 Nadia Cattouse album he produced. My mum was impressed because she'd actually heard of her and had seen her on the telly. The Liverpool Scene and Nadia Cattouse versions were considerably different to the one we did. I found a whole 3 over 2 way of playing the accompaniment, and Iain arranged a lovely cascading harmony, reminiscent of the work he did on 'Raider' on the *Amelia* record. I also got plenty of dulcimer onto it, which for me was always a bonus. I love my dulcimer.

Iain Matthews: For the record, there is an outtake from the album. A song of mine called 'That's All It Could Amount To'. I'm not sure why it's not on the album. I like it a lot but have no idea who or what it's about.

> He wasn't blind
> He couldn't see
> He touched on mutilation
> He turned a stone and down we went
> Enough to flood a nation

Andy Roberts: The lyrical approach on that song bears the stamp of Richard Fariña's writing. It is an extraordinary piece of writing. Iain never shied away from stark, confrontational words, whereas I would have run a mile from anything as explicit. What was the boy going through? Mutilation, blindness, floods, sacrifice, decomposition, remorse, fate – all in three short verses.

Sandy Roberton doesn't recall any tension in the studio in the recording of the album, but when trying to come up with a title for it, it's clear the band were pre-occupied by the fact they were a player short. Andy suggested the deliberately oblique *Plainsong 3*, Iain preferred *Now We Are 3*; he was a fan of the Christopher Robin stories by A. A. Milne and liked a book of verse called *Now We Are Six*.

Andy Roberts: I think that Iain's writing and singing on this album was phenomenal. His phrasing, and the whole direction we were going in was overwhelmingly extraordinary. I do wish we had sorted out the feels on some of the tracks. If only we could have ironed out the wrinkles. Our version of 'Swinging Doors' had no place on this Plainsong record, that I will admit, and as a consequence it caused a lot of damage. It handed Jac Holzman a stick to beat us with, which he did, unmercifully.

Iain Matthews: I have always been a searcher. I believe I get it from my mother, who was never happy with the status quo and always looking. She was a big Jim Reeves fan, but that didn't stop her searching for other music. She became a fan of a gospel group called The Deep River Boys, even went to see them in concert at Hull. Like her, I find no appeal in the status quo. The least little thing can set me off. Back in the Fairport days when

Joe Boyd brought the latest songs from the West Coast it would start me on a quest to find more. Then when I heard Ian & Sylvia for the first time I started on a new quest. I didn't see myself as a historian. That's where I differed from Andy. He heard country and really dug back into the tradition. With me I would get to a certain point and whether through boredom or because I'd hit on something new I would stop. I loved country, but never reached the wellspring; the Carter Family and people like that. Once I found a songwriter I liked I stopped digging. At first I liked The Dillards, by the time I was with Plainsong I dug Gene Clark and John Hartford. Andy was with me most of the way but made some choices that I couldn't understand, and David was stuck with his Grateful Dead records like *American Beauty* and *Workingman's Dead*. He wanted us to cover a Dead song called 'Sugar Magnolia', we had it in the live set for a couple of concerts. If it had been left to David we would have been doing nothing but Grateful Dead songs. The second album was a mess of conflicting styles and ideas, old musical ideas. I thought the point should be to take those old ideas and express new things. That's where the tensions were. On the first Plainsong album the stars were all aligned and we made an album that we all agreed was special. When it came to the second album the stars were out of line. We had neither compass nor chart and just following our hearts wasn't going to get us there. In the studio for that second album I couldn't get it out of my head that we were making an acoustic country album and putting limitations on ourselves. Throughout my career I have always tried to make the second album better than the first. Due to the tensions over material, this was never going to happen. In order to sort out these tensions, Sandy organised a series of meetings with the three of us. They were not easy meetings. David would come in with a certain look on his face from the start. A mean, intimidating look. I became really uncomfortable with him. I shied away from conflict. I tried to look to Andy as an ally, but eventually I couldn't do that.

Andy Roberts: My notebook tells me that we recorded 'Urban Cowboy' on 7th December and we went back to the studio on

19th December to record 'All Around My Grandmother's Floor', and that was the last thing the original Plainsong ever recorded in the studio. By then there was a deep sense of 'this is going nowhere'. I really didn't know what the problem was. I always thought Plainsong was a way forward, I wanted to stick with it, because I was doing proper music. Up to then I had been role playing. And when it came down to it, there was no arguing over the music. Even though we were spiralling down out of control we were still making great music in the studio and for all the tensions between David and Iain, David still knew what a phenomenal singer Iain was. The tensions came at the gigs.

Iain Matthews: For me, Plainsong was in all respects a group effort, despite what David Richards may or may not have voiced. Admittedly, it was primarily Andy and myself calling the shots, but everyone had a voice. David's taste in music was not mine, so I never looked to him for song suggestions.

14. Like Icarus Ascending

In the autumn of 1976, Iain did an extended and very open interview with John Tobler for *Zig Zag* magazine. The interview was published over three issues. Iain spoke to Tobler about the unreleased second Plainsong album.

Iain Matthews: As a three piece we decided to make an album as much like the stage act as possible without using a drummer. So the first 'drafts' were done without drums and it sounded terrible – so stark, so boring and so long – so we decided to add a drummer to certain numbers. I wanted to add a drummer all the way through pretty much, give or take a couple of songs, and one of the others didn't want to add a drummer at all, and I think Andy wanted to add a drummer on certain songs. Then we put drums on some of them, and then we wanted to add B.J. on dobro – we were just disagreeing all the time and it got out of hand and it got sloppy, and we forgot why we were making it. It turned out a mess, a complete mess.

The third part of John Tobler's *Zig Zag* interview with Iain came out in December of 1976, around the same time as Joni Mitchell's album *Hejira* hit the record shops. The word 'Hejira' originally referred to the journey the prophet Mohammed and his followers made from Mecca to Medina, but has since come to mean any journey that is a flight from danger. Mitchell did away with the melodies of her previous well-known records to reveal a joy in the natural rhythms of words and the sounds they make. The album was loaded with transient, dreamlike lyrics and fragile metaphors. On one song, 'Amelia', she reflected on a break up with a partner while making reference to Amelia Earhart's last flight.

> A ghost of aviation
> She was swallowed by the sky
> Or by the sea, like me, she had a dream to fly
> Like Icarus ascending
> On beautiful foolish arms
> Amelia, it was just a false alarm

Most of the songs on the LP were written as Joni undertook a journey from the East Coast to the West Coast. A journey that started with Woodstock now finding a new home in California.

In December 1972, after they had completed recording on their second album, Plainsong had two gigs left to fulfil and a recording session for BBC Radio 1.

John Cornelius: Iain stopped performing some of the songs from the *Amelia* album and dug deeper into the more obscure and depressing ancient country songs; 'Miss the Mississippi' and 'Nobody Eats at Linebaugh's Anymore' were two. Fate occasionally threw me into a one-to-one conversation with each member of the band. They all said they were pissed off. It was easy for me to see from the outside what was wrong. It was the same thing that was right for Plainsong: Iain Matthews. He was an extremely gifted singer and songwriter, both lyrically and melodically. The *Amelia* album was almost perfect and he was leading the band upward and outward, but he could be bloody awkward. On the one hand he was a prima-donna but he was also diffident. Once on a cross channel ferry I saw a waiter fawning all over him. He was uncomfortable with it. Another time we were lounging in the rehearsal room in the Old Kent Road. Someone opened up one of the music papers. There was an article where Robert Plant had named Iain as one of his all-time favourite singers. Iain just mumbled 'That's nice of him' and hardly bothered to look up. He had a reputation but he never used it for the benefit of the band.

Iain Matthews: A lot of things came together to prevent Plainsong from making it. The choice of repertoire was one. I became disillusioned with it, just too much country music. Yet I had helped to drive that, so I was to blame. Then there was a problem with David. He got more and more frantic about the band identity. He hated it when people called it my band. I tried to explain to him that we couldn't control that, it was just how it was and you can't stop the press seeing it like that. He just got angry and said, 'It's not Iain's fucking band.' Andy was torn. He had known David before he knew me and didn't want to take sides. He stayed neutral when I wanted him to back me up. A lot of it was my fault. It was who I was at the time, selfish and driven. I knew that I was the cash cow for a number of people, but I didn't always consider how what I did might affect the others. At that time I left behind a trail of tears wherever I went. When it came to Plainsong, you just knew that it wasn't going to end well.

John Cornelius: The shows were becoming really boring. I have some copies of live recordings Plainsong made towards the end of 1972 and you can almost hear the gloom descending. The songs they were singing said nothing about their lives, never mind the lives of their audiences. They certainly didn't do much hanging around in honky-tonks, which were themselves a bit thin on the ground in Gospel Oak where Iain lived and virtually unknown where Andy lived in Hertfordshire. It would have been more to the point if they had been singing about cocoa and ping-pong and the virtues of an early night. They were playing country stuff like a bunch of wizened old timers, when they were actually the same age as their burgeoning contemporaries, the likes of Rod Stewart, Marc Bolan and David Bowie. Yet they felt duty-bound to strum the dulcimer every night and blow the dust off an old gospel song called 'I'll Fly Away'.

Andy Roberts: Harry decided he was going back to work with Jon Hiseman and Allan Holdsworth in a band they had formed called Tempest. In some ways that was the beginning of the end for Plainsong. He had been our organiser, our photographer, our driver and bookkeeper; he did everything apart from wipe our arses.

John Cornelius: Harry Isles was no fool and he could smell on the wind the way things were going. He broke the news to me one day in the van. 'They're splitting up you know.' There was a pause. He went on, 'What will you do?' I felt like a straw on that wind. 'I suppose I'll go back to Liverpool.' I started waking up every day feeling lonely and took to spending my wage in the pub on every non-Plainsong night. As Christmas approached I started to notice huge, white advertising boards going up all around Piccadilly Circus. The boards proclaimed 'Happy Xmas (War is Over) Love John and Yoko'. In the White Star, the DJ was pumping out two current hits, 'Back Stabbers' by The O'Jays and the strange Rod Stewart song under the name Python Lee Jackson, 'In a Broken Dream'. I reeled home to bed with lines from that song going round in my brain. 'Right now is where you are, in a broken dream.' I became seriously depressed. I even found myself after a tedious rehearsal session at Wood Green stuffing my pockets with cheese rolls that the band had taken one bite out of and discarded. After a Barnstaple gig I was cornered in the snug of a bar by David Richards. I didn't resist because he was buying the ale. David was a gap-toothed, twitchy sort of fellow. He always seemed to wear the same denim jacket and jeans and like the rest of the band clomped around in clogs. He was a good bass player, a jobbing musician who seemed to do well enough. He lived on a houseboat with his girlfriend. You reached it by shuffling along a series of planks and other boats to get to his tub. He was indifferent towards me, but now and again he would let his frustration with Plainsong come out. He told me that he was pissed off with the stinking band and wished he had a proper job. He then moaned that playing bass and piano were his only skills. I should have said 'The only skills I have got are drawing, painting, writing, guitar playing, songwriting, singing and here I am humping your gear and wiping your arse for fifteen quid a week.' But I didn't. By the time of the Glasgow show Plainsong were hurtling towards a brick wall. We drove through a bleak and wintry landscape to the concert hall.

The first of two gigs before Christmas was at Glasgow City Hall on 21st December.

Andy Roberts: I went up to Glasgow with David. Iain was supposed to fly there to join us. I can't recall him arriving. The promoter talked to us and was happy for us to go on as a duo.

The support act was an up-and-coming Billy Connolly, who had been a member of The Humblebums with Gerry Rafferty but had embarked on a solo career that year at the Edinburgh Festival.

Andy Roberts: The promoter told us that Billy had a strong enough local following to be promoted to top of the bill, so we exchanged places and David and I went on first to do a forty-five minute set. Then Billy went on and brought the house down. It wasn't the first time Iain hadn't showed or walked off after two numbers because he wasn't satisfied. I made allowances because Iain is obviously a world-class singer, one of the best voices you are going to hear in your life.

Almost a year to the day after forming as a band, on Friday 22nd December 1972 the original Plainsong played their last live gig together. By then a threesome with two barely on speaking terms, they fulfilled an engagement at Liverpool St George's Hall. It was on this day that two Uruguayan rugby players emerged from the Andes Mountains to announce that they and fourteen others had survived a plane crash some three months previously. Some of the survivors later admitted that they had resorted to eating the flesh of their dead comrades in order to survive.

John Cornelius: The final gig was in my home town of Liverpool. Iain decided to go on the train with his box of sandwiches and his jumbo Martin guitar. David's parting shot to him was 'When you get to Lime Street Station, you'll find a taxi rank. Ask them to take you to St George's Hall.' I wish I had been there to see Iain ask a Liverpool taxi driver to take him across the street.

Iain spent Christmas at home in Gospel Oak with his wife Chris and baby Darcy. They talked about his plan to record with Michael Nesmith in California.

Iain Matthews: I was hesitant about broaching the idea of moving to California with Chris and with good reason. Chris was devoted to her mom and vice versa. She visited her mom every Sunday and Grandma was besotted with baby Darcy. I knew that a move to Los Angeles several thousand miles away would not be well received. If we moved, it was going to severely dent that mother/daughter relationship. I was constantly touring and recording, which meant I was rarely home. Moving to Los Angeles would be no different, but I so desperately wanted to go. I had been listening to contemporary North American singer-songwriters since the late 1960s and it had long been my dream to go to California and be a part of the scene. I naively thought a fresh start in California might be just the cure for us.

The last act of Plainsong played out almost like a tragedy. On Friday 29th December, Iain, Andy and David arrived at Maida Vale Studio 5 at the BBC to record a session for the Radio 1 programme *Sounds on Sunday*. The producer was Frances Line and the presenter Alan Black. *Sounds on Sunday* was a half hour programme of songs and chat in the form of an interview. Plainsong performed eight songs.

Andy Roberts: This radio session was done in one day. I'm pretty sure the format was that we recorded all together, with piano, guitars and some bass parts. Then overdubs were added after that. Not every track has them, but guitar solos and harmonies were additional, plus bass parts where necessary. We worked very fast by that time. I doubt there were many second takes, if any. It is clear to me that the pianos were integral to the master recordings, so the basses must have been added. Iain might have played some rhythm guitar on these radio tracks but in the studio he barely played guitar at all. He tended to back off from playing because it was a more efficient use of time to have me play it all, as I wouldn't have needed a second take on almost anything because I was such an experienced session player by then. After recording the songs, we then chatted to the presenter. The interview was constructed to suggest that it was being done in segments, but this wasn't the case. The interviews were done in one unbroken take.

The interview section was edited for broadcast, but it is as interesting for what the musicians don't say as for what they do say. The lyrics of the songs the band chose tell a different story; there is an almost unbearable poignancy here in the light of what was going on within the band and no doubt inside Iain's head.

The show kicks off with a return to an early live show favourite, the Commander Cody song 'Seeds and Stems'. The third verse of that song starts with the lines, 'Now everybody tells me there's other ways to get high, they don't seem to understand I'm too far gone to try.' We have to bear in mind the sensitivities of the BBC over lyrics including the phrase 'get high', so Iain chooses to sing 'Everybody's telling me there's other ways to get by, but I'm too far gone to try' and in doing so brings a whole new depth of meaning.

The band is introduced and the first question is 'You all write songs don't you?' David is quick to respond, 'Except me. I don't do anything except play bass.' It's meant to be a joke, but it falls a bit flat. The interviewer then says, 'But you do record other songwriters' material?' Again David is first to respond, 'There's no point doing all your own material as a be all and end all, when there are so many other people doing good things.' Andy seems to want to explain further, 'We always have a predisposition to doing our own songs if they are there to be used, but when there are other people writing songs that nobody has heard at least you can give them a chance by doing their songs.' The group then perform Paul Siebel's 'Any Day Woman' with a segue into Nils Lofgren's 'Take You to the Movies Tonight'.

There is talk then about 1972 being a successful year. Andy says, 'We've done two albums, well we're in the process of doing a second one, which we hope are nice albums. It's difficult to know what we intend, you see we have all been in the business so long that we don't want to be stars and be incredibly successful and all that sort of thing. We probably wouldn't go on *Top of the Pops* if they asked us, but they haven't asked us. What we want to do is be a working unit and enjoy ourselves, do nice shows and make nice records.'

The next song is Don Gibson's 'Blue Blue Day'. Iain sings 'It's been a blue blue day, I feel like running away, I feel like running away from it all.' After the song, the interviewer says he wants to ask about influences and particularly country music influences. He directs his question at Iain, 'You're very much a country music buff.' Iain just says 'Yeah' then pauses. 'Well it comes out in your singing and the music.' Iain says 'Yeah' again. The interviewer moves swiftly to Andy, 'You have moved into country music as well.' Andy says, 'Mainly through working with Iain, I'd always rejected it as a style of music, then Iain gave me a Merle Haggard album because he didn't like it and I really liked it, that was what sparked it off. That started me wanting to be in that kind of a country band that Plainsong was when we recorded that first album.'

Jimmie Rodgers's 'Miss the Mississippi' is next with its lines about mockingbirds singing around the cabin door. There are no yodels at the end of the song; Iain finishes on a high and plaintive falsetto. This is followed by 'I Work For Jesus in the Personnel Department'. Iain had collected that song during the American tour with Andy and Richard Thompson. It had been written by a young man called Jerry Leichtling, who was introduced to Iain by Bud Scoppa.[8]

Alan Black suggests 'Plainsong is a singing band, you all sing don't you?' This time Iain tries a wisecrack, 'Those of us who can.' Again the joke falls a bit flat. David suggests the best thing the band could do is to play a twelve-foot square room without amplification and recalls two memorable gigs, one at Les Cousins and the other at the Folk Fairport cafe in Amsterdam 'after a fairly

---

[8] At the time Leichtling was driving a New York cab. He later moved to the West Coast to become a screenwriter. Jerry got rich in the 1980s when he wrote a film called *Peggy Sue Got Married* which was directed by Francis Ford Coppola.

naff gig at the Paradiso'. Iain agrees and says, 'They're probably the two most enjoyable gigs we've done.' David adds, 'Just because you can relate so well when there's no electronics between you and the audience, but it's just not economically feasible.'

Next up is 'I Don't Want to Talk About It', a song written by Danny Whitten of Neil Young's band Crazy Horse. Andy mentions that the band wanted to perform the song in memory of Danny who had recently died at the tragically young age of 29. Whitten had died six weeks earlier in Los Angeles from a combination of alcohol and drugs which he had been taking to relieve severe rheumatoid arthritis. There is great pathos in Plainsong choosing to pay tribute with their arrangement of this song, but the sadness becomes almost palpable. Andy's guitar and David's piano work together to slowly introduce the song and then Andy sings with a beautiful harmony from Iain:

> I can tell by your eyes
> that you've probably been crying forever
> And the stars in the sky
> don't mean nothing to you they're a mirror

Iain then comes in with a perfectly pitched:

> And I don't want to talk about it
> how you broke my heart
> If I stay here just a little bit longer
> if I stay here won't you listen to my heart

Plainsong manage to wring six minutes and four seconds of sadness and sorrow out of the song, a call and response conversation between bandmates who seem to know that something has gone wrong and it's easier to sing about it than it is to talk about it.

With one more song to come, Black asks about the new album and if they have a title for it. Iain says 'We're not really sure, we thought we had, but we're not really sure are we?' The band then play 'Save Your Sorrows', one of Iain's songs slated for the second album.

> Where's the point in us bringing the doctor in here?
> Where's the sense in you holding my arm?
> Where's the smile when my funny irregular scene
> works a charm?
> And where's the end if we can't find a place to begin?
> Where's the money? I've done what you said
> And where's the need for my face
> in this Albion race up ahead?

In the closing moments of the programme Alan Black announces 'Thank you very much, you've been listening to *Sounds on Sunday* with Plainsong. My name's Alan Black, the producer was Frances Line. Radio 1 now joins Radio 2 and we reopen again tomorrow morning with Tony Blackburn. Goodnight.' And that should be it. Except that it isn't, the producer decides to go out on a twenty-five second coda, a return to 'I Don't Want to Talk About It'; not the vocal part, but Andy and David on guitar and piano, the last notes played by Plainsong. If its purpose is to allow us to take in what we have just been listening to, it works.

If it wasn't for the existence of the radio session from 29th December, it would be hard to believe that a band falling apart could convene to perform with apparent harmony; at least with musical if not personal harmony. It's not clear at what point Iain told his bandmates that he was leaving for California. The programme was transmitted on Sunday 7th January, by which time Iain was gone.

In an interview for the sleeve notes of a Plainsong reissue CD in 2005, Pat Thomas asked Iain why Plainsong ended.

Iain Matthews: Mostly because I let Jac Holzman convince me that I was a solo artist. California was like a magnet for me and when the chance to be there came, I couldn't wait to dive right in. I didn't know how to tell the guys, so I just sort of snuck away.

In the winter of 1976, Andy was interviewed by Andrew Finney for the specialist music magazine *Fat Angel*.

Andy Roberts: Jac Holzman made Iain a very good solo offer, you know, 'Come over to the States and I'll make you a star.' So Iain left for the States within a day of telling me he was leaving. It was that quick.

Finney suggested to Andy that he had heard a rumour that Iain had rung from Los Angeles to say 'Hi, I've left.'

Andy Roberts: It was a bit like that. The thing is that he had known that it was all being set up for him to go to the States for about two months. I feel sorry for Iain, he can't help the way that he is, he's just a classic Gemini – split right down the middle. When Iain is up and enthusiastic he's charming and really nice, but then he'll throw these terrible moodies. You just don't know where you are with him. It's such a shame because he is one of the finest singers anywhere in the world today, there's no doubt about that. He has an immense amount of taste, but just gets carried away on these slightly sort of hare-brained schemes.

Sandy Roberton: I think he had gone to see Holzman behind all of our backs. I certainly didn't know anything about it. Iain was just looking out for himself and when he was offered to sign to Elektra on his own he jumped. I suppose it was greed and lack of loyalty on his part. I don't think he liked David Richards. Ronga was gone so he probably realised he didn't want to be in a trio with David Richards so when he got the offer of a solo album he jettisoned the other two and me and left. It was David who told me that Iain had gone, he was already in America by then. It was all very underhand of Iain.

Andy Roberts: I was holding back and holding back. I hid away, shut my eyes and put my hands over my ears. I just wanted to make music. I don't know if Iain ever did tell me what his reason for leaving was.

The first newspaper to break the story that Iain was going to leave for America was *Sounds* on 13th January 1973. Ray Hammond was the journalist who Iain entrusted with the exclusive. Under the headline 'Ian Packs His Bags', Hammond informed his readers, 'Britain is going to lose a major contemporary music force this week. Ian Matthews packs his bags, wife and child and goes west to live permanently in Los Angeles.' Iain spoke to Hammond about the break up of Plainsong, revealing that leaving had been on his mind for a while.

Iain Matthews: My actual decision to leave has been quite sudden, but I've been working on the idea for some time. Plainsong broke up two weeks ago and even before we broke up we had decided to come off the road for a few months, it was getting a bit pointless.

Hammond put it to Iain that *In Search of Amelia Earhart* had been exceptionally well received by the critics and the music business but it missed out on getting across to the public.

Iain Matthews: It didn't sell any; I think it sold about 3,000. I thought it was the best album I've ever done. I've a feeling that maybe it was thought of too much as Amelia Earhart and not as Plainsong. I think a mistake from my point of view, perhaps, has been burying myself so much with Plainsong. If it had been Iain Matthews and Plainsong a few more people might have come to see us. We worked for half the life of Plainsong with no record out. That started to kill it off because nobody knew who we were and we didn't pull crowds. I went over to the States about three weeks ago, really just to see what the situation was. I visited Paul Siebel, who is an amazing writer. I met with Mike Nesmith and we clicked straight away, rather like Andy and I did. We have a completely compatible attitude to music and it's been arranged now that I'm going to make an album in LA with Mike producing. I don't think I'll be back for at least a year.

In that same month *Disc* magazine published a letter from Tony May of Barnet, Hertfordshire. He wrote, 'How frustrating it was to read in *Disc* that the Plainsong LP *In Search of Amelia Earhart* had only sold 4,000 [sic] copies. Of course they should have messed around covered in glitter on *Top of the Pops* and had their music played 500 times a day on Radio 1 instead of expecting the so-called discriminating public to recognise class – all on their own.'

Iain's move to California even made news in his hometown newspaper. Nick Cole, reporting in the *Scunthorpe Evening Telegraph* under a headline that read 'There's No Need for Ian to go California Dreaming', wrote with almost undisguised envy, 'Braving the Californian sun while the rest of us weather the coal strike, the three-day week, petrol increases and the general election is Scunthorpe's most famous son in the recording world.'

Iain Matthews: Chris had a hundred reasons to not go. 'What about the house?' I thought we should probably hang on to it and try to rent it out. 'What about Mom, my friends, my life?' I was torn. The musician in me simply had to go. The husband and father in me understood and felt her concerns. Was I being selfish and opportunistic, or was I being realistic about our future? The voice in my head kept telling me, 'This could fix things. This could make things right again.' Chris was resistant and for a while we sparred around it. I explained that apart from it being a wonderful career move, it could also be a new beginning for the two of us. We'd leave our mounting problems behind us in England and begin again. Darcy could grow up with wall-to-wall sunshine. I knew I'd be tearing her away from her home and friends but, selfishly, my career was my main concern. I felt that Europe had run its course for me and I needed new musical challenges. Finally she agreed and I prayed I'd done the right thing convincing her. We made plans. I would leave in January, make the album and set things up for them to follow on. Rather than sell our lovely house, we agreed to keep all of our belongings and rent it out as is, on the off chance that things didn't work out...

In early January 1973, Iain boarded a west bound 747 to fly to Los Angeles. On arrival he walked out of the airport and climbed into a car being driven by Phyllis, the wife of Michael

Nesmith. Phyllis drove him north on Interstate 405, heading for The Countryside Ranch recording studio where he would meet up with Michael and the musicians who were to work on Iain's first solo Elektra album. Phyllis steered the car onto the long dirt driveway that swept up to the studio ranch house. The sun was shining, as it tends to do in California even in January. After all, as Albert once sang, 'It never rains in California.'

Iain asked Nesmith which of the musicians that he'd requested had he managed to secure? His reply came as a bit of a shock. 'To tell the truth,' he said, 'I couldn't get any of them, but no worries, I have a terrific house band and they're excited to be working with you. What do you think?'

15. Fallout

Phyllis Nesmith found Iain a house in an area of Los Angeles called Van Nuys and he set to work immediately on his first Californian solo album. The album contained three songs from the aborted second Plainsong album: 'Keep on Sailing', 'Old Man at the Mill' and 'Save Your Sorrows'.[9] Iain called the album *Valley Hi* and it was very well received by the critics. To this day, many of Iain's fans cite it as their favourite album of his. Jac Holzman remains very fond of the album too.

Jac Holzman: I frequently re-listen to LPs I was intimately involved with many decades ago and sometimes find myself feeling as if I'm hearing the music for the first time – a performance that soars off the vinyl bringing happy shivers to the entirety of you. Listening to Iain's *Valley Hi* today is an outstanding example of timeless music that caresses your ears and warms your heart. When the quality of song excellence and performance blend, the impact is far greater than the sum of its parts because your inner emotions contribute to the listening experience.

Iain wasn't alone in recycling discarded Plainsong tracks. Andy's solo album *Urban Cowboy* included two of his songs from the abandoned album too, though his album credited the musicians involved.

Andy Roberts: After the collapse of Plainsong, Sandy quickly thrashed out a solo deal for me with Elektra UK. *Urban Cowboy*, the first release of the two-record contract, comprised all of the

---

[9] The album also contained a version of Steve Young's 'Seven Bridges Road'. The beautiful close-harmony arrangement created by Iain and Michael Nesmith was controversially lifted in its entirety, uncredited, by the Eagles and released on their *Eagles Live* album in 1980. It wasn't until years later that Glenn Frey finally gave credit to Iain for the arrangement in the liner notes of an Eagles greatest hits package.

tracks we had recorded over the past year and a bit, including 'Urban Cowboy' and 'All Around My Grandmother's Floor' from the second Plainsong album. It came out on Elektra around April 1973.

Valley Hi was released in August 1973 in the States, by which time Iain's wife Chris and baby Darcy had joined him at his house in the San Fernando Valley, with its yellow stuccoed walls and open-air swimming pool. Early issues of the album carry a tribute on the sleeve: 'Dedicated to Chris – for tearing up her roots'. Sadly the uprooting to live in America was not good for Chris. Iain went straight out on tour following the critical success of his album leaving Chris alone with the few friends she had managed to make. Chris fell ill, leading to a big discussion about the future for their relationship. Iain wanted to stay in California, Chris wanted to go home to London. They came to a gut-wrenching decision. Iain would stay and she would take Darcy back home to London.

Iain Matthews: To this day I get a thick, tight, emotional knot in my stomach whenever I think about that time and the decision we made. I so clearly see now that I should have cancelled the tour, stayed with them and helped them integrate. Nothing is as important as family. I know that now. But I was young and overflowing with ambition. I chose to pursue my own dream and let my family go. In doing so, I missed seeing my little girl grow up.

Amidst all the upheaval of leaving England for America and the emotional stress of first reuniting and then saying goodbye to his family, Iain still had to deal with the fallout with his former bandmates.

Iain Matthews: David Richards was enraged by my decision. He was convinced that it had been my plan all along to use Plainsong as a vehicle to further my own career. This was far from the truth and I denied it. He called me at the studio in California when I was recording with Michael and let his still festering feelings be known. 'I'll get you back,' he said, 'I'm gonna fuck your wife.' I laughed it off but I knew it would be just like him to try.

Another member of the Plainsong team who wasn't going to take Iain's disappearance lying down was Sandy Roberton. He was well versed in the wranglings of the music business. Above all the emotional upheaval felt by the rest of the band, Sandy's eyes were focused on the contracts. He took action letting WEA know that they were obliged to accept a third Plainsong album, which obviously carried a $50,000 advance. Iain was pushed to make himself available, but eventually it all fizzled out. Action was also pursued against Iain for lifting the tracks wholesale from the original Plainsong recording and using them, uncredited and unpaid for. In addition to the three tracks on *Valley Hi*, Iain's second Californian album, *Some Days You Eat the Bear*, which might be viewed as the third album of the Elektra contract, included a further two of his songs from the aborted Plainsong album, 'Home' and 'The Fault', plus yet another take of 'Keep on Sailing'. Sandy, Andy and David began legal proceedings, but they proved expensive and came to nothing.

David spoke to *Dark Star* magazine in 1978 about the fallout from Plainsong, and it's clear that his anger was still burning.

David Richards: I was really pissed off with Iain, it was a cunt's trick. He fucked up what was quite a nice deal. And to fuck it up by dint of saying that the record was a bummer and then to use five of the songs and four of the backing tracks! It couldn't possibly be anything to do with Elektra or Holzman saying that he didn't like that album, otherwise... there's four of the tracks that Iain used and two that Andy used – that's half the album gone out already. The band was probably untenable in any case with the attitudes that there were kicking about at that time and it probably was vindictive on our part to take legal action.

Sandy and Andy were not quite as sympathetic as David in their assessment of Jac Holzman's role in Plainsong's demise.

Sandy Roberton: At the same time as Plainsong signed the WEA agreement they signed one with me agreeing that I would be the 'sole' producer for the term of the WEA agreement and would not engage the services of another producer. Clause 16 is the crucial clause saying 'The members of the group are jointly and severally bound by the terms and conditions of this agreement.' I was entitled to one fifth share of advances and royalties for all albums delivered under this deal. To this day I have not received a single royalty accounting from WEA Records or Plainsong for *In Search of Amelia Earhart* or the tracks on the second Plainsong album. These days, lawyers certainly know their law a lot better than in 1973. A good lawyer today would have gone after Jac Holzman and Elektra for Tortious Interference and the three other members of Plainsong and their producer would have received a substantial settlement from Elektra and Holzman for encouraging Iain Matthews to leave Plainsong and go to California to pursue a solo career. I've come a long way since those days and learnt a lot about the law, friendships and how to deal with situations like this. Elektra, Holzman and Iain could have dealt with this in a much better way and looking back it pains me to see how friends on a musical journey ended up with such legal disharmony.

Andy Roberts: I met Jac Holzman briefly, twice. Once was at the WEA sales conference at the Selsdon Park Hotel, when we played on a bill with Véronique Sanson. I believe it was at that hotel where Holzman made his first overtures to Iain. The other time was at the Royal Festival Hall, when we played on a bill with Harry Chapin and Mickey Newbury. I'd never met Jac before we were signed, and he made it quite clear after the band finished that he was only ever interested in signing Iain and he took Plainsong because it was the only way he could get him at the time. He worked on Iain to leave the band and move to the States, so he was undermining Plainsong by the autumn of 1972. I believe that Iain resisted it at first, but eventually Holzman got Iain where he wanted him. He got what he wanted, and was quite open about this. His quote later that he only paid for two UK acts, Dennis Coulson and a quarter of Plainsong, was hurtful and unnecessary. I have no time for him at all, since he never had a single consideration for myself or the other members of the band, apart from Iain. I know we were in trouble several months before Iain left, and we were drifting apart musically, though most of the problem was personnel, not music. I don't have anything much to say about Jac, and I'm damn certain he won't have much to say about me. I ran all this past Mick Houghton when he was compiling *Forever Changing – The Golden Age Of Elektra Records*, the box set that Rhino put out in 2006. In fairness to Mick, he correctly reflected the sourness I felt about the Elektra deal, generally, once it was over. The way I feel about Jac is a matter of history, and it certainly didn't extend to Ian Ralfini at WEA or Jonathan Clyde at Elektra UK. They were both lovely. It is obvious that Jac retained the affection and respect of many of his artists. He ran a very successful leftfield operation for 23 years, worked hard, hired good people, and reaped the benefits. My reaction is of very little consequence. But, fuck him!

16. Reconciliation

Iain recorded *Some Days You Eat the Bear* in December 1973 and January 1974 at Elektra Sounds in Hollywood. By this time Jac Holzman had relinquished control at Elektra and Iain had to answer to David Geffen, the businessman who had founded Asylum Records.

Iain Matthews: Once again, the record received wonderful reviews, but failed to sell in any significant numbers, giving David Geffen reason enough to not want to renegotiate my contract.

Before passing on Iain, Geffen had suggested that he go into the studio and record some new demos, which he made in Hawthorne with Emitt Rhodes producing. It was these recordings that secured Iain a two-album deal with Columbia Records. He travelled to Nashville to make an album called *Go for Broke* which was released in 1976. It was around this time that Iain bumped into an old friend.

Andy Roberts: I saw Iain again for the first time when I toured the States with Roy Harper in 1976. I was staying at the Oakwood Apartments on Barham Boulevard in Universal City, Los Angeles. Out of the blue Iain turned up at the apartments. He must have heard I was in town. The last time I had seen him he had bad English teeth and he didn't know how to drive a car. He turned up with a set of California pearly whites and he was driving a TR7 sports car.

Iain Matthews: It was a brief encounter. I believe Andy was already on his way to the show with Roy Harper and we spoke in the parking lot.

Later that year, in his interview with Andrew Finney for *Fat Angel*, Finney asked Andy if it was a great disappointment to him and the rest of the band that Plainsong broke up.

Andy Roberts: Yes, I believed in Plainsong and so did Iain in his own way. From what I've heard from various parties I think that Iain thinks that the working relationship with me at any rate was the thing he most enjoyed doing, was most into doing, but he didn't realise that at the time.

Iain's second album for Columbia, *Hit and Run*, followed in 1977. Columbia however, like David Geffen before them, were thinking about numbers. When the record didn't sell in huge amounts, Iain's contract wasn't renewed. In the four years since leaving Plainsong for his new life in LA, Iain had made four albums for two major labels and now he found himself without a deal.

Iain Matthews: I arrived in Los Angeles wide-eyed and full of verve. Four short years later, that shine had worn off. It's that kind of place. The sun is always shining, but by the same token it's a cold, dog-eat-dog town where you have to be competitive or forget it. Some stay and get a real job. I was ready to take my leave.

Iain moved north to Seattle with his new partner Judith Caldwell. Back in England, Sandy had formed a label called Rockburgh Records and signed acts as varied as Wilko Johnson, Allan Taylor and the Irish master fiddler, Kevin Burke from The Bothy Band. Sandy somehow found Iain's phone number in Seattle and gave him a call with a view to renewing their working relationship.

Sandy Roberton: I got over the disappointment and disillusionment of Plainsong and just decided to reach out to Iain and offer him a deal. I signed him to Rockburgh in 1978. We made an album called *Stealin' Home*. From memory we never mentioned or talked about Plainsong.

Sandy made a deal to license the album in North America to Mushroom Records in Vancouver. Mushroom were enthusiastic about a particular song on the album called 'Shake It'. They released it as a single and, following massive radio play, it made the Top 10 across North America, giving Iain a hit with an American sounding song that was actually recorded in rural Oxfordshire. A touring band was put together off the back of the album and toured for the next two years across Europe, America and Japan. The band reunited Iain with his old Matthews Southern Comfort bandmate Mark Griffiths.

Mark Griffiths: I stayed with Iain in Seattle when we toured in support of the Beach Boys. Sandy produced four albums for Iain and I was invited to play on three of them: *Siamese Friends, Spot of Interference* and *Shook*.

The tragic death of Mushroom Records' driving force, Shelly Siegel, in 1979 meant that Iain lost an important promoter of his work in North America and the subsequent records didn't reach the same level of success. By 1990 Iain had moved on again and had settled in Austin, Texas where he begun to reboot his career with a more independently-minded approach. After releasing an album called *Pure and Crooked* (and changing the spelling of his name from Ian to Iain) he came to the UK for a tour with his friend and producer from Austin, Mark Hallman.

Andy Roberts: I was in Brighton with my then girlfriend Sally, who I have been with for over 30 years now. I opened the local paper and saw that Iain Matthews had a gig that night in a pub called The Richmond. I said to Sally, 'I once worked with Iain Matthews, but I don't think it will be the same one.' We went along to the gig anyhow and to my surprise it was Iain, he was touring Britain with a musician from Texas called Mark Hallman. It was a fabulous reunion.

Iain Matthews: Mark and I took the stage and powered through our opening song and as I thanked the crowd at song's end, there standing directly in front of me was my old pal and Plainsong partner Andy Roberts. I hadn't seen Andy for a long time, and there he was like a friendly ghost from the past flashing that inimitable Andy 'hiya' in my direction. It felt so damned good to see him again. We met him and Sally for a drink after the show and did some brief catching up. I felt elated, rejuvenated and more than a little relieved as the angst of our musical break-up all those years earlier seemed to melt away. I nervously invited him to come join us in London the following night and to bring his guitar, which he joyfully accepted.

Andy Roberts: I travelled up to London for the gig at The Cricketers the following night. We rehearsed a few songs in the soundcheck and backstage. We played some Plainsong material that night. The first song we sang with the three of us was 'Keep on Sailing', and when we hit the first harmony chorus, I naturally took the low line. Mark was used to singing high, so we had a perfect three-part blend right from the off. I remember the glow of recognition I felt. This was how Plainsong had sounded back in the day. Our friendship was rekindled and we have been like brothers ever since.

Andy and Iain resumed their musical partnership at the Cambridge Folk Festival in 1990 and toured together afterwards. A live recording made at the Bonington Theatre in Nottingham in 1991 was released as an album in 2021. It includes two songs from their Plainsong days, 'Yo Yo Man' and 'I Don't Want to Talk About It'. The following year, Andy and Iain joined together with Mark Griffiths and singer-songwriter Julian Dawson and reignited Plainsong.

Mark Griffiths: The first album by the reformed Plainsong was called *Dark Side of the Room*. We made it at Outrider Studio just up the road from me in Northampton. The guys stayed at my house while we were recording.

Dark Side of the Room featured a return to the Amelia story in a song written by Iain and Andy called 'Sweet Amelia'. It was a song slightly critical of the continuing search for the aviator and had the refrain 'Oh sweet Amelia, all these years on your own Cloud Nine'. Two further albums with this line-up followed with *Voices Electric* in 1994 and *Sister Flute* in 1996. This time around, Iain and Andy didn't repeat the mistake of burying themselves in Plainsong and continued with their solo careers in tandem with recording and touring as Plainsong.

Plainsong got together again in 1999 for an album called *New Place Now*, with Julian Dawson replaced by Clive Gregson. The album featured Gregson's song 'Following Amelia', in which he pays tribute to Linda Finch, who in 1997 successfully completed a rerun of the round the world flight that Amelia Earhart had been so close to completing before 'flying into yesterday' at Howland Island.

By this time Iain was tiring of his life in Texas and was looking to move on. The tour with Plainsong to support *New Place Now* gave him the impetus he was looking for.

Iain Matthews: When we got to England I was looking around to find my new home. We played perhaps two-dozen dates the length and breadth of Britain in arts centres and small theatres to enthusiastic audiences. It felt like a coming home. For me it was a new beginning and everywhere we played I found myself consciously wondering, 'Is this the sort of town I could settle down in? Is this where I'm meant to be?' I was searching for a feeling, a vibe, a sign of some kind, but sadly we reached the end of the tour and that vibe, that sign, never appeared. At tour's end I flew to Amsterdam and upon walking out of the airport terminal the strangest feeling came over me. I suddenly felt as though I had come home.

Iain moved to The Netherlands in 2000 and has remained there ever since. In 2004, he married his Dutch bride Marly and asked Andy to be his best man. The following year Andy returned the compliment when he and Sally were finally married. Around that time, Andy and Iain were recording demos and invited David Richards to join them on bass.

Andy Roberts: I'd always stayed in touch with David and played with him in a band called GRIMMS straight after Plainsong. In some ways I think David was more hurt by my decision not to go with him as a bass player on my record *Andy Roberts and the Great Stampede* later in 1973 than he was with what happened with Plainsong. I greatly respected Pat Donaldson and Gerry Conway as a rhythm section, and I wanted to use them together on that record. But David and I continued to tour together happily and to make records with GRIMMS, and he was on several radio sessions of mine into the mid-seventies. He consciously 'retired' from active performing when he began a working association with Derek Rowe, and turned his efforts to computing; a rare occupation at that time. Later still he was mini-cabbing in Surbiton. He eventually started playing again in the Richmond area, with a bluegrass band called Tabasco. They did a couple of my songs in the eighties.

Iain Matthews: I first saw David again briefly at some point in the 1990s. I was on tour in the UK and playing a folk venue somewhere near Richmond. I'd just finished my soundcheck when in waltzed David. He was very friendly, but I was caught off guard and wasn't quite sure what to make of it. We chatted and nothing came up about the past. I considered bringing it up, to check where we were on it, but left well enough alone. He stayed for my first set, but was nowhere to be found in the break. The last time I saw David was when Andy was living at Villa Helene in Brighton. We recorded a demo of a song Andy and I had written called 'Randolph Scott'. We invited David down to put a bass on it. I guess this was in 2005. We'd given him the track to listen to with a few days notice and when he arrived he seemed to have no idea what to play, which seemed strange to Andy and me, but we got on fine and he stayed several hours. Nothing of the break-up of Plainsong was raised, but I felt tense. Maybe that was just me and my own insecurities.

Hazel Richards: Music was very important to David. He was more than passionate about it. He was also a very loyal person, the sort who would never dream of letting someone down. He was also sensitive and easily hurt and didn't really like to talk about what happened with Plainsong. Later in his life David went to Ireland and immersed himself in the egalitarian attitude they have over there to music. He liked the idea that you can be an amazing musician, as he was, without having to be famous. It was enough to come together to make music.

Andy and Iain had also made an attempt to reunite with Bobby Ronga in the early 2000s.

Andy Roberts: I lost contact with Bobby completely until one day I was playing at the Tønder Festival in Denmark. I talked to an old musician friend Allan Taylor. We spoke about Bobby, and I said I thought he had died. Allan told me he hadn't and gave me a number. I managed to have one or two conversations on the phone with him. He was still bitter about Plainsong and carried the bitterness until the day he died.

Iain Matthews: When Andy and I were back together performing, he contacted Bobby with a view to him rejoining us. He was settled back in New York by then, but he was still bitter and adamant that he would have nothing more to do with Plainsong. I never got the chance to talk to Bobby again.

Bobby Ronga died at The Westchester County Medical Centre on 11th November 2012 at the age of just 65. His lengthy obituary published in *The Daily Freeman*, a morning newspaper published in Kingston, New York, makes no mention of the part he played in Plainsong. David Richards died on 16th January 2019. His ashes were committed to the River Thames, near where he had moored his houseboat in the early 1970s, on 4th March 2019 at a celebration attended by friends and family, including his sister Hazel, Andy, Sandy and Paul Kent.

The latter-day version of Plainsong had made a self-declared final album in 2003 with a returning Julian Dawson. They gave it the anagrammatic name *Pangolins*. With Plainsong retired for the second time, Iain looked to reboot Matthews Southern Comfort. He pulled together a band and began work on a Matthews Southern Comfort album in 2005. Not quite liking what he heard, and with a new baby on the way, Iain put the tapes to one side and for five years scratched his itch to make jazz music with a series of collaborations with pianist Egbert Derix. In 2010, Iain found the tapes in a drawer and decided he liked what he heard after all and asked the band to help him finish what they had started. *Kind of New* was released that year and was taken out on the road for a one-off tour. Matthews Southern Comfort were again reformed in 2017 with an exclusively Dutch line-up of musicians, with BJ Baartmans and Eric Devries on guitar and Bart de Win on keyboards. This band made two highly-praised albums and toured extensively across Europe.

From the 1990s onwards, Iain has switched between being a member of a band and a solo artist frequently, never being tied down to one thing, always keeping his options open, seeking out new creative partnerships, and always keeping working.

Iain Matthews: Throughout my entire life, the role of bandleader or musical director hasn't come naturally. The creativity and vision comes instinctively, but assuming the role of leader is something I have struggled to come to grips with. Okay, I've had a fair amount of success and sustained a long career. Many musicians seem drawn to me because of my history, but often what they don't realise is that I am also attracted to working with them because they are far more musically knowledgeable and adept than I am. There's the rub. I'm not sure this will ever change. I think it is rooted somewhere deep in my childhood psyche, from my mother urging me to stay small. I guess all human beings have their moments of self-doubt, none of us are immune, it's part of the condition. We each have our ways of resolving it too.

In 2012, Plainsong decided to make one last farewell tour, finishing with two dates in Japan. They released the album *Fat*

Iain and Andy, Plainsong farewell tour, Union Chapel, Islington, 2012.

Lady Singing, a live-in-the-studio retrospective that looked back across the history of Plainsong. And that should have been that, except it seems that like the search for Amelia, the need to return to Plainsong continues. In 2015, Iain, Andy and Mark Griffiths recorded an album of Richard Fariña songs, a project that allowed Iain in particular to go right back to the beginning. It made sense for them to call the band Plainsong. This line-up played Fairport Convention's Cropredy Festival in 2017. In his memoir, Iain tells a story about something that happened at the signing tent after their performance.

Iain Matthews: People queued for two-and-a-half hours to get their CDs signed. The question most asked by the folk in the queue that day was, 'Is Plainsong really over?' I hadn't thought to prepare an answer for that one. I guess only time will tell.

At the heart of everything that has ever been produced under the name of Plainsong is the musical partnership of Iain Matthews and Andy Roberts. In August 2021, Iain and Andy did a short English tour. Fifty years on from forming their band, they referred to themselves as Plainsong.

Plainsong Concert Dates 1972

Mid-late January dates at Les Cousins, Soho, London.

28th January	Colchester Youth Club
29th January	Leeds University
1st February	Kent University, Canterbury
5th February	Croydon Tech
18th February	Westfield College
20th February	Roundhouse, Chalk Farm, London
24th February	Liverpool University
25th February	Cory Hall, Cardiff
3rd March	Bristol University
4th March	Southampton University
9th March	Winter Gardens, Penzance
10th March	Van Dike, Plymouth
11th March	Loughborough University
12th March	Cherry Trees Motel, Alcester
15th March	Hampstead Country Club
17th March	Salford University
19th March	Roundhouse, Chalk Farm, London (Implosion event)
24th March	Demos, Eindhoven
25th March	Paradiso, Amsterdam
26th March	De Kolk, Assen
28th March	Eksit Club, Rotterdam
29th March	De Harmonie, Tilburg
30th March	Stadsschouwburg, Nijmegen
31st March	De Harmonie, Leeuwarden
1st April	De Prins van Oranje, Goes
2nd April	Stadsschouwburg, Winterswijk (midday)
2nd April	Tin Pan Alley, Kerkhoflaan (evening)
3rd April	Extase, Bergen (midday)

3rd April	De Ark, Maassluis (evening)
April	Three consecutive nights at Music Workshop (The Scotch of St. James)
25th April	Paradiso, Amsterdam (evening)
25th April	Folk Fairport, Amsterdam (after hours)
28th April	London School of Economics (with Sandy Denny, Third Ear Band, Camel and more)
29th April	Reading University
30th April	Théâtre de l'Alhambra, Bordeaux
1st May	Le Théâtre Bobino, Paris
2nd May	Lady Mitchell Hall, Cambridge
5th May	Aberdeen University
6th May	University of St Andrews
12th May	Liverpool University
13th May	Leicester University
19th May	Leeds Polytechnic
20th May	Manchester University
22nd May	Pinkpop Festival, Geleen
24th May	Ship and Rainbow, Wolverhampton
27th May	ICA, London (for French TV)
28th May	Cherry Trees Motel, Alcester
2nd June	Goldsmiths College, London
3rd June	King's Cross Cinema, London
10th June	Gainsborough Town Hall
11th June	Redcar Jazz Club
7th July	Sporthalle, Oostburg
16th July	Kasteellaan, Wijchen
1st September	Elektra Sales Conference, Selsdon Park
5th September	Eksit Club, Rotterdam
7th September	Paradiso, Amsterdam
8th September	Breda
9th September	Groningen show and rest of tour cancelled due to Andy Robert's appendicitis.
29th September	Canley College, Coventry
30th September	St Albans City Hall
1st October	Newcastle Polytechnic

5th October	Leeds University
6th October	Queen Elizabeth College, London
8th October	Roundhouse, Chalk Farm, London
12th October	Palais de Danse, Nottingham
13th October	Victoria Rooms, Bristol
17th October	Kudos Boathouse, Kew Bridge, London
20th October	Queen Elizabeth Hall, London
21st October	Cardiff University
1st November	Bath University
19th November	Wake Arms, Epping
21st November	Cambridge College of Arts and Technology
26th November	Chancery Hall, Chelmsford
2nd December	Southampton University
3rd December	Cherry Trees Motel, Alcester
14th December	Queen's Hall, Barnstaple
15th December	The Gardens, Penzance
16th December	Plymouth Polytechnic
21st December	Glasgow City Hall
22nd December	St George's Hall, Liverpool

Plainsong Radio and TV Appearances 1972-1973

John Peel Session, BBC Radio 1
TX: 1st February 1972
REC: 24th January, Playhouse Theatre
Producer: John Waters
Songs: Tigers Will Survive, Seeds and Stems, Spanish Guitar, Any Day Woman.

Sounds of the 70s with Bob Harris, BBC Radio 1
TX: 21st February
REC: 15th February, Maida Vale
Producer: Jeff Griffin
Songs: That's All it Could Amount To, Time Between.

The Old Grey Whistle Test, BBC2
TX: 7th March
REC: 7th March, Studio B, TV Centre (with Dave Mattacks on drums)
Presenter: Richard Williams
Producer: Michael Appleton
Songs: Raider, Call the Tune.

Sounds of the 70s with Bob Harris, BBC Radio 1
TX: 3rd April
REC: Date unknown, probably late March, Maida Vale
Songs: Raider, Call the Tune, I'll Fly Away.

Top Gear with John Peel, BBC Radio 1
TX: 6th June
REC: 24th April, Studio T1, Kensington House
Producer: John Walters

Songs: Truck Driving Man, Amelia Earhart's Last Flight, Yo Yo Man, I'll Fly Away, True Story of Amelia Earhart (TX: 15th August).

Sounds of the 70s with Pete Drummond, BBC Radio 1
TX: 15th June
REC: 31st May, Maida Vale 4
Producer: Malcolm Brown
Songs: Me and Mr. Hohner, Poison Apple Lady.

Sounds of the 70s with Pete Drummond, BBC Radio 1
TX: 27th July
REC: Unknown
Songs: Diesel on My Tail, For the Second Time.

Sounds of the 70s with Bob Harris, BBC Radio 1
TX: 7th August
REC: 19th July, Aeolian Hall
(The contracts suggest that this session is likely to have been recorded with Martin Jenkins instead of Bobby Ronga.)
Producer: Jeff Griffin
Songs: I'm So Lonesome I Could Cry, Miss the Mississippi, Louise, Wreck of the Old '97, Carolina Moon, Old Kent Road.

The Old Grey Whistle Test, BBC2
TX: 17th October
REC: 17th October, White City (with Roger Swallow on drums)
Presenter: Bob Harris
Producer: Michael Appleton
Songs: Even the Guiding Light, Bold Marauder.

Sounds of the 70s with John Peel, BBC Radio 1
TX: 30th November
REC: 27th November, Langham 1
Producer: Bernie Andrews
Songs: Nobody Eats at Linebaugh's Anymore, Old Man at the Mill/Charlie, Save Your Sorrows, Home.

In Concert with Bob Harris, BBC Radio 1
TX: 16th December
REC: 30th November, Paris Theatre
Producer: Jeff Griffin
Songs: Nobody Eats at Linebaugh's Anymore, Home, Miss the Mississippi, Old Man at the Mill/Charlie, First Girl I Loved, Bold Marauder, The Goodnight-Loving Trail (with Rab Noakes).

Sounds on Sunday, BBC Radio 1
TX: 7th January 1973
REC: 29th December 1972, Maida Vale 5
Presenter: Alan Black
Producer: Frances Line
Songs: Seeds and Stems, Any Day Woman/Take You to the Movies Tonight, Blue Blue Day, Miss the Mississippi, I Work For Jesus in the Personnel Department, I Don't Want to Talk About It, Save Your Sorrows.

Plainsong In Concert, BBC2
TX: 15th February 1973
REC: 30th October 1972, Shepherd's Bush (with Roger Swallow on drums)
Presenter: Noel Edmonds
Producer: Stanley Dorfman
Songs: Amelia Earhart's Last Flight, Any Day Woman/Take You to the Movies Tonight, Poor Ditching Boy, Even the Guiding Light, True Story of Amelia Earhart, Raider, Miss the Mississippi.

Acknowledgements

Thanks to the following for their contributions to this book:

Iain Matthews, Andy Roberts, Sandy Roberton, Richard Thompson, Harry Isles, John Cornelius, Jac Holzman, Jonathan Clyde, Mark Griffiths, Hazel Richards, Roger Swallow, Frank van der Meijden, Peter Cowley, Richard Jeffrey, Ron Fritts, Nick Lambert, Richard Lewis, Bob Young, Ron Yaxley, Barry Eaton, Susan Sondheimer, John Wood, Jo Peeters, Arthur Lancaster, Derek Aslett, David Mattacks, David Suff, Geoff Jukes, Max Hole, Jerry Boys, Andy Finney, John Tobler, Peter Kay, Stuart Lyon, Tim Renwick, Keith Skinner, Pat Thomas, Emily Parsons, Anne Foulkes and Jon Mitchell.

A special thank you to Liverpool John Moores University Special Collections & Archives who look after the Andy Roberts Archive, which has been invaluable in the making of this book.

Ian Clayton is an author and storyteller from Featherstone, West Yorkshire. His stories are about making sense of where we come from. His books include *Bringing It All Back Home*, a bestselling book about music; *Song For My Father* about his lifelong search for a father figure; *Our Billie* about loss; and *It's The Beer Talking*, about adventures in public houses. *Right Up Your Street* is a compilation of columns he wrote for *Pontefract and Castleford Express*. He is the co-author of Anne Scargill and Betty Cook's memoir *Anne & Betty*, and Iain Matthews's *Thro' My Eyes*.

For more on this book, and Route's full book list, visit:
www.route-online.com